The story of DEATH TRAIN was conceived by Alistair MacLean—author of the world-famous bestsellers *The Guns of Navarone, Where Eagles Dare* and *Santorini*—and was completed as a novel after his death. During his lifetime, two of his other story outlines, HOSTAGE TOWER and AIR FORCE ONE IS DOWN, were written as thrillers and published to great acclaim.

His millions of loyal readers will be happy to know that with DEATH TRAIN the Alistair MacLean tradition of fast-paced action and pulse-pounding suspense continues.

ALISTAIR MACLEAN'S
DEATH TRAIN

Alastair MacNeill

FAWCETT CREST · NEW YORK

A Fawcett Crest Book
Published by Ballantine Books
Copyright © 1989 by Devoran Trustees Ltd.

ISBN 0-449-21748-5

This edition published by arrangement with William Collins
Sons & Co. Ltd, London.

Manufactured in the United States of America

First Ballantine Books Edition: January 1990

PROLOGUE

On an undisclosed date in September 1979 the Secretary-General of the United Nations chaired an extraordinary meeting attended by forty-six special envoys who, between them, represented virtually every country in the world. There was only one point on the agenda: the escalating tide of international crime. Criminals and terrorists were able to strike in one country then flee to another but national police forces were prevented from crossing international boundaries without breaching the protocol and sovereignty of other countries. Furthermore, the red tape involved in drafting extradition warrants (for those countries who at least had them) was both costly and time-consuming and many an unscrupulous lawyer had found loopholes in them, resulting in their clients being released unconditionally. A solution had to be found. It was agreed to set up an international strike force to operate under the aegis of the United Nations' Security Council. It would be known as the United Nations Anti-Crime Organization (UNACO). Its objective was to "avert, neutralize, and/or apprehend individuals or groups engaged in international criminal activities."* Each of the forty-six envoys was then requested to submit one detailed *curriculum vitae* of a candidate its government considered to be suitable for the position of UNACO Director, with the Secretary-General making the final choice.

UNACO'S clandestine existence came into being on 1 March, 1980.

* UNACO Charter, Article 1, Paragraph 1C.

ONE

It was to be the culmination of months of planning. The assassination of General Konstantin Benin.

Dawn on Monday morning shone only a bleak grey light over Moscow and it looked as though the weathermen would be right in their predictions of rain by midday. The national six o'clock news had just begun when the blue transit van pulled into one of the numerous lay-bys on the hard shoulder of the southbound ringroad. Lena Rodenko killed the engine and turned off the monotonous drone of propaganda. She pushed a cigarette between her dry lips then fumbled in her coat pocket for a lighter and, cupping her trembling fingers around the flame, lit it and inhaled deeply. She was naturally attractive but took no interest in her personal appearance. Her short red hair was crudely shaped in a wedge and her pallid cheeks and small chin were peppered with unsightly acne. She glanced at her brother sitting beside her and managed a weak, nervous smile. Vasili was twenty-two, three years her senior. His hair, by contrast, fell untidily to his shoulders and his patchy beard looked as though it had been stuck on at random. She took a cassette from her pocket and slid it into the machine. The tape was of an English band, given to her by Vasili for her last birthday, which had become her most cherished possession. Neither of them understood the words but the music represented all that was fair and just. Democracy. As she sucked thoughtfully on the cigarette her mind wandered back to the contents of the dossier they had prepared on Benin.

A graduate of the Red Army Academy in 1950 he was recruited by the KGB four years later but first came to prominence in 1961 as one of the architects of Fidel Castro's *Direccion General de Inteligencia*. The two men were to remain lifelong friends. He then spent several frustrating years as a military attaché in Brazil, a move rumoured to have been spearheaded by his superiors fearful of their own positions, before returning to Moscow as head of the Surveillance Unit. He then spent a brief spell on the staff at the Gaczyna spy school before being sent to Angola in 1974 as a senior military adviser; three years later he took over as commandant of the notorious Balashikha, a centre on the outskirts of Moscow used for the training of international terrorists. He was subsequently appointed deputy director of Directorate S, the most sinister division within the KGB. Its functions were abduction, assassination, sabotage and terrorism, both at home and abroad. He was promoted to director in

1984. It was said, even within the confines of the Politburo itself, that he was responsible for sending more people to their deaths in the Siberian concentration camps than any other KGB officer in living memory.

They had encountered one setback while compiling the dossier. Apart from his graduation picture there was no other known photograph of Benin. In retrospect Lena could see the ingenuity of his ploy. He had become just another faceless bureaucrat. This had initially seemed to be an insuperable problem until someone said that his face might not be familiar but they certainly knew his car. More like a bulletproof tank, someone else said; it would take an anti-tank missile to get at him. She hadn't heard the rest of the conversation. In her mind she was already formulating a plan of action . . .

She looked at the cracked face of her cheap wristwatch and swallowed nervously. It was almost time. As though in response to her thoughts the two-way radio in Vasili's lap crackled into life. They had the all-clear sign. She struggled to start the van and just when she thought she had flooded the engine it spluttered into life and she eased out into the road. She stopped the van seventy yards further on beside a steel drum and slipped the gear into neutral, leaving the engine idling. Vasili checked the time. They had a little over four minutes. They climbed out and hurried round to the back of the van to open the doors.

Gennadi Potrovský still found his good fortune hard to believe. Two days earlier he had been driving troop carriers at Kuchino, one of the KGB's training centres outside Moscow, and now he'd been asked to drive for

General Benin no less. He had been ordered not to tell anyone, not even his pregnant wife, until the letter of appointment made it all official. She would be the first to know, then he would throw a party to tell his friends who had graduated from the Red Army Academy with him the previous year. They would celebrate with him but he knew they would be envious. After all, Benin was *the* legend of the academy.

It was Potrovsky's first day of official duty. The previous day he had had to drive the route over and over until he knew it perfectly. There was to be no inconvenience to the General, he had been repeatedly told. Not that he had even *seen* Benin, hidden behind the opaque dark windows in the back of the Mercedes. Even the partition between the front and back seats had been blacked out. Benin was there, though, always preferring to be in the car first. An aide had told him it was just one of Benin's little idiosyncrasies. Potrovsky had waxed and polished the car the night before and had even gone as far as to iron the two pennants which flew on either side of the bonnet. He was determined to impress Benin.

He touched the brake gently as the Mercedes reached the bend and although he saw what lay ahead of him he had only a split second in which to react—a blue transit van parked in the slow lane of the dual carriageway and, kneeling beside it, a youth partially hidden behind a tripod-mounted anti-tank launcher. Potrovsky stamped on the brake pedal violently and the Mercedes was still slewing across the icy road when the missile struck it broadside. The car disintegrated in a sheet of searing flame and chunks of contorted metal were flung hundreds of feet into the air, landing in the snow-laced pine forest on either side of the carriageway. All that remained was a deep, jagged depression where the Mercedes had once been, encircled by burning fragments of mangled debris.

Lena was transfixed by the gaping trough in the road. Vasili shook her shoulders violently then slapped her across the face. A single tear escaped from the corner of her eye but she made no move to look away. He pushed her aside and unclipped the 33lb launcher from the tripod then carried it to the back of the van where he dumped it on to the grey blanket which they had used to cover it. He tossed the tripod in after it and banged the doors shut. Grabbing Lena's hand he pulled her to the front of the van and bundled her into the passenger seat. In his haste to get away he grated the gears and the wheels shrieked in protest when he failed to balance the changeover between clutch and accelerator. The van jerked forward but he managed to keep the engine from stalling and within seconds they had turned into a sharp bend and the grotesque crater was no longer visible in the rearview mirror. He glanced at Lena. She was still in a state of shock, her eyes locked on to an imaginary spot in the centre of the windscreen. He had always said she was too young to be involved but had taken her with him at her own insistence. The bitter irony was that the whole plan had been her idea right from the start. His main priority now was to get them to safety. Safety being a dacha in Teplyystan, a village ten miles south of Moscow. The dacha was owned by a doctor who, Vasili reasoned, would be able to snap Lena out of her trance; then the two of them could set off for Tula on the banks of the River Don where they would lie low until, with time, the investigation wound down.

He suddenly became aware of a white Mercedes behind them. Where had it come from so quickly? Road signs were supposed to have been erected at the mouth of the carriageway as soon as Benin's car had passed through, warning motorists of an impending dynamite blast and rerouting them on to another section of the motorway. His eyes continually flickered towards the rearview mirror as he monitored the Mercedes' progress with mounting apprehension. He willed himself not to panic: surely there was a logical explanation? The moment he emerged on to a flat stretch of road after negotiating a particularly tight corner the explanation was obvious. A roadblock. A Mercedes and a Zim, bumper to bumper, blocking both lanes of the carriageway and behind them the menacing silhouette of a T-72 tank, its barrel aimed directly at the oncoming van. Vasili glanced over his shoulder, his foot already on the brake and his hand dipping towards the gear lever. The Mercedes had straddled the road, hemming him in, its two occupants now standing beside it, AK47 rifles in their gloved hands. Four of the five men manning the roadblock were similarly armed. Vasili reluctantly switched off the engine and the unarmed man stepped forward and pulled open the driver's door. No sooner had Vasili's feet touched the ground than a pair of tight-fitting handcuffs were snapped around his wrists. He watched helplessly as Lena was hauled from the passenger seat and she too was handcuffed before being led away to the waiting Zim. The unarmed man then produced a buff-coloured plastic ID card and held it up in front of Vasili. Directorate S.

The back door of the Mercedes opened and a tall, craggy-faced man climbed out. He tugged a fur-lined hat over his cropped white hair as he approached the transit van, his eyes riveted on Vasili's face.

"Let me introduce myself. General Konstantin Benin."

Vasili wasn't surprised. The whole plan had gone horribly wrong, but when? He voiced the question.

Benin reached into the van, turned the music off and ejected the cassette before answering. "Women and drink should always be treated as chalk and cheese in this business. Fortunately one of your colleagues didn't know that."

"Who?" Vasili instantly regretted having risen to the bait.

"You'll find out soon enough. Most of your fellow conspirators are already in detention."

"How long have you known?"

"Right from the beginning. Your flat's been bugged for the past two months."

"General, take a look at this." The unarmed man was gesturing to the back of the van. "It's not one of ours, sir."

"No, indeed." Benin peered inside the van and ran his hand over the British-made Carl Gustav missile launcher.

Benin turned back to Vasili then gripped the cassette in both hands and snapped it in half, allowing the tape to spill out on to the road. He stuffed the two pieces into Vasili's anorak pocket.

"Anatoli?" he called out after Vasili had been led away to the Zim.

Benin's deputy hurried round from the back of the van. "Yes, sir?"

"I want you to deal personally with the Potrovsky widow. Make sure she's entitled to a state pension."

"I sent the details off last night."

"Good. Oh, and send her some flowers on my behalf, usual wording."

"Yes sir. What about a press release?"

"Make it brief. Give them some story about how an unexpected delay saved my life. Mention the missile but not the make. You can also add that the two youths involved were shot while resisting arrest. Get it to Tass some time this morning."

"Aren't you going to make a show trial out of it, sir?"

"It did cross my mind, but how can I when there are no defendants?" He patted Antatoli's arm then returned to the Mercedes.

The driver closed the door behind him and moments later the car drew away from the roadblock, heading south. It only slowed down on nearing the outskirts of Teplyystan where it turned off on to a narrow road leading into the Bittsevsky forest park, a panoramic landscape of ravines and gorges layered with fir, oak and pine plantations. The hoarding at the entrance was ominous enough: HALT! NO TRESPASSING. WATER CONSERVATION DISTRICT. The driver eased the Mercedes to a halt in front of a boomgate a couple of hundred yards further down the road and extended his ID card to the KGB duty officer, who immediately waved them through. The road ended in a cul-de-sac after another quarter of a mile and the driver turned the car into the adjoining parking bay, almost deserted at that time of the morning.

Benin climbed out and crossed to the guardhouse where he showed his ID card to the nearest of three armed sentries. The sentry checked its authenticity then activated the electronic turnstile. All three saluted as Benin passed but, as always, he ignored them. He made his way along a footpath flanked by spacious lawns and spectacularly colourful flowerbeds (rumoured to contain plastic flowers to ensure a year-round display), up a flight of steps and through the double doors of the tri-star-shaped glass and aluminum building. The newsstand was not due to open for an hour but after showing his ID card to a guard Benin asked that a copy of *Pravda* be delivered to his office the moment it arrived.

He rode the lift to the seventh floor and walked the length of the deserted corridor to the last of the suites of offices. Being on the top floor with its breathtaking view of the surrounding forest was one of the job's many perks. He activated the lock with his magnetic strip ID card, then repeated the action on the inner door leading into his private office, closing it securely behind him. After switching on the light he sat down behind his solid oak desk (made, on his orders, from Bittsevsky oak), opened his leather-bound diary and scanned the day's agenda. One name was missing. The name of his most trusted and valued European operative, whose identity appeared nowhere in his office documentation. The operative he had come in especially early that morning to contact. He closed the diary and swiveled round in his chair to unlock the

wallsafe. From it he removed a set of keys and selected one, using it to unlock the bottom left-hand
drawer of his desk. It was divided into two sections,
the back section secured behind yet another lock. He
opened that one too and withdrew a telephone. In a
world of bugs and surveillance he considered an occasional trump card imperative to keep a winning
hand. He dialled out, and as he waited for it to be
answered he knew he was using a line more private
than anything set up between the Kremlin and the
White House. Monitoring the telephone conversations
of the Kremlin hierarchy had become one of his pet
projects over the last few years. What he knew about
their private lives . . .

The receiver was lifted at the other end.

"Brazil," Benin said.

"1967," came the reply.

The codewords matched. Benin continued. "Were
there any problems loading the cargo on to the train?"

"None at all, the cover worked perfectly."

"And the train?"

"It left on schedule. The men are all in position,
it's running according to plan."

Benin replaced the receiver and locked the telephone away, then, after securing the drawer, put the
keys back in the wallsafe, closed it and spun the dial.
He sat back in his chair, his hands clasped behind his
head. The assassination attempt on his life had been
thwarted and his master plan on the Continent was
going exactly to plan. It was going to be a good week.

TWO

Karl-Heinz Tesselmann liked to think of himself as a wanderer. Words such as tramp, hobo and vagrant offended him, terms bandied about by an unsympathetic society. His parents had been killed during the Berlin blitz and after being shunted from one set of foster parents to another he had run away at the end of the war. At seventeen he joined a travelling band of gypsies who taught him the finer skills of pickpocketing until an accident to his hand six years later put paid to what would have been a very lucrative career. The gypsies, having no more use for him, threw him out. He tried to go solo but was quickly apprehended and subsequently jailed. On his release all the doors seemed to close in his face. He was a jailbird. So, at the age of twenty-six, he took to the road. That was thirty-two years ago.

Winter was closing in fast over Europe and, as always at that time of year, he was travelling south to avoid the worst of the weather. It was the first time in fourteen years that he was travelling alone, his best friend having died of pneumonia only weeks before. Although not unexpected, his death had still come as a shock. Hans had never really recovered from a near fatal case of tuberculosis as a child which had subsequently left him susceptible to infection. Now all Tesselmann had left to remind him of Hans was a faded wool-lined overcoat. A last gift from a true friend. He looked from the overcoat to the grimy, torn green flannels and the scuffed brown shoes laced with uneven lengths of string, then felt in his pocket for the cigarettes he had bummed off a group of Swedish students in Bonn a few days earlier. He had been hoping they might be filled with something a little stronger than tobacco (having heard stories about Scandinavian teenagers) but was disappointed when they turned out to be regular cigarettes. Beggars can't be choosers. His smile faltered when he withdrew his hand. It was the last of the cigarettes. He contemplated a few drags until he realized he was down to his last three matches, and reluctantly put the cigarette back in his pocket.

He had left his hometown of Kiel in northern Germany and covered the distance to Wissembourg on the Franco-German border in the space of ten days but he was still uncertain where he was ultimately headed. It all depended on the availability of goods trains in any particular station at any particular time. Hans and he had spent the last winter in Nice and it was the only place he wanted to avoid; the memories were still too painful. Perhaps the following year. His only concern right now was to board the Berne-bound goods train within the next few minutes. It was a matter of dodging the security guards then hiding in one of the freight cars. Although he had done it countless times before there was always a risk involved, especially since the introduction of guard dogs trained to sniff out illegal stowaways like himself. He had only ever been discovered once and still bore the scars on his wrist from the Alsatian's razor-sharp teeth. He made his way across the first set of tracks and reached the tail-end of a dozen coal-laden wagons. Pressing himself against the last wagon he peered around the side for any sign of the guards. No one. The Berne-bound goods train was standing on the next track down; all he had to do was cover the twenty yards between the two tracks and find himself an empty freight car. He had covered half the distance when a loud, commanding voice rooted him to the spot. He immediately thought of the dogs. His feet felt like lead and slowly, fearfully, he turned to look in the general direction of the voice. Again, nobody. Then he saw the signalman leaning out of the signalbox window, a pipe clenched between his teeth. The signalman removed the pipe and his loud voice boomed out again as he shared a joke with one of the engine drivers, both men totally oblivious to Tesselmann's nervous stare. The signalman guffawed at his own punchline then disappeared from view, closing the window after him. Tesselmann sighed deeply.

The train shuddered and edged forward. It was leaving ahead of schedule! As he hurried towards the nearest freight car, he heard the dreaded sound of a dog barking furiously behind him. He glanced over his shoulder in time to see a guard, down on one knee, fumbling with the leash to release the straining animal. Tesselmann grabbed at the handle of the freight car and hauled himself off the ground, his legs swinging precariously in the air as he tried to clasp his other hand around the handle. He could see the dog bounding towards him, its fangs bared, its tail flashing from side to side. With the strength that can come only from fear he managed to draw his legs up until his heels were touching his buttocks. The dog leapt up at him, twisting in mid-air, its jaws snapping shut inches from his calves. The dog landed awkwardly on its hindlegs, losing its balance, and he looked away sharply as it tumbled under the wheels. Allowing his legs to relax, he worked at unlatching the twin bolts and eased the door open, clambering inside where he dropped to his knees, exhausted, his chest heaving as he sucked in mouthfuls of air. Not until he had regained his composure did he crawl over to the side of the car and slump down against it, wiping the sweat from his forehead with the back of his hand. They would be waiting for him at the train's next scheduled stop, the guard would see to that. Except he had no idea where or when the train would next be stopping. He tried to scan his surroundings but the interior was too gloomy so he kicked the door open a bit further, flooding the freight car with light. It was stacked with the usual assortment of crates and containers, impregnable behind an ingenious array of clamps and locks. Security had changed drastically over the years. He could remember the days when a simple penknife would open the majority of crates and boxes being transported across Europe. Their contents had usually turned out to be machine parts but there had been a couple of times when he had found something a little more palatable—once a case of French Burgundy, on another occasion a case of German hock.

He hugged himself against the sudden freezing wind then scrambled to his feet as it whipped the first drops of rain through the open door. A storm was imminent. Over the years he had become as used to the rocking and swaying of a train as an experienced sailor is to the pitching and rolling of a ship. He made his way easily to the door and was about to close it when he caught sight of something tucked into the corner of the car between two wooden containers, out of sight from where he had been sitting earlier. A sage-coloured tarpaulin. It would come in useful. He braced himself against the now torrential downpour and grabbed the door handle with both hands, hauling the sliding door back across the opening but stopping short of banging it closed. Instead he pressed his foot against it while reaching over to pull a crate towards him. He took his foot away and pushed the crate into place where it acted as a stop to prevent the door from sliding back open again. The wind still managed to find a way through the hairline crack, whistling eerily around the interior of the freight car. He shivered. When he removed the crates to get at the tarpaulin he realized it was covering something, further stimulating his interest. He gathered in the tarpaulin as a yachtsman might a spinnaker and dumped it behind him before peering into the semi-darkness. Beer kegs. No wonder they had been covered up. He counted them by tapping each with his forefinger. Six in all. They were made of metal and this presented him with a major problem. How to open them? He looked around for an implement to use and although his eyes were by now accustomed to the gloom he could see nothing suitable. Not that this deterred him; he was determined to break one open and quench his thirst. He only wished Hans were with him, not just as a drinking partner but also because he had always been the brains of the duo. Hans would have had an answer to the current predicament. A thought suddenly came to mind. The fire extinguisher! He turned to the wall where it should have been hanging but there was only an empty bracket. He cursed and was about to turn away when another idea sprang to mind. He inspected the bracket more closely. It had rusted and one of the three screws was missing. All it needed was a good tug. He gripped it in both hands and pulled. It held firm. He twisted it, trying to prise loose the remaining screws, but although brittle from corrosion they refused to snap. He gripped it again with both hands and yanked hard. It came away from the wall and he had to grab on to a crate to stop himself overbalancing. He held it up triumphantly as though it were a trophy then knelt beside the nearest keg and traced his finger around the seal of the small bung. It would have to be knocked out. When he had seen it being done by publicans a mallet and a stake had been used, but all he had was a rusty bracket. Nevertheless he steadied his aim and brought the bracket down on to the bung. All it did was leave a dent. The seal had been reinforced. He decided to change his tactics. Instead of striking the middle of the bung he would concentrate on the seal itself. If he could first weaken the seal, a solid blow to the middle might be enough to break it open.

For the next five minutes he pounded frustratingly at the seal lining, the task not made any easier by the rhythmic rocking of the train as it sped through the rain. Of the blows delivered, barely half found their mark. He finally slumped against the nearest crate and stared at the dimpled area around the bung. Had he made any sort of impression? He gripped the bracket in both hands and repeatedly pounded the bung. It suddenly buckled inwards, the bracket disappearing into the newly formed aperture. There was no splash. Instead, a cloud of luminous white powder blew up through the hole. Instinctively he waved it from his face before getting to his feet and brushing it from the lapels of his overcoat. He waited until the cloud had settled before returning to the keg to peer inside. It was full of powder. Baffled, he scratched his greasy white hair and wondered what it could be and why it should have been stored in a beer keg. Suddenly the train began to slow. He hurried to the door to see where he was and immediately recognized the goods yard. Strasbourg. Then he remembered the guard back at Wissembourg and knew he had only a limited time to cover his tracks. After pushing the open keg back into place he covered all six kegs with the tarpaulin and replaced the other crates around it. He then went back to the door to check for any sign of the security guards he was certain would be waiting for him. The area was deserted. His luck was in, at least for the moment, but he had already decided not to tempt fate again. The odds were stacked too heavily against him. He waited for the train to shudder to a halt before jumping from the freight car and closing the door as quietly as possible behind him.

The storm was over and he regarded that as a good omen.

Josef Mauer had been with the Austrian police for eighteen years, the last eleven as a sergeant stationed in Linz, but despite numerous attempts by his superior to change his mind he had never been interested in promotion, preferring the everyday excitement that came with riding the streets in a police car to struggling with a mound of paperwork in some closeted office. His original partner had been killed in a shootout four years earlier but instead of taking on a new partner Mauer now worked with the rookies, showing them the ropes and generally helping them to settle into the daily routine at the Mozartstrasse precinct as quickly as possible after their graduation from the Police Academy in Vienna.

Ernst Richter was the latest recruit from the academy, having arrived the previous day, and he had been assigned to work with Mauer for the first month so that his temperament and personality could be assessed to ensure that later on he would be paired with the right partner.

"What's the drill for today, sir?" Richter asked when the two men reached the police car.

"Sergeant, not sir," Mauer said tugging the peak cap over his thinning blond hair. "Your main priority is to get to know the city as quickly as possible, so we'll be acting mainly as back-up for the first few days. It'll also help you to get to grips with police procedures.'' He held up his finger as Richter opened his mouth to speak. ''I know, you've already learnt all about police procedures at the academy. You all say that but the truth is, the theory and the practice are worlds apart. It's one thing to sit in a classroom writing down notes but it's quite another to come face to face with an armed murderer or a cornered rapist, you mark my words.''

Mauer had barely swung the police car out into Mozartstrasse when the radio crackled into life.

''Can I answer it, Sergeant?''

Mauer smiled to himself. Rookies were all the same in the beginning, eager to please and desperate to be judged favourably by their superiors, but within the space of a few months they had become as bitter and cynical as the seasoned policemen they had been trying to impress. Richter would learn soon enough: there were no heroes, only survivors.

As soon as Mauer knew their destination he switched on the siren and within minutes they had reached Landstrasse, drawing to a halt opposite the Landerbank. They scrambled from the police car and headed down a narrow alleyway, their hands resting lightly on their sheathed batons.

A bald man in a tuxedo was standing in a doorway halfway down the alley. Seeing the approaching policemen, he hurried forward.

''He's over there, amongst the dustbins,'' he said with a vague flick of his hand. ''I can't have him lying

there, I've got a restaurant kitchen through that door.
It's not hygienic, is it?''

Mauer looked distastefully at the half-dozen overflowing bins and wondered where the man got the
nerve to talk about hygienic conditions. Another two
bins had been knocked over and a crumpled figure lay
motionless between them, his right arm extended as
though trying to reach out for something.

''I thought he was dead but he moaned when I
touched him. Probably drunk. I can't have him lying
there.''

''So you said. Thank you for your assistance, we'll
take it from here.''

The man saw the determination in Mauer's eyes and
returned to the kitchen, closing the door behind him.

''Looks like a vagrant,'' Richter said. ''The overcoat doesn't look very old. Probably stolen.''

''More than likely,'' Mauer replied, then squatted
down beside the body. He screwed up his face at the
appalling stench but made no move to draw back.

The vagrant's hands were covered by woollen gloves
and his face was hidden underneath a navy-blue balaclava.

''Can you hear me?'' Mauer asked, prodding the
vagrant with the tip of his baton.

Tesselmann's fingers twitched but when he tried to
speak it escaped from his lips as a gurgle. Mauer un-
masked him.

Richter stumbled back and retched against the wall.
Mauer jerked his hand away. His legs were trembling
as he ran back to the police car to radio for immediate
medical help.

THREE

Whatever did happen to chivalry? The question crossed Sabrina Carver's mind as she stood with her left hand looped through the handle hanging from the rail above her in the aisle of the packed subway train as it hurtled through the cavernous tunnels beneath New York. Her attitude towards feminism was ambivalent. She certainly believed in equality between the sexes, especially in the work place, but felt there was always room for courtesy and manners in what was becoming an increasingly uncaring society. As she looked around she felt a twinge of sadness that in a carriage where 70 per cent of the commuters were men there were five women forced to stand in the aisle.

She had a sneaking suspicion that she knew why the men had not given up their seats. From where they sat they were able to study the women in detail. Especially her. She was twenty-eight years of age with the

kind of breathtaking allure normally associated with
the cover of a glossy fashion magazine. Her features
were classically beautiful: the perfectly structured high
cheekbones, a small nose, sensual mouth and mes-
merizing oval-shaped green eyes. Her shoulder-length
blonde hair, tinted with auburn highlights, was pulled
back tightly from her face and secured at the back of
her head with a white ribbon. Her designer clothes
were from the pages of a glossy fashion magazine. A
Purificación Garcia (her favourite designer) white cotton Jacquard tabard, a knee-length black cotton skirt
and a pair of Kurt Geiger black suede high-heeled
shoes. She hated excessive make-up and had applied
just enough to emphasize her striking looks. Her one
fixation was fitness and she kept herself in peak phys-
ical condition by attending aerobic classes three times
a week at the Rivereast Health Club on Second Avenue, where she also helped put housewives through
their paces in the basic skills of karate. She had successfully gained her own black belt four years previously. Although ever watchful of her enviously slim
figure she was not obsessive, and loved to dine out.
Once a fortnight she and a gaggle of friends would go
Dutch at one of their three favourite restaurants: either
steaks at Christ Cella's, cordon bleu cuisine at Lutece's
or her own personal favourite, a tandoori mixed grill
at Gaylord's. This was invariably followed by a session
of late-night jazz at Ali's Alley downtown in Greenwich Village.

As far as her friends were concerned she worked as
a translator in the United Nations. It was the prefect
cover story. She had a degree in Romance languages

from Wellesley and after doing her postgraduate work at the Sorbonne she had travelled extensively across Europe before returning to the States where she was recruited by the FBI, specializing in the use of firearms. She had joined UNACO two years ago.

She alighted from the train at Central Park North and whistled softly to herself as she walked the hundred yards down Manhattan Avenue from the subway to her ground-floor bachelor flat. The concierge doffed his hat to her as she crossed the black and white tiled foyer and after smiling at him she unlocked the door of her small flat and entered directly into the sparsely furnished lounge. She kicked off her shoes then crouched down in front of the stereo and traced her fingernail along the impressive collection of compact discs, selected one, and fed it into the machine. A David Sanborn album. It immediately reminded her of the unforgettable night at Ali's Alley when she had met Sanborn, her jazz idol, who had then discreetly found out from her friends which of his songs was her favourite and made an impromptu appearance on stage to play it especially for her.

The telephone started to ring. She turned the music down and picked up the receiver. Her only contribution to the phone conversation was an occasional monosyllable. After replacing the receiver she sat down on the edge of the coffee table and smiled to herself. An assignment. The team was now officially on standby with a briefing session scheduled for later that afternoon.

Of the other two operatives making up the team, she had always enjoyed a special rapport with the phleg-

matic C. W. Whitlock. His equanimity was legendary
amongst his colleagues and he had gone out of his way
to make her feel a part of the team when she first
arrived at UNACO. Furthermore, he had always related to her on an intellectual level, unlike the majority
of men she knew who saw her as just another pretty
face (to try a line on), and although she and Whitlock
never mixed socially, only ever meeting up at work,
she had come to regard him as one of her few real
friends.

After turning the volume up again she disappeared
into the kitchen to make herself a pastrami on rye.

New York was swathed in sunlight and the heat
would have been stifling had it not been for a gentle
easterly breeze blowing in from the Atlantic. The perfect weather for a barbecue.

C. W. Whitlock emerged from the living-room on
to the balcony of his sixth-floor Manhattan apartment,
picked up the pair of tongs hanging beside the portable
barbecue and prodded the simmering charcoal briquettes through the bars of the grill. It was hot enough.
He placed the marinated chops and sausages on the
grill then stood back and wiped the sweat from his
forehead with the towel draped around his neck. A
loud guffaw boomed out from the lounge and he
glanced through the doorway, thankful to be out of the
way. Dr. Charles Porter was, as usual, centre stage.
He didn't dislike the man; he just found him a bore.
Porter, one of the country's most respected authorities
on paediatrics, had taken a shy Puerto Rican intern
called Carmen Rodriguez under his wing twenty years

ago and given her the confidence to start up her own practice soon after graduating from medical school, and she was now one of New York's most popular and in-demand paediatricians. She had become Carmen Whitlock six years ago. Whitlock looked at his wife sitting at an angle to the doorway, her face in profile. Someone had once described her as "willowy," a description he thought suited her to perfection. Her eyes flickered towards him and she playfully stuck out her tongue. Whitlock smiled at her then looked beyond her at the couple on the sofa. Carmen's sister Rachel and her German husband, Eddie Kruger. The sisters had similar features but Rachel was shorter and stockier. Kruger was typically Teutonic. Blond hair and blue eyes. They had remained firm friends ever since their first meeting.

Whitlock turned his attention back to the barbecue and prodded each chop with a steak knife to find out if they were properly cooked. After turning the sausages and prodding the briquettes again he rested his arms on the railing and looked out over Central Park, his eyes screwed up against the sun even though he was wearing a pair of prescription sunglasses. It was that kind of day.

He was a forty-four-year-old with a light complexion for an African-born black, his grandfather having been a British Army major stationed in Kenya at the turn of the century. The sharp nose and thin lips gave his angular face a harshness which was softened by the neatly trimmed black moustache he had worn since his early twenties. He had been educated in England and after graduating from Oxford with a BA (Hons) he returned to his native Kenya where, after a short spell in the national army, he joined the Intelligence Corps. In his ten years with the Intelligence he rose to the rank of colonel, but his superiors' prejudice against his British ancestry and education became unbearable and he resigned to take up the post offered to him with UNACO. To all intents and purposes he was an attaché with the Kenyan delegation at the United Nations and the only person outside UNACO who knew the truth was his wife, and even she had only been briefed in the vaguest possible terms. He never discussed the nature of his work with her.

"I thought the chef might like a beer."

Whitlock smiled and took the Budweiser from Kruger.

"Don't lie, you've just had enough of Dr. Kildare." He had never lost his distinctive public school accent.

"I don't know how Carmen can put up with him."

"Carmen?" Whitlock snorted. "Spare a thought for me. At least I've got an excuse to miss today's lecture." He picked up the tongs to check the meat. "Carmen regards him as a kind of guru and I'm the first to admit he's been an invaluable catalyst in her career, but I wish he could talk about something other than medicine."

Kruger grinned then moved to the railing where he watched two female joggers passing beneath him, their bronzed legs moving in rhythmic unison. When they disappeared he turned his attention to a couple of girls who were laughing and giggling as they flung an orange frisbee at each other.

"You should get yourself a telescope C.W. You could spend the whole day stargazing."

"I'd see a lot more stars when Carmen hit me over the head with it. Anyway, those two aren't much older than Rosic."

"None of us are getting any younger," Kruger replied wistfully.

"How is Rosie? We haven't seen her around here for a while."

Kruger put a hand on Whitlock's shoulder. "I know We were counting on her coming with us today but she'd already made plans to meet some friends in Times Square."

"Come on Eddie, it's hardly fair to expect a fifteen-year-old to give up her Saturday, especially one like today, to sit around with a bunch of old fogeys. It's only natural she should want to be with kids her own age."

Carmen appeared in the doorway, her hands pushed into the pockets of her flared skirt. "How's the food coming on?"

"A few more minutes yet. Is school out already?"

She rolled her eyes then returned inside.

Kruger stared after her. "It's weird, a paediatrician without kids of her own."

"I don't see why," Whitlock replied without looking up from the grill. "You can have too much of a good thing."

The telephone rang in the lounge and Carmen answered it on the extension in the kitchen.

"C.W., it's for you," she called out, her hand cupped over the mouthpiece.

He went through to the kitchen and knew immediately who the caller was by the apprehension in her eyes. She handed the receiver to him and left the room without a word, closing the door quietly behind her.

When he emerged Carmen was absently rearranging the chrysanthemums in the crystal vase on the table in the hallway. As he approached her he thought of Mike Graham, the third member of the team, who had lost his family so tragically the year prior to his recruitment by UNACO. What if Carmen's life were put at stake as a direct result of a UNACO assignment? Would he react as Graham had done? He dismissed the question as so much supposition, but when he tried to give her a reassuring hug she wiggled free and went out on to the balcony to join the others.

The question stayed in the back of his mind.

"Get rid of the bum!" Mike Graham snapped when the radio commentator announced the second strike against the batter. He leaned forward, his forearms resting on his knees, his eyes riveted to the portable radio at his feet as he waited for the pitcher's next delivery.

"Strike three, side out," the commentator shouted above the disparaging cries of the partisan crowd.

"Why the hell didn't they sell you to the Angels when they had the chance?" Graham hissed angrily.

It had been an indifferent season for the New York Yankees, the team he had followed faithfully for thirty years, and, at 4-1 down to the Detroit Tigers with two innings left, defeat seemed to be on the cards for a third successive game.

As the commentator began to analyse the Yankees' seasonal batting averages Graham looked around slowly at the tranquility of his surroundings. In front of him, as far as the eye could see, was the serenity of Lake Champlain, and all about him were the lush verdant forests of southern Vermont. The panoramic grandeur of the place seemed a world away from New York, which had been his home until two years before. New York was 230 miles away and, apart from business trips, he only ever returned there to compete in some of the city's more gruelling and arduous marathons. He lived alone in a log cabin beside the lake, his only company a portable radio and television. The nearest town was Burlington and he travelled the five miles there each Monday morning in his battered white '78 Ford pick-up to collect enough supplies to last him through the week. He had always been friendly but reserved with the townsfolk who, in the main, accepted his reclusive lifestyle without question. He never spoke of the tragedy which had driven him into seclusion.

He was thirty-seven years old with tousled collar-length auburn hair and a youthfully handsome face marred by the cynicism in his penetrating pale-blue eyes. He kept his firm, muscular body in shape with an hour's run every morning followed by a demanding work-out in the small shed adjacent to the cabin which he had converted into a mini-gym soon after arriving from New York.

Sports had played a significant part in his life. He was granted a football scholarship to attend UCLA and after graduating with a degree in Political Science his dream was realized when he signed for the New York Giants, the team he had supported since childhood, as a rookie quarterback. A month later he was drafted into Vietnam where a shoulder wound abruptly put an end to his promising football career. He subsequently became involved in the training of Meo tribesmen in Thailand and joined the élite Delta antiterrorist unit on his return to the States.

His dedication and expertise with Delta were finally rewarded after eleven years when he was promoted to leader of Squadron B, with sixteen men under his command, but while he was on assignment in Libya his wife and five-year-old son were abducted by Arab terrorists in New York. Despite a nationwide search by the FBI he never saw either of them again. He was immediately given extended leave to undergo psychiatric therapy but refused to cooperate with the medical staff and was retired from Delta at his own request a month after he returned to work. At the suggestion of the Delta Commander he applied for a post at UNACO and was finally accepted six weeks later after a succession of exhaustive interviews.

The spinner dipped under the water. He had a bite. As he reeled the fish in he listened with a growing sense of dismay and despair to the baseball commentary on the radio. The score was unchanged and the Yankees were batting in the ninth, and last, inning. He landed the fish without any difficulty. A five pound pike, hardly worth the effort. The bleeper attached to his belt suddenly shrilled into life and after silencing it he eased the hook from the mouth of the pike thrashing about at his feet and brushed it back into the water

with the side of his boot. The game ended in jeers and
abusive chants. He resisted the temptation to kick the
radio in after the fish then sprinted the forty yards to
the cabin where he made a telephone call to acknowl-
edge the bleeper.

It was answered at the other end after the first ring
by a friendly, but formal, female voice. "Llewelyn
and Lee, good afternoon."

"Mike Graham, ID 1913204."

"I'm putting you through, Mr. Graham," came the
immediate reply.

"Mike?" a deep voice boomed down the line a moment later.

"Yes, sir."

"Code Red. I've chartered a Cessna from Nash,
saves us sending a plane from our end. He's waiting
for you at the Burlington airstrip. Sergei will be waiting for you at JFK."

"I'm on my way, sir."

"And Mike, pack some warm clothes. You'll need
them."

He replaced the receiver then hurried back to the
water's edge where he gathered together his tackle before returning to the cabin to pack.

Sergei Kolchinsky was the stereotyped image of a
chain smoker. Early fifties, thinning black hair, the
unmistakable signs of middle-age spread and the sort
of doleful features that gave the impression he was
carrying the troubles of the world on his shoulders.
The strange thing was that he derived no real enjoyment from smoking. It had just become a costly, and

addictive, habit. Yet behind those melancholy eyes lay
a brilliant tactical mind.

Following a distinguished career with the KGB, including sixteen years as a military attaché in a succession of western countries, he was appointed as Deputy
Director of UNACO after his predecessor had been
sent back to Russia in disgrace for spying. He had
been with UNACO now for three years and although
he still suffered from bouts of home-sickness he never
allowed those feelings to interfere with his work. His
clinical approach to his job had always been one of
complete professionalism.

"This cab free, *tavarishch*?"

Kolchinsky looked round sharply at the face peering
through the open passenger-door window. He smiled,
then scrambled from the white BMW 728, crushing
the half-smoked cigarette underfoot. "Hello Michael,
I wasn't expecting you for another twenty minutes."

Kolchinsky was the only person Graham knew who
called him Michael. Not that it bothered him. After
all, it was his name.

"I told Nash to step on it. The boss sounded agi-
tated when I spoke to him over the phone."

"He's got reason to be," Kolchinsky replied, opening the boot so Graham could deposit his two black
holdalls.

"When's the briefing?"

"As soon as we get to the UN," Kolchinsky answered, then snapped his seatbelt into place. "Sabrina
and C.W. should be there already."

"Have you been briefed yet?"

Kolchinsky started the engine, glanced in the side

mirror, and pulled away from the kerb. "Naturally. And no, I'm not telling you anything."

"I never said a word."

"You didn't have to. Put some music on; the cassettes are in the glove compartment."

Graham found three tapes, holding up each one in turn. "They're all Mozart. Haven't you got anything else?"

"Mozart's the perfect driving music," Kolchinsky replied, lighting another cigarette.

Graham reluctantly pushed one of the cassettes into the system, waved the cigarette smoke irritably from his face, then turned his attention to the New York skyline and started to name the numerous skyscrapers to himself in an attempt to pass the time.

Officially, UNACO didn't exist. Its name was absent from all the directional boards in the United Nations foyer and none of its thirty telephone lines was listed in any of the New York directories. When someone did ring one of the numbers it was answered by a recep tionist on behalf of "Llewelyn and Lee". If the caller could identify himself either by an ID number or a codeword his call would be transferred to the relevant extension. If it was a wrong number, no harm had been done. Not surprisingly "Llewelyn and Lee" were also unlisted in the city directories. The receptionist presided over a small office on the twenty-second floor of the United Nations Building, its unmarked door locked at all times and only accessible to authorized personnel. Apart from her desk and swivel chair, the only other furniture was a burgundy-coloured couch and two matching armchairs. Three of the walls were papered in a light cream colour and decorated with a selection of framed sketches of the Dag Hammarskjold Plaza, commissioned by the Secretary-General himself. The fourth wall was constructed of rows of teak slats, incorporated into which were two seamless sliding doors, impossible to detect with the naked eye and only capable of being activated by miniature sonic transmitters. The door to the right led into the UNACO command centre, manned round the clock by teams of analysts monitoring the fluctuating developments in world affairs. Massive multi-coloured electronic charts and maps plotted the vacillating movements in known trouble-spots, computer print-outs updated existing material and VDUs displayed detailed information on known criminals at the touch of a button, feeding off the thousands of names stored in the system's central memory bank. It was the nerve centre of UNACO's highly sophisticated world operation. The door to the left could only be opened by one person. It was the Director's private office.

Malcolm Philpott had been the UNACO Director ever since its inception, having spent the previous seven years as head of Scotland Yard's Special Branch. He was in his mid-fifties with a gaunt face and thinning wavy red hair.

There were 209 employees working for UNACO, thirty of those being crack field agents siphoned off from police and intelligence agencies around the world. Ten teams, each with three operatives, able to cross international boundaries without fear of breaking the law or breaching protocol. There was no pecking order; each team had its own individuality and style.

That was certainly the case with Strike Force Three. Of all his field agents Philpott had known Whitlock the longest, having personally recruited him for MI5 at Oxford University. He had liaised closely with him as a handler until his transfer to the Operations Planning Department, but Whitlock never really got on with his new handler and jumped at the chance to work with Philpott again. Whitlock was the master of patience; nothing ever seemed to rile him, which was just as well considering the simmering tension between Sabrina and Graham. When Sabrina's dossier had arrived on his desk from the FBI Director he was initially sceptical about her abilities but quickly changed his mind after meeting her. She was both friendly and intelligent with none of the vanity so often associated with beautiful women. Then he had been treated to a display of her marksmanship, involving both moving and stationary targets. She was, without question, the finest shot he had ever seen. He had never regretted the day he welcomed her to UNACO. Graham, on the other hand, had nearly slipped through the net. The Delta Commander had contacted the Secretary-General instead of Philpott to put Graham's case forward. The Secretary-General rejected Graham on the basis of his psychiatric report. Philpott had then been contacted by Graham personally on the advice of the Delta Commander. Philpott had been furious that the Secretary-General had failed to consult him and after several meetings with Graham overruled the decision, accepting Graham on to the team on a probationary basis, on the understanding that he would be subjected to periodic re-evaluation. Graham still bore the mental scars of his tragedy but he had proved to be an excellent operative and Philpott had no intention of letting him go.

Philpott pressed a button on his desk intercom. "Sarah, send them through."

Although he had left his native Scotland as a boy his voice still contained traces of his Celtic background.

He pointed the miniature transmitter at the door and pressed the button. The door slid open. When they had all come in he closed it again. He indicated the two black leather couches against the wall and Kolchinsky was the first to sit down, immediately lighting up a cigarette.

"If you want tea or coffee, help yourself," Philpott said, waving in the general direction of the dispenser to the right of his desk.

"Milk, no sugar," Graham said to Sabrina then eased himself on to the couch beside Kolchinsky.

Sabrina glared at him, arms akimbo. "I'm not your personal maid."

Whitlock saw the anger in Philpott's eyes and stepped forward with a placating smile. "Let Uncle Tom get it. My ancestors had plenty of practice, it's second nature to me by now."

"It's okay, C.W., I'll get it," she muttered.

"Sabrina!"

She turned to Philpott, who was pointing at the couch behind her. She sat down without a word and shook her head when Whitlock asked if she wanted coffee.

Whitlock poured two cups of coffee then returned to his seat with one after handing the other to Graham.

Philpott opened the file in front of him. "As I said to you all over the phone, it's a Code Red operation. Time isn't on our side. There isn't much to go on but these are the facts as we know them. A vagrant was discovered yesterday in Linz, the skin on his face and hands severely burnt almost as though he had been in a fire. On further examination at the hospital it was discovered that he had lost most of his teeth and hair and there was irreparable damage to the stomach and intestines as well as to the central nervous system. The doctors were unanimous in their diagnoses. Somatic radiation poisoning. An instantaneously absorbed dose of five grays would prove fatal within the space of two weeks. The autopsy revealed he had absorbed three times that amount."

"What are grays?" Graham asked.

"It's the SI unit to measure absorbed doses of radiation," Whitlock answered without looking at him.

Philpott nodded, then continued. "He managed to give the authorities a few sketchy details before he died. He jumped a freight train at Wissembourg on the Franco-German border and found six beer kegs in the car, but when he broke one of them open he was showered in fine powder. He then covered the kegs with a tarpaulin and left the train at Strasbourg. Three days later he was found in Linz."

"Have the doctors identified the radioactive substance?" Whitlock asked.

"Plutonium-IV."

"Used in the manufacture of nuclear weapons," Whitlock added grimly.

"So the kegs could be anywhere in Europe by now," Sabrina said.

Philpott tamped a wad of tobacco into his briar pipe and lit it carefully before looking up at Sabrina. "Correction. Those kegs could be anywhere in the world by now. They must be found, and quickly."

Kolchinsky got to his feet and paced the length of the room before turning to face the others. "That damaged keg's a time bomb. You've heard what happened when a few particles came into contact with the vagrant. Imagine the consequences if its entire contents were to escape into the atmosphere. Chernobyl's still fresh in everyone's mind. It's absolutely imperative that we avoid another nuclear disaster."

Philpott paused before speaking to give added impact to Kolchinsky's words. "Mike, Sabrina, you'll work together to trace those kegs. And for God's sake bury the hatchet."

They both nodded sombrely.

"What about finding out who's behind the shipment?" Graham asked, breaking the brief silence.

"Your only concern is to find the plutonium." Philpott jabbed the stem of his pipe towards Whitlock. "Anyway, with luck C.W. will come up with something there. We've run a series of programs through the computer in the Command Centre and it's almost certain that the plutonium originated from the nuclear recovery plant outside Mainz in West Germany. It's the only reprocessing plant in Western Europe which specializes in the production of grade-IV plutonium. I've organized your usual undercover role as a free-lance reporter; see what you can dig up. Initial enquiries at the plant have so far uncovered nothing. There's no record of any shipments or thefts so we're obviously dealing with a professional outfit.

Kolchinsky picked up the three manilla envelopes from Philpott's desk and handed them out. They contained the standard kit for any UNACO operation. A résumé of the assignment (to be destroyed after reading), airline tickets, maps of their ultimate destinations, written confirmation of hotel reservations, contacts (if any) and a sum of money in the appropriate currency. There was no limit to the amount of money which could be used during any given assignment but at the end of it each operative had to account to Kolchinsky for his or her expenses in tabular form, supplying the relevant chits to back up the figure-work. Kolchinsky's pedantic approach towards the expense accounts had given rise to a joke amongst the field operatives that it would be better to lose a life than a chit.

Graham held up his envelope. "C.W.'s bound for Mainz. Where are we going?"

Philpott exhaled, blowing the smoke upwards. "Strasbourg."

FOUR

Strasbourg, the capital of the French province of Alsace, is situated close to the border with Germany on an island formed by the two arms of the River Ill. It is a picturesque city of cobbled pedestrian streets and timber-framed houses, dominated by the Cathedral Tower, a Gothic building constructed of red Vosges sandstone and standing over 320 feet tall. The Cathedral, which can be seen even from the furthest peaks of Alsace, is regarded by the Alsatians as a proud symbol of their heritage.

As Sabrina stood outside the hotel on the Place de la Gare staring up at the Cathedral's spire silhouetted against the dark, sombre skyline, she let her thoughts drift back over the hours since their departure from New York's John F. Kennedy Airport. The flight to Paris had been punctuated by periodic bouts of turbulence and consequently neither of them had managed to get much sleep. Before disembarking, the passengers had been reminded to put their watches forward by six hours to be in line with Continental time, which had served to add disorientation to fatigue. A Piper Chieftain, belonging to UNACO, had been waiting at Orly Airport to fly them on to Strasbourg. Although desperately tired both had pushed any thoughts of sleep from their minds, though after checking in at the hotel, the Vendôme (chosen for its proximity to the station), they had each taken a long, refreshing shower before meeting up again for a late breakfast in the dining room.

Graham's appearance brought her out of her reverie and they walked the short distance to the station, where she approached the information desk to ask for directions to the stationmaster's office. She had never learnt to speak Alsatian, a dialect closely related to Old High German, so she spoke in faultless German instead. The clerk even asked where in Germany she came from. She answered Berlin; it was a city she had come to know well over the years.

The stationmaster's office turned out to be ideally situated overlooking the busy concourse. She knocked on the door.

"Herein!" a voice commanded from inside the office.

She opened the door. It was a spacious room with wall-to-wall carpeting, a teak desk and three imitation leather armchairs against the wall to the right of the door. The shelves on either side of the window behind the desk were stacked with files, directories and timetables.

"*Entschuldigen Sie*, Herr Brummer?" she said, addressing the silver-haired man standing by the window.

He turned to face them. "*Ja. Kann ich Ihnen helfen?*"

Graham held up his hand before she could reply. "*Sprechen sie Englisch?*"

Brummer nodded. "Of course. Can I help you?"

"I'm Mike Graham. This is Sabrina Carver."

"Ah, yes, I was told to expect you. I have the invoices you'll want over here." He indicated the five bulky files on his desk. "All the transactions of goods loaded and off-loaded at Strasbourg in the last ten days."

Graham eyed the mountains of files with dismay. "You must be running a pretty busy operation here."

"It is, Mr. Graham. Because of its strategic position Strasbourg has become the rail centre of Europe. We also have an ever-growing harbour complex, with the result that over half the city's workforce are dependent on the transportation industry for their livelihood. So as you can see, it is imperative for us to attain a constant turnover to maximize profitability."

Sabrina opened the top file and leafed through the first few invoices. "Are they all in French?"

"Yes. It is for the benefit of the inspectors who come up from Paris for the biannual audits. None of them speaks Alsatian."

"Thank goodness for the Parisian inspectors. How are the invoices for the loaded and off-loaded goods filed? Separately or together?"

"Separately, but on a daily basis for easy reference.

All invoices also state the consignment's ultimate destination. For insurance purposes, you understand.''

"Thank you for your help," Sabrina said with a quick smile.

"If there's anything you need don't hesitate to ask."

"Coffee," Graham said abruptly.

"I'll have some sent up straight away."

"And some privacy to work," Graham added.

"If you need me I can be contacted on the phone. Extension seven."

Sabrina waited until Brummer had left then selected a ballpoint pen from the holder on the desk and wrote on a scrap piece of paper. She handed it to Graham.

"What's this?" he asked suspiciously.

"*Tonnelets à bière et tonneaux à bière*—the French for beer kegs and beer barrels. You don't exactly speak the lingo, do you?"

The meticulous scrutiny of each invoice proved to be both tedious and time-consuming, especially for Graham, who had the disadvantage of not understanding anything he was reading. He finally resigned himself to memorizing the translated words, hoping to come across a matching entry on one of the invoices. It was wishful thinking.

They managed to keep their lassitude at bay with regular coffee breaks every hour and when lunch arrived unexpectedly just after midday, courtesy of Brummer, they were grateful for the nourishment and the respite. Lunch consisted of *garbure*, a thick vegetable soup, followed by veal *à la forestière* and *pot-au-chocolat* for dessert. Although momentarily tempted by the seductively rich chocolate dessert Sabrina's willpower held firm and she gave it to Graham. With lunch over they reluctantly returned their attention to the files.

It was 3:20 when Sabrina finally closed the last of her three files. She stood up, stretched, then moved to the window and looked out over the busy concourse. "Are you nearly finished?"

He gripped the remaining invoices between his thumb and forefinger in an attempt to judge their numbers. "About fifty to go."

"Give them to me, it'll be quicker. You get the gear from the locker downstairs."

Their weapons would have been deposited in the locker the previous night by a UNACO operative. The key had been left at the hotel pending their arrival. It was a standard UNACO procedure.

"Why the hurry?" His eyes narrowed. "You've found something, haven't you?"

She shrugged. "Perhaps. Give me the file."

"We are *supposed* to be working together."

She rubbed her eyes wearily. "I had my reasons. We had to go through all those invoices, regardless of what we found. If I'd told you about the entry earlier on it might have lulled you into a false sense of complacency. It was you, after all, who was going on at breakfast about the perils of lapses in concentration."

"Your faith in me's touching," he said tersely.

"It works both ways, Mike," she replied, holding his stare.

He bit back his anger and left the office. The concourse was packed and he struggled to control his temper as he was jostled and shoved by passengers rushing for the boarding gates the moment their trains were announced over the Tannoy. On reaching the lockers he found the area around them occupied by a crowd of students, their rucksacks and kitbags strewn across the unswept floor. He removed an envelope from his anorak pocket, slit it open with his finger, and dropped the key into his hand. He unlocked the relevant locker and removed the pale-blue Adidas holdall; but when he turned away he found his path blocked by an attractive teenager in scruffy jeans and a baggy floral T-shirt. The glazed expression in her eyes told him she was on drugs. She offered him the half-smoked burnie but he batted it angrily from her fingers before heading back towards the concourse. It was then he saw the approaching gendarme. For a moment he thought the gendarme had seen the incident and he instinctively gripped the holdall tighter. He would have a lot of explaining to do if he were asked to open it. The gendarme stopped in front of the scattered luggage and prodded the nearest haversack with his foot, ordering the students to stack their belongings in a tidy pile against the wall. As the students came forward to claim their luggage the gendarme watched them closely, randomly checking passports and train tickets. Graham noticed the fear on the girl's face as she crouched against the wall, her eyes flickering nervously around her. He crossed to where she was squatting and hauled her to her feet.

"You speak English?" he asked sharply.

She nodded.

"Put these on," he said pressing his sunglasses into her hand.

She glanced at the gendarme. "You're not going to . . ."

"Put them on!" he interposed irritably. "Now, where's your luggage?"

"The orange haversack."

Graham hoisted the haversack over his shoulder and noticed the gendarme watching him. "My daughter's. Is there some problem?"

He never knew whether the gendarme understood him or not but felt relief flood over him when he was dismissed with a curt wave of the hand.

"Who are you?" the teenager asked after he had led her into the main concourse.

"That's not important. How old are you?"

She bowed her head. "Eighteen."

"Student?"

"Princeton."

"You're young, pretty and obviously intelligent so why the hell are you trying to screw up your life? All it takes is one conviction to make you a criminal. You'll have to carry that stigma around with you for the rest of your life. It's not worth it."

"You've done drugs," she said softly.

He held out his hand. "You're safe now. My sunglasses."

She took them off and gave them back to him. "Thanks. I owe you."

"You owe yourself." He pushed the sunglasses into his shirt pocket then disappeared into the seething mass of afternoon commuters.

Sabrina looked up when he returned. "You took your time."

He grimaced. "It's a jungle out there." He pointed to the file in her lap. "Find anything?"

"Just that one entry."

He put the holdall on the table then moved behind her chair to look over her shoulder at the entry she was underlining with a fingernail.

"It's got a nine written in the margin," he said.

"Don't forget the vagrant was heavily sedated when he spoke to authorities. Even if he did count six kegs, who's to say there weren't more stacked away in another part of the freight car?"

"Where were they shipped from?" he asked.

"Munich. They were unloaded here five days ago. Local address."

"Ties in roughly with the time the vagrant jumped the train. It could also be a wild-goose chase."

"Could be, but it's the only lead we've got."

He unzipped the holdall, took out a couple of Boyt shoulder holsters and dropped them on to the table before delving into the holdall again for two handguns carefully wrapped in strips of green cloth. Both were Beretta 92s, the official handgun of the United States Army. The Beretta 92 had always been Sabrina's favourite handgun but Graham still secretly hankered for the Colt .45 he had first started to use in Vietnam. He had only changed to the Beretta after joining UNACO. All UNACO operatives were allowed to choose their own handguns and, although he had initially used a Colt .45, there had been one main reason for his converting to the Beretta; its magazine capacity—fifteen rounds as opposed to the Colt's seven. Eight extra bullets in a tight spot could mean the difference between life and death. And not only for him.

After strapping on her shoulder holster and snapping a magazine into the Beretta, Sabrina checked the hold-all to make sure the radiation detection counter had also been included. It was a portable Geiger-Muller detector, one of the most popular and reliable devices on the market. It was also one of the most economical, which was why Kolchinsky would have purchased it in the first place. She smiled to herself. Kolchinsky was used to the gentle ribbing he got from the operatives about his cost-cutting exercises but when it came to the crunch he would never put any of their lives at risk for the sake of the budget. He demanded, and got, only the best, invariably at a knockdown price after cleverly playing the manufacturers off against each other.

"Ready?"

She nodded. "Have you got a plan in mind?"

"Not yet. Let's see the place first."

The address on the invoice turned out to be a three-storey house on the Quai des Pêcheurs, its reflection perfectly mirrored in the tranquil waters of the River Ill. Its white walls contrasted vividly with the black shutters latched into place over the numerous windows, and the heavy curtains drawn across the three dormer windows jutting out from the unpainted corrugated-iron roof only added to its forbidding atmosphere.

"They're certainly hiding something," Graham said as he climbed out of the rented Renault GTX.

"I think, under the circumstances, we should call in our contact," Sabrina said at length.

He looked over the car roof at her, his eyebrows furrowed questioningly. "What circumstances?"

"We can hardly go in demanding a guided tour without any kind of official search warrant."

"You know the rules, Sabrina: we only use contacts if it's absolutely necessary. We can handle this ourselves."

"How? You're not going to go storming in there like a bull in a china shop again? You know how pissed off Kolchinsky was when he got the bill the last time you did that."

"No, I've got a more subtle approach in mind. The damsel in distress."

"I might have guessed. Okay, let's hear it."

A minute later Sabrina swung the Renault into a narrow alleyway beside the house and emerged into a cobbled courtyard closed in on all sides by faded white walls, the paint peeling off in unsightly flakes to reveal greyish plaster underneath. She climbed out and rapped the knocker on the black wooden door. A judas hole slid back and a youthful face peered out at her. She explained her predicament to him in French, occasionally gesturing at the Renault behind her. As she spoke he leaned closer to the grille to get a better view of her. Skintight jeans tucked into a pair of brown leather boots and a terrific figure. He could hardly believe his luck and unlocked the door to admit her. Once inside in the long, dimly-lit corridor she withdrew a photostat copy of the invoice from her pocket and handed it to him. His salacious grin faltered then

disappeared and he glared at her, furious with himself
for being tricked so easily. His eyes flickered past her
and he smiled faintly before turning back to her and
loudly questioning the validity of the original invoice.
His clumsy attempt to distract her attention was all the
warning she needed. She waited until the last possible
moment before pivoting round to challenge the approaching figure. As the figure closed his fingers
around her lapels she clenched her fists together and
forced her arms up between his arms until her hands
met in front of her face, forcing him to loosen his grip.
She then brought her clenched fists down viciously on
to the bridge of his nose. He screamed in agony and
fell to his knees, cradling his broken nose between his
bloodied hands.

The youth snaked his hand behind the door but as
his fingers curled around the hilt of the sheathed poniard Graham appeared behind him and pressed the
Beretta into his back. He stiffened in terror then let
his hand drop to his side. Graham pushed him away
from the entrance and reached behind the door to unsheath the poniard. He extended it towards the youth,
hilt first, daring him to take it. Sabrina intervened by
taking the poniard from Graham's hand and slipping
it down the side of her boot.

"Did you pick up any readings on the outer building?" she asked, removing the Geiger-Muller counter
from the holdall he had brought with him.

He shook his head. "It's clean."

She switched it on and traced its sensitive receiver
over the door and surrounding floor area. The needle
never moved. When she approached the youth he took

a hesitant step back but froze to the spot on seeing Graham's threatening look. She tried to get a reading first off the youth then off his whimpering colleague. Both readings were negative.

"You speak English, boy?" Graham demanded.

The youth pressed his back against the wall, his eyes wide with fear.

"*Parlez-vous anglais?*" Sabrina translated.

The youth shook his head. She asked him about the beer kegs and he pointed to a flight of wooden stairs at the end of the hall.

"What about him?" Graham asked, indicating the injured man.

"He won't be going anywhere in a hurry."

The wooden stairs led down into a narrow corridor illuminated by a single naked bulb dangling at the end of a piece of frayed flex. The only door was situated at the end of the corridor, secured by a bulky padlock. She made her way to the door but again the counter failed to give a reading. She told the youth to unlock the door but he shook his head. Graham, having understood the conversation by Sabrina's gesticulation towards the padlock, shoved the youth roughly in the back towards the door. When the youth swung round he found himself staring down the barrel of Graham's Beretta. He fumbled to unclip the keys from his belt and his fingers were trembling as he tried to unlock the door. It took him three attempts to insert the key into the padlock. He dropped the padlock on to the floor then pushed the heavy door open and reached inside to switch on the light. Sabrina followed him into the room, still unable to get any sort of reading on the

Geiger-Muller counter. Hundreds of crates of beer were stacked against three of the whitewashed walls but the fourth, and longest, wall was hidden behind rows of wooden racks lined with bottles of both local and imported wines. The youth led them through a brick archway into a second room overflowing with cardboard boxes, many of them open to reveal their contents. Whisky. He pointed to the nine beer kegs standing in the centre of the room.

Sabrina traced the counter over the kegs. The needle never moved. She switched it off and squatted beside the kegs to read the labels. "Four kegs of *Heller*, five of *Dunkler*. Both are beers native to Munich. It's bootleg."

"A goddam shebeen," Graham snapped angrily.

"So it was a wild-goose chase after all."

"Yeah. I only hope C.W. comes up with something more constructive."

Whitlock had come up with something a lot more constructive and was on his way to verify its authenticity.

His flight had left New York three hours after the Paris flight and by then the worst of the turbulence over the Atlantic had dissipated so he had been able to sleep for most of the journey. Once at Frankfurt's Rhine-Main airport he had collected the keys of a Golf Corbio from the Hertz desk and driven the twenty-four miles on the A66 to Mainz where he checked in at the Europa Hotel on Kaiserstrasse. Like Graham and Sabrina he too had been left a holdall, containing a Geiger-Muller counter and his favourite handgun, a

Browning Mk2, in a locker at the main railway station where he had spent three hours studiously checking the invoices for all the freight loaded at the goodsyard over the past ten days.

One invoice had fitted all the requirements perfectly. Six metal beer kegs loaded on to a Swiss-bound goods train which had stopped at Strasbourg on the same day the vagrant had claimed to be there. Although it was hardly conclusive proof they were the same kegs as those discovered by the vagrant, all the signs pointed to it being more than just a coincidence. There was only one sure way of finding out and that was to visit the local address given on the invoice to test for radiation levels.

It was already nightfall when Whitlock crossed the Heuss Bridge over the Rhine and turned the Gulf Corbio into Rampenstrasse, his eyes screwed up behind his tinted glasses as he tried to distinguish the numbers, many of them faded and indistinct, on the rows of warehouses lining the river bank. He found the warehouse which corresponded to the number on the invoice lying beside him on the passenger seat and slowed the Golf to a halt in front of it. He grabbed the holdall from the back seat and climbed out. The only other cars were the five parked outside a brightly lit Italian restaurant on the other side of the street. Not only was it gaudy in appearance but the smell wafting from the kitchen was distinctly malodorous. He walked over to the warehouse. The unpainted doors were padlocked and above them he could vaguely make out the name Strauss, the paintwork having been abraded over the years by the weather. He glanced around, then took

a nailfile from his pocket and set to work on the padlock. Moments later it opened and he unfastened the
chain securing the two doors together and eased one
of them open wide enough for him to slip inside. After
trying several switches he succeeded in lighting a bulb
in the far corner of the warehouse. Rusted hooks hung
from antiquated iron girders above him, the windows
had long since been vandalized and the faded walls
were daubed with obscene graffiti. Even the concrete
floor had cracked with age and clusters of weeds had
grown up through the uneven apertures. The whole
place reeked of desolation and neglect. He unzipped
the holdall, removed the Geiger-Muller counter, and
switched it on. The needle immediately showed a
reading, which then strengthened and weakened as he
moved about the warehouse. He switched it off, satisfied that the kegs had, at some stage, been stored
there.

"Was wünschen Sie?"

Whitlock swung around. The man standing at the
entrance was in his late twenties with greasy blond
hair and a stained apron tied loosely around his fat
stomach. Whitlock thought of the Italian restaurant and
moved closer to get a better look. The impression was
overwhelmingly one of weakness. He believed strongly
in physiognomy and his instincts were rarely wrong.

"Do you speak English?" Whitlock asked.

"I speak a little. We must, we have plenty of English people come here."

Whitlock assumed "here" meant Germany and not
the restaurant. Surely no tourist would venture there.
Then again . . .

"I take it you work in the restaurant across the road?"

The man nodded.

"How long?"

"Nearly two years."

Whitlock reached into his pocket and withdrew a roll of banknotes which he turned slowly in his hands. The weak were always the easiest to bribe. He hated bribery because it was the hardest of all expenses to try and explain to Kolchinsky.

"I'm after information and I'm willing to pay well for it."

"Who are you? British Police?"

"Pay me and I'll tell you. Otherwise let me ask the questions."

"What do you want to know?" the man asked, wiping his palms on his apron, his eyes never wavering from the banknotes in Whitlock's hand.

"Have you seen anyone around this warehouse in the last six months?"

The man ran his tongue over his dry lips and nodded. "Sometimes they come and eat in my restaurant. Three of them. One only come in the restaurant once but I'm sure he's the boss. The other two were—" he looked up at the roof as he struggled for the word "—how you say, scared of him? My wife say he's handsome." He shrugged as though her opinion was irrelevant.

"What did he look like?"

"A big man with black hair. And he have different coloured eyes. One brown, one green. I see when he come to pay the bill. He speak good German but he not born here.''

''Did you recognize his accent?''

''No.''

''And the other two?''

''One is small with short red hair. The other an Ami—an American. Blond, like me. He have a moustache.''

''Did you ever hear their names mentioned?''

The man shook his head. ''They always sit in the corner. They like to be alone.''

''Any activity around the warehouse?''

''I see a van come here sometimes. That's all.''

''Was there anything written on it?''

''I didn't see.''

Whitlock peeled off several notes from the roll and the man snatched them from his fingers and stuffed them into his pocket.

''What is that?'' the man asked, watching Whitlock replace the Geiger-Muller counter in the holdall.

Whitlock zipped the holdall and stood up. ''Pay me and I'll tell you.''

''You smart.''

''Yeah?''

Whitlock waited for the man to leave the warehouse before following him out and padlocking the chain.

''You come eat in my restaurant. I make you a good lasagne.''

''We have a saying in English. 'When in Rome, do as the Romans do.' We're in Germany.''

''You not like lasagne?''

Whitlock glanced at the restaurant. "As you said, I'm smart."

He returned to the Golf and picked up the invoice from the passenger seat. The cargo's ultimate destination had been printed neatly in black pen in the bottom left-hand corner of the page.

Lausanne.

Whitlock telephoned them the moment he returned to the hotel but when Sabrina contacted Lausanne station she was told the only afternoon train had already departed. Both she and Graham agreed there was little else they could do that night and when he telephoned through to report to UNACO headquarters he was told a company Cessna would be waiting at six o'clock the following morning to fly them on to Geneva, the nearest airport to Lausanne.

They both settled for an early night.

FIVE

The Cessna arrived at Cointrin Airport, Geneva, at 7:30. Graham rented the fastest car Hertz could offer, a BMW 735i, to take them the seventy miles to Lausanne. Sabrina, with a string of saloon car races under her belt, felt she would be best qualified to drive until Graham tactlessly reminded her of her near fatal crash at Le Mans. She bit back her anger, for it was neither the time nor the place to start an argument. She let him drive.

An hour later they arrived at Lausanne station where the stationmaster had been told to expect them. He made several internal calls then announced, somewhat relieved, that he had tracked down the porter who had overseen the off-loading of the freight train the previous day. Graham asked him not to summon the porter to his office. He believed strongly in the psychology of home territory, which invariably put witnesses at their ease and made them more likely to remember little details they might otherwise forget or overlook in strange or foreign surroundings. He had seen it work while at Delta.

The porter was standing on the platform, his hands dug into his overall pockets.

"You speak English?" Graham asked.

The porter nodded hesitantly.

"We'd like to ask you some questions," Sabrina said.

"What's in it for me?"

"Your job," Graham replied tersely.

"Well, if you put it that way . . ." the porter said with a nervous chuckle.

"Recognize this invoice?" Sabrina asked, holding up the one given to her by the stationmaster.

The porter pointed to the name printed in the top left-hand corner. "That's me. Deiter Teufel. Teufel means "devil." Deiter the Devil, especially with the women."

"I don't give a damn about your social life," Graham snapped. "So you dealt with this particular cargo when it arrived here yesterday?"

"It's my name, isn't it?"

"I don't need your sarcasm, boy."

"I was here but . . ."

"But?" Sabrina prompted.

"I could lose my job," Teufel said, staring at his unpolished shoes. "I should have known it wouldn't work."

"You're on the verge of losing it anyway unless you start coming up with some answers."

"Hang on, Mike." Sabrina stared at Teufel's bowed head. "Look, we're not interested if you've broken some internal disciplinary code. All we want to know is what happened to the cargo."

"I don't actually know," Teufel replied, stubbing his toecap absently on the concrete platform.

"I promise you it won't go any further than the three of us," Sabrina said.

"You promise?"

"I promise," she answered with a reassuring smile.

"About forty minutes before the train was due to arrive this man came up to me and asked if I'd be interested in making five hundred francs. Naturally I jumped at the chance."

"What man? Had you seen him before?" Graham asked.

"I'd never seen him before. Well-built, black hair, spoke good German. He knew somehow that I was dealing with this section and gave me the serial number of a wagon and told me not to go anywhere near it. He said it contained his own private cargo and that he wanted to unload it himself. I know it's against the rules but I wasn't going to argue, not for that kind of money."

"Then what happened?" Sabrina pressed.

"A white van was reversed up to the wagon."

"Did he have any accomplices?" Graham asked.

"I only saw the driver but there could have been others inside the wagon."

"Describe the driver," Graham said.

Teufel shrugged. "I didn't really take much notice of him. I just remember he had a moustache. There was something strange though. After the van had been loaded it drove to another loading bay and backed up against a second wagon. It must have been there for at least an hour. Then it returned to the original wagon and backed up against it again. Both trains left about the same time.

"Did you check either of the freight cars before they left?"

"No, sir, but I did check my invoices afterwards. Both wagons were down as empty."

"Where were the trains going?" Graham asked.

"The one from Mainz goes on to Rome. I'm not sure about the other one. I'll check if you want."

"Check," Graham said.

Teufel disappeared into a booth and returned a minute later. "The other train's bound for Zurich via Fribourg and Berne. It's stuck in Fribourg at the moment. Mechanical problems. I've also written down the serial numbers of the two wagons if that will be any help to you."

"Has the cargo been transferred to another train in Fribourg?" Sabrina asked, taking the slip of paper from him.

"No, the train's scheduled to leave Fribourg later this afternoon. The cargo will still be on board."

"So you never went near either of the freight cars?" Sabrina asked.

"I stayed well clear. I wanted the money."

"Thanks for your help. And don't worry, we won't say anything to the stationmaster about yesterday."

"Thanks," Teufel muttered, then smiled knowingly

at Graham. "You're lucky to have such a beautiful assistant."

"Partner," Sabrina said sharply.

Teufel touched his cap apologetically. "Excuse me, I've got work to do."

Sabrina watched him disappear back into the booth. "So crime does pay sometimes."

"Meaning?" Graham asked as they walked back towards the main concourse.

"He'd be irradiated if he'd turned the bribe down and gone to the freight car."

"True enough," Graham answered, then chuckled to himself.

"What?"

"Assistant. I like it."

"I bet," she replied, then pointed to the station café. "Come on, I'll buy you breakfast."

He had bacon, eggs and sausages. She settled for a continental breakfast, substituting two slices of freshly baked *tresse*, a plaited white loaf, for the conventional croissant.

"What do you make of these latest developments?" Graham asked as they sat down at one of the few vacant tables.

She stirred her coffee thoughtfully before answering. "They found out about the damaged keg and had to repair it secretly; that *must* be why the van was backed up to the freight car."

"Not to mention the fact that someone in a protective white suit might just attract the wrong kind of attention," Graham added between mouthfuls.

"They must know they're in the frame otherwise why the decoy?"

"Not necessarily. We're dealing with professionals. It's only natural they should cover their tracks after a setback like that." He forked the remaining bit of sausage and dipped it into the runny egg yolk. "Which train do you think is the decoy?"

"The original one bound for Rome," she replied without hesitation.

"They've fooled you," he said, his mouth full.

"Really? And what makes you so certain?"

"Intuition."

"Intuition? Of course, why didn't I think of that?" she said sarcastically.

Graham banged his fist angrily on the table. A couple at the next table scowled at him but looked away when he glared back at them. He leaned forward and tapped his finger on the table. "I already had six years' experience of the criminal mind by the time you graduated from the Sorbonne as a spoilt little brat."

"The spoilt little brat. I was wondering when we would get round to that. What about the rest of it? The poor little rich girl who got into the FBI through her father's influence and who would now be married to some rich Miami socialite had it not been for the timely intervention of Colonial Philpott, who was pressed into giving her a job with UNACO. You should try playing another track, Mike, that one's already beginning to stick."

"The truth hurts."

"And you should know." She immediately regretted her words. "I'm sorry, Mike, I didn't mean that."

"You wouldn't have said it if you didn't mean it." He rubbed his hands over his face. "Can we get back to the case?"

"It could actually be a blessing in disguise."

"What could?" He pushed his plate aside.

"Our difference of opinion. We'll have to check out both trains."

"True, but we need a second Geiger counter and there isn't time to wait for them to send us another one."

"You take it; I shouldn't find it too difficult to buy another."

"Well, we're wasting time sitting here," he said and stood up.

"And as the boss keeps reminding us, it's a Code Red. The proverbial race against time."

The hoarding at the entrance to the sliproad leading off the A643 five miles out of Mainz warned of the penalties which could be imposed on any unauthorized personnel attempting to gain illegal entry into the Nuclear Fuel Reprocessing Plant a mile further down the road.

Whitlock swung the Golf Corbio on to the sliproad, past the hoarding, and as he reached the crest of the first rise he saw the plant laid out before him, hemmed in behind ten-feet-high fencing crowned with layers of barbed wire, all of which he later discovered could be electrified at the flick of a switch. Towering above the numerous box-shaped buildings were three unsightly cooling towers, each belching out plumes of thick, grey smoke which drifted up into the low, threatening rainclouds overhead. As he drew to a halt in front of the boomgate he thought about the unacceptable quantities of low-level toxic waste being expelled daily into the atmosphere by avaricious chemical companies with scant regard for the safety and welfare of future generations. They treated little embarrassments such as their role in the gradual destruction of the ozone layer in the same way that the Vatican dealt with internal corruption: by brushing it under the carpet and pretending it never existed. It had always distressed him that the West and the Eastern bloc could both budget so generously for what he considered to be the evils of the nuclear industry while millions in the Third World were left wanting for food. Whatever the questions he really wanted to ask at the reprocessing plant, though, he would never allow his personal feelings to interfere with an assignment.

A guard emerged from the hut behind the boomgate and approached the Golf. Whitlock noticed the holster affixed to the guard's belt, then glanced down at the leashed Doberman sitting obediently beside him. He wound his window down and thought momentarily of his brother-in-law, Eddie Kruger, who had taught him all the conversational German he knew. It wasn't much, but enough to get by on.

"Morning. The name's Whitlock. *New York Times.* I've got an appointment with—" he paused to look at the name at the foot of the letter which had been included in his holdall at the station "—K. Schendel. Nine o'clock."

The guard traced his finger down the typed list of names attached to his clipboard, found the name, then asked Whitlock for some kind of identification. Satisfied with Whitlock's passport, the guard returned to the hut to telephone through to reception. He opened the boomgate and Whitlock gave him a friendly wave as he drove past on his way to the visitors' car park.

The reception area had obviously been designed to impress, with its mushroom-coloured Anton Plus carpet imported from America, its three-tiered Czechoslovakian glass crystal lights, its brown leather armchairs and its crushed velour curtains draped ornately on either side of the plate glass window facing directly out on to the car park.

He approached the oak-panelled reception desk and returned the receptionist's smile. "I've an appointment with Mr. Schendel at nine."

"Miss, actually. Karen," a female voice said in English behind him.

When he turned his first thought was that she too had been designed to impress. Contradicting and yet somehow enhancing the pinstriped jacket and skirt she was wearing, her sable-coloured hair was coiled up on her head, accentuating her fine features and her perfect neck. Her movements were graceful and elegant and her handshake firm without losing any of its femininity.

"My apologies," Whitlock said, deciding to stick to English.

Her English seemed infinitely better than his beleaguered German.

"What for?" she asked with a frown.

"For assuming you'd be a man."

"It's a natural assumption for a man to make. Come through to my office. I was about to order myself some coffee."

Her office, situated off the corridor leading directly out of the reception area, was spacious and subtly feminine. Pastel walls formed a tasteful background to a selection of mounted Sara Moon prints, fresh flowers were arranged in a crystal vase, and there was a pink shade on the small desk lamp. She indicated the white leather armchair in front of her desk, then sat down in her swivel chair and reached for the telephone.

"Tea or coffee?"

"Whatever you're having."

"Why are men always so evasive? It's not a difficult choice. Tea or coffee?"

"Coffee," he replied, then, as she gave the order, leaned forward to look more closely at a framed photograph of a freckle-faced boy on her desk. "He's pretty cute."

"My son, Rudi," she said, replacing the receiver. "He and his father were drowned off the Costa Brava four years ago."

"I'm sorry," Whitlock said.

"Thank you."

"How long had you been married?"

"Oh, we weren't married. Childhood sweethearts. I met Erich when I was fifteen. We would have been together nineteen years this year."

"I can honestly say you don't look a day over twenty-five."

She laughed. "I've got a feeling we're going to get along just fine, Mr. Whitlock."

"C.W., please."

"What do the initials stand for?"

"Nothing, they're just initials."

He had never forgiven his parents for naming him Clarence Wilkins.

Karen poured the coffee when it arrived and let Whitlock help himself to milk and sugar.

"What sort of article do you want to write?" she asked.

"I was hoping to get an insight into the people who work here. So much has already been written about the operational side of the industry that the public tend to take for granted the workforce whose expertise makes it all possible."

"The human angle, in other words?"

Whitlock nodded. "Also, with Chernobyl still fresh in everyone's mind I thought it might be a good idea to show that workers in the nuclear industry are just like the rest of us. They have families and mortgages and are just as worried about the possibility of a radiation leak as the next person."

"More worried. Not only would our livelihood be at stake if there was a shutdown but we'd also be the first to be irradiated." She paused to take a sip of coffee. "So why come to Mainz?"

"We've been deluged with stories about the American nuclear industry over the past few years. People want to read about something different and with Mainz central to the rest of Europe this is both an important and controversial plant site. Fallout from here could contaminate the whole continent.''

''The melodrama of journalism,'' she said with a smile. ''How long are you planning on being here?''

''Two, three days,'' he replied.

''Good, then I'll be able to show you personally just how stringent our safety regulations are. Unfortunately I'm going to be busy for most of today lecturing to a group of Japanese businessmen, so I'll have to leave you in the hands of my assistant. He'll give you a general tour and you can decide who you'd like to interview after that. I'll set up the interviews for you.''

''Sounds fine,'' Whitlock replied.

''I'll organize a dosemeter badge for you,'' she said, reaching for the telephone.

''A what?'' Whitlock asked, affecting ignorance.

''It's a badge containing a strip of masked photographic film worn by all personnel working within the plant itself. When the film's subsequently developed the degree of darkening reveals the radiation dose received.'' She replaced the receiver and gave him an apologetic smile. ''Sorry about having to rush off like this but I promise I'll be free tomorrow.''

''Duty calls,'' he said with a wry grin.

She scribbled something on her memo pad and slid the paper across the desk to him. *Ask me out tonight.*

He looked up in bewilderment and noticed the self-assurance had gone from her eyes. She looked frightened.

''I was wondering, would you be free tonight?''

''Yes,'' she replied, injecting a little hesitancy into her voice.

"I thought we could go out for a meal," he said folding the paper and slipping it into his jacket pocket.

"That would be nice. Did you have anywhere in mind?"

"I'll leave the decision to you."

"The Rheingrill at the Hilton's about the best in town."

"Eight o'clock?" he said.

"I shall look forward to it. You'll have to excuse me now, I've still got a few things to see to before my audience arrives. My assistant will be with you shortly."

He slumped back in the armchair after she had left. What the hell was going on?

It had taken Sabrina forty minutes to drive from Lausanne to Fribourg and another fifteen minutes to find the isolated goodsyard where Teufel, the porter at Lausanne, had said she would find the freight cars. She parked the hired Audi Coupé in front of the wire fence then reached into the back for the holdall containing the Geiger-Muller counter which she had managed to buy after numerous telephone calls to a succession of Lausanne retailers. The icy wind cut across her face as she opened the door and she zipped her anorak up to her throat and tugged the protective hood over her head.

The gate was padlocked from the inside. She slipped the holdall straps over her shoulder and effortlessly scaled the fence, jumping nimbly to the ground when she was halfway down the other side. She crouched down behind a row of freight cars and took in her surroundings: to her right a goods shed, to her left two sets of parallel track and a rusted freight car, its wheels barely visible through the tangled mass of overgrown weeds. The whole area was completely deserted. She transferred the Beretta from her shoulder holster to her anorak pocket then moved down the row of freight cars, checking for the serial number which corresponded with the one Teufel had written down for her. It was stencilled in white paint on the freight car fourth from the front. She took the Geiger-Muller counter from the holdall but couldn't get a reading from around the seal of the door. She then ran her finger along the narrow groove between the door and the frame to check for wires in the unlikely event of it having been booby-trapped. Her fears were groundless and she slid the door back. She saw the shadowy movement out of the corner of her eye and she was still reaching for her Beretta when she was struck heavily on the shoulder, knocking the Geiger-Muller counter from her hand. It smashed against the rusted freight car behind her, shattering the glass exterior and buckling the sensitive anode.

The ginger tomcat glared up at her, its tail lashing furiously from side to side. She waited until it had stalked away before picking up the remains of the Geiger-Muller counter and dropping them into the holdall. Her grim smile was triumphant when she turned back to the open freight car. Its sole contents were six metal beer kegs. She clambered up into the car to take a closer look at them, careful though to remain at what she considered to be a safe distance. All six bungs were sealed and there was no evidence that any of them had ever been damaged. Even a master welder would have left some traces of his craftsmanship. It had to be a trap.

The bullet smashed into the nearest keg. She flung herself to the floor and rolled to safety behind the half-opened door, the Beretta clenched tightly in her gloved hand. Although the gunman had her pinned down he wasn't her immediate threat. Her heart was pounding fearfully as she slowly looked over her shoulder. The bullet had torn a jagged hole in the side of the keg but there was no sign of the deadly plutonium she had imagined would be seeping out into the atmosphere. She let out a deep sigh of relief. These were the decoy kegs after all—Mike had been right. From the angle at which the bullet had penetrated the keg it had to have come from the direction of the shed. The door of the freight car was useless as an escape route: the sniper would have it covered. She noticed one of the wooden struts on the opposite wall had snapped off leaving an aperture the size of a football in the corner of the car. It solved the mystery of how the cat had managed to get inside. She pressed her back against the wall and shuffled on the seat of her jeans to the aperture, her eyes continually flickering towards the open door to ensure she was still out of sight of the shed. Rot had already set into the damp wood and she was able to break chunks off the strut as though they were bits of soggy cardboard. The strut above was more durable but the nails came loose when she struck it firmly with the heel of her boot. She kicked out again, this time cracking it a couple of feet from the juncture with the adjacent wall. The third kick splintered it enough for her to break it off. She peered out through the hole but all she could see was the perimeter fence thirty yards away. Sweating with fear she wriggled through the hole, then ducked under the freight car and crawled slowly forward on her belly between the two sets of rails. Although she couldn't be seen herself, neither could she see the shed or, more importantly, the exact location of the sniper.

She was only a few feet away from the buffer when a rat darted in front of her, and although she jerked her head back sharply its wet tail brushed against her cheek as it disappeared into a gap between the two lengths of corroded track. She bit her lower lip to stifle the cry in her throat and felt the goosepimples bristling across her skin. Where was the damn cat when she needed it most? She had always prided herself on her resoluteness and fortitude but there was one fear she had never managed to conquer—a fear of rats which dated back to an incident when she was three years old. She had been inadvertently locked in a disused cellar and the only sound she heard while cringing in a darkened corner was the incessant stratching as the rats scurried across the concrete floor around her. When she had finally been rescued some two hours later it was discovered that the hem of her frock had been chewed away.

She winced painfully as a burning sensation spread across her cheek, and jerked her hand away from her face. Without realizing it she had been rubbing the area of skin which had touched the rat's tail. She began to crawl forward again, her eyes continually flickering between the tracks on either side of her. Rats, like rabbits, were notorious breeders. She reached the buffer and rolled out from underneath the freight car, safe in the knowledge she was on the sniper's blindspot. Only it worked both ways. The shed was at least twenty yards away and there was no cover.

She took several deep breaths, then broke cover and sprinted in a zigzag weave across the open ground. The first bullet struck the earth behind her, spitting up a mound of soil. The second bullet followed almost immediately, this time in front of her, and she had to fling herself the last few feet, landing heavily against the side of the corrugated-iron door. She massaged her collarbone gingerly and tried to calm her ragged breathing. The bullets had followed each other too quickly from different angles for them to have been fired by the same person. She had an idea where the first sniper had been but in any case he could have moved. The second sniper could be anywhere. She knew it would be tantamount to suicide to try to go in through the open doorway so she made her way cautiously around the side of the building, careful to duck low enough under the shattered windows to avoid detection. There were two doors at the back of the shed, one partially open, its frame warped from years of neglect. It was the only way in. She pressed herself against the wall inches away from the door and used a piece of corroded piping at her feet to ease it open. A volley of bullets immediately peppered the ground directly in front of the doorway, confirming her worst fears. They were armed with semi-automatics, not sniper rifles. Her view of the interior of the shed was limited but what she did see raised her hopes. It was the first bit of luck she had had all afternoon. A faded yellow skip stood a couple of feet from the door, well within diving distance.

She launched herself through the doorway and was safely behind the skip by the time the first bullets rattled against it. There was a vehement curse in German, then silence. The German was somewhere on the H-shaped catwalk on the opposite side of the shed. The other sniper was crouched behind a rusted workbench close to the main doorway. Two black Honda scramblers were parked close to the workbench and her first thought was to put them out of action, but she doubted whether she could get in a clear shot without exposing her head. She heard footsteps on the catwalk and peered up into the semi-darkness trying to get a fix on the German's movements. It was too dark for her to see anything, but from where he was, twenty feet up, she would be perfectly silhouetted against the open door. He was closing in for the kill. She bit her lower lip anxiously, her eyes scanning the darkness above her in a desperate attempt to catch a glimpse of movement. It was all she needed to give her a chance to retaliate. A sudden burst of gunfire from behind the workbench riddled the wall harmlessly behind her. She saw the German at the last possible moment. He was down on one knee, the FN FAL semi-automatic rifle resting lightly on the railing. Its barrel was pointing straight at her. She had no time to aim and fired off four shots in rapid succession. One of the bullets struck his forearm and he cried out, dropping the rifle which clattered noisily on to the concrete floor below.

She was expecting to be pinned down by a concentrated bout of gunfire to give the German a chance to retreat but instead the second sniper swung his FN FAL on the unsuspecting German and gunned him down. He then sprayed a fusillade of bullets across the front of the skip as he pushed one of the scramblers out through the doorway. He kick-started the motorbike and continued to fire wildly behind him as he sped away. By the time she reached the doorway he was out of firing range. She moved cautiously up the corroded metal steps on to the catwalk and knelt beside the German, the Beretta pressed into the nape of his neck. There was no pulse. She pushed the Beretta into her anorak pocket then rolled him on to his back and pulled off his black balaclava. He was in his late thirties with thinning brown hair and a rugged, weatherbeaten face. She went through his pockets but all she found was a spare clip for the FN FAL. She wiped the clip on her anorak, then removed his leather gloves and pressed his fingers on either side of its shiny surface. If he had a criminal record UNACO would have a set of fingerprints. After slipping the clip carefully into her anorak pocket and zipping it closed she descended the steps and scooped up the fallen FN FAL. She ejected the clip and threw it amongst the pile of discarded wooden crates in the corner of the shed, then buried the rifle under a mound of rubble in the pockmarked skip.

Sensing she was being watched, she spun around to face the doorway, the Beretta gripped tightly at arm's length. Immediately she lowered the gun. The two boys were no older than six, their eyes wide and fearful as they stared at the gun hanging limply at her side.

"Are you making a film?" one of them asked innocently in French.

She pocketed the Beretta, her hands still trembling as she thought of how close she had come to firing on the turn. She crossed to the doorway and led them away from the shed.

"Yes, we're making a film," she replied in French, then squatted down in front of them, her hands resting lightly on their shoulders. "What are your names?"

"Marcel."

"Jean-Paul. What's your name?"

"Sabrina."

"Are you really a film star?" Marcel asked.

She nodded, then put a finger to her lips. "Don't tell anyone though, we're filming in secret."

"Where are the cameras?" Jean-Paul asked, looking around him.

"They'll be here later this afternoon. We're just rehearsing at the moment."

"Will you be on television?" Marcel asked.

"Next year," she replied with a smile.

"See, I told you it was a movie," Jean-Paul said and pushed Marcel playfully.

"Didn't," Marcel replied and pushed Jean-Paul back.

"I saw a man here the other day. He said he was also in the film." Jean-Paul gave Marcel another push. "You weren't here. You were sick."

Sabrina stared at Jean-Paul. "What man?"

"He said I wasn't to tell anyone but I guess it's okay seeing you're also in the film. He wasn't as friendly as you."

"Did he say who he was?"

Jean-Paul shook his head. "But I bet he's the baddie."

Sabrina decided to play her hand. "I think I know who you mean. A big man with black hair?"

"Yes. Is he the baddie?"

Sabrina nodded. "What was he doing?"

"He and another man were putting some barrels into that wagon over there. He said it's part of the film."

"How long have those wagons been standing there?" Sabrina asked, trying to bring Marcel back into the conversation.

He shrugged and glanced at Jean-Paul. "Since we started playing here."

"How long's that?"

He shrugged again. "A long time."

"Will you be here tomorrow?" Jean-Paul asked.

"I don't know yet," she lied. "How about you?"

"We play here every day," Jean-Paul replied, then gave Marcel a playful shove before running away towards the fence.

Marcel scowled then ran after him.

She waited until they were out of sight before returning to the shed. The German was too heavy for her to drag down the steps, so she reluctantly decided to push him off the catwalk. She cupped her hands underneath him and eased him over the edge. She felt momentarily nauseated as the body struck the concrete floor but quickly regained her composure and, after hurrying down the steps, she scanned the shed for a suitable place to hide the body. A row of corroded steel drums caught her eye but she quickly discounted

them. Even if she could have got him into one, which
she very much doubted, there was no guarantee it
could hold his weight without breaking. A tattered
brown tarpaulin bundled in the corner of the shed? Not
only would it be an obvious place to look but she was
uneasy about what might be living underneath it. A
picture of the rat crossed her mind and she instinctively rubbed the back of her hand across her cheek.
The workbench? She crouched down and jerked open
the two doors, fully expecting the cupboard to have
been converted into a homely little rat lair. Plenty of
cobwebs but no rats. The space was divided in two by
a metal shelf, which she managed to dislodge and pull
out. Then she dragged the body to the workbench and
pushed it into the cupboard, head first. There was
enough room for the body, except for the left arm. No
matter how she tried she couldn't prevent the arm from
flopping out on to the floor.

With a lot of effort she finally managed to close the
left-hand door and bolt it into place, then pushed the
arm against the dead man's chest and forced the other
door over, sliding the remains of a file through two
loops where the handles had once been to keep it shut.
She piled a mound of rubble in front of it, then took
the FN FAL from the skip and hid it in a length of
hollow piping above the catwalk. The scrambler was
next. It was too big to conceal in the shed so she
wheeled it outside and hid it in the freight car containing the metal beer kegs. It would only be a matter
of time before it was discovered but it was the best
she could do in such a short time. She knelt beside the
damaged keg and peered through the serrated bullet

hole. The keg was empty. She then tested its weight against the individual weights of the other five kegs. They too were empty. After jumping nimbly from the freight car she closed the door, picked up her holdall, and hurried towards the fence.

She would phone her report to Philpott as soon as she got back to the hotel.

The Rome-bound train had been unavoidably delayed in Montreux after a small avalanche had blocked the track five miles further up the line. It was due fifty minutes late in Martigny, its next scheduled stop, twenty-five miles south of Montreux.

Graham had already budgeted on being in Martigny ten minutes prior to the train's scheduled arrival so when he reached the station he found he actually had an hour to kill. He decided to while it away in the station cafeteria and was already on his third cup of coffee when the train's approach was announced over the Tannoy.

He picked up his two black holdalls and went out on to the platform to watch the train pull into the station. The locked wheels shrieked as they slid along the rails and the train finally shuddered to a halt in a cloud of hissing steam. He made a mental note of the number of coaches and freight cars. Six coaches and eight freight cars.

He crossed to the guard and tapped him on the arm. "How long is the train due to stay here?"

"Twenty minutes," the guard replied, then hurried away to help someone with his luggage.

A movement caught his eye and he looked back at the man standing on the steps of the rear coach.

The man was in his early forties with jet-black hair combed back from a cruel menacing face and the kind of muscular physique usually associated with a body-builder. He alighted from the coach, seemingly oblivious to his surroundings, and walked the length of the freight cars, stopping beside the last one. He unlocked the bulky padlock and eased the door open. The man who climbed out of the freight car was at least six feet five inches high, a couple of inches taller than the other man, with a horrendously scarred face and a dyed blond pigtail dangling grotesquely from the back of an otherwise shaven head. The black-haired man slid the door shut but refrained from padlocking it.

Graham waited until the two men were seated in the cafeteria before moving down the platform to the freight car. He glanced around, satisfied that nobody was taking any notice of his suspicious behaviour, then opened the door fractionally and peered inside. A nylon Firebird sleeping bag was laid out on the floor directly in front of the door, obviously being used as a makeshift pillow. There was an overwhelming stench of stale urine and sweat from inside the freight car but Graham swallowed back the rising bile in his throat and eased the door open further to see what else it might contain. A sealed wooden crate, twelve feet by six, with *WERNER FRACHT, ERHARDSTRASSE, MÜNCHEN* stencilled in black paint across its facing side. He placed the holdall inside the freight car and activated the Geiger-Muller counter inside it. The counter emitted a monotonous crackle. The freight car was contaminated.

He heard the approaching footsteps on the gravel behind him.

"Cosa desidera?" The flush-faced man was in his mid-fifties with a thick grey moustache and a pair of pebble glasses perched precariously on his bulbous nose. He was dressed in a pale-blue tunic and trousers with a red trim around the sleeves and lapels.

"What did you say?" Graham asked casually as he zipped up the holdall.

"I asked what do you want? This is private property."

"Really, and here I thought trains were for the public."

The man struggled to marshal his thoughts and translate them into English. "They are, but this wagon is private property."

"You're making sense now." Graham pointed to the crate. "Whose is this?"

"I ask the questions! What are you doing here?"

"Looking."

"Looking? Are you a passenger?"

Graham nodded. "And what are you?"

"I'm the conductor. Show me your ticket."

"Sure, when I'm on the train."

Graham picked up his holdalls and walked away to the cafeteria, where he changed a couple of Swiss francs into loose change then made a call on one of the public telephones, positioning himself in such a way so he could study the two men as he described them to Philpott. He replaced the receiver, having been given his new instructions.

Stay with the train at all costs.

The two men left the cafeteria when the train's departure was announced over the Tannoy. The black-haired man closed his accomplice in the freight car again, padlocked the door, then glanced round as the conductor hurried towards him.

"Excuse me, sir, you said I was to tell you if anyone came snooping around the wagon while you were in the cafeteria," the conductor said excitedly in Italian.

"So?" came the nonchalant reply.

"There was somebody, sir. An American."

"Excellent. What was he doing?"

The conductor removed his peak cap and scratched his wiry hair thoughtfully. "He had something hidden in his holdall. I couldn't see what it was but it made a funny crackling noise."

"So where is he now?"

"On the train, sir. Do you want me to watch him for you?"

"If I did I'd tell you."

"Yes, sir," the conductor replied obsequiously.

"Point this American out to my friend on the train. Tell him you've already spoken to me."

"Yes, sir."

The man peeled off two bank notes from the roll in his pocket and stuffed them into the conductor's tunic pocket.

"Thank you, sir," the conductor said, then scurried away.

The man stood thoughtfully on the platform as the train slowly pulled out of the station.

The bait, in the form of the unlocked freight car, had been taken. The plans would have to be altered accordingly and that meant first attending to some unfinished business at Lausanne station.

The prospect of a candlelit dinner with a visiting British nurse had had Dieter Teufel glancing at his wristwatch all day. With less than twenty minutes of his shift remaining he had already decided on the clothes he would be wearing for the special occasion. A Roser Marce blue linen suit and a cream Christian Dior shirt. Not that he could ever have afforded to buy those kind of designer clothes on his meagre wage but with the money he had received to throw the American and his beautiful assistant, or rather partner, off the scent he had been able to splash out for once in his life. All he had done was follow instructions. He had no idea what any of it was about but who was he to complain when he was being paid so well? And, according to the black-haired man, there would be more to come . . .

He watched the approaching passenger train from Interlaken. It contained his least favourite type of commuters, the Yuppies with their expensive skiing gear and false tales of bravado which were shouted, rather than spoken, to relatives on the platform. He pushed past a group of waiting relatives (why people insisted on waving when the train was still so far away had always been a mystery to him) and glanced round sharply at a teenage girl who elbowed him accidentally, but painfully, in the back. She smiled ruefully, then continued to wave frantically at the approaching train.

The engine was less than five yards away when he felt a hand shove him hard in the small of the back. He stumbled then fell on to the track, his scream silenced abruptly as he disappeared beneath the screeching wheels.

Karen Schendel walked into the Hilton foyer punctually at eight o'clock. Whitlock, who had been watching the entrance from the comfort of an armchair for the past ten minutes, got to his feet and shook her extended hand.

"Thanks for coming," she said with a smile. "I thought you might have written me off as a crackpot after my performance this morning."

"Hardly, but I do admit to being both baffled and intrigued. I must say you're looking lovely tonight."

She was wearing a turquoise silk dress, her newly washed black hair spilling on to her narrow shoulders.

"Thank you," she said softly, fidgeting with her pearls.

"Well, shall we go through or would you prefer a drink first?"

"Let's go through to the restaurant, we'll have more privacy to talk there."

The maître d'hôtel beamed at her. *"Ah, guten Abend, Fraulein Schendel."*

"Guten Abend, Franz. I believe Mr. Whitlock booked a table for us," she said, subtly switching to English.

"Please don't change to English just because I'm here. I do speak German, only it needs a major overhaul to set it right."

"Your German was word perfect when we spoke earlier, Mr. Whitlock," Franz said.

"I should hope so. I practised it enough times in the car coming here," Whitlock replied with a grin.

Karen chuckled. "Hidden talents?"

"Some talents are better left that way," Whitlock replied as they followed Franz to a table for two in the corner of the restaurant.

"Is this one of your regular haunts?" Whitlock asked after their order had been taken.

"When the company's paying. I'm not really one for dining out. You might find this hard to believe but I'm the kind of person who likes nothing more than to potter about the house in a pair of jeans and a sweater and eat spaghetti Bolognese. I guess I never really grew out of the tomboy stage."

"Where did you pick up your English?"

"In Britain. After graduating from Mainz University I went over there for three years as a lab assistant, first at Dounreay then at Calder Hall. I only became interested in public relations once I had come back to Germany."

"How long have you been involved in PR work?"

"Five years now, the last two as head of PR here in Mainz. I'm also in charge of the hiring of the plant's non-technical staff. Guards, drivers, cleaners, personnel like that."

The wine steward presented the wine bottle for Whitlock's inspection. He nodded.

Karen watched the steward opening the bottle at the sideboard. "How long have you been with the *New York Times*?"

"About four years."

"Then you'll probably know a friend of mine. John Marsh?"

He shook his head. "Can't say I do, but you must remember I'm only there in a freelance capacity. I've never been on the permanent staff."

"Of course, it said you were a freelance writer in your introductory letter. So, as you'd say in journalism, you're a stringer."

"Right," Whitlock replied, returning her smile.

The wine steward returned with the open bottle and poured a measure for Whitlock to taste. On receiving the customary nod he filled both glasses and left the bottle in the ice bucket by the side of the table.

"You're not really a journalist, are you?" she said quietly.

Whitlock felt cornered. His stomach was churning but he knew he could elude her if only he could remain calm and call her bluff. "You're an intriguing person. This morning you mysteriously slide me a note telling me to ask you out and now you claim I'm not really a journalist even though my credentials were thoroughly checked out by your plant manager before he let me near the place. I feel as though I'm disintegrating before my very eyes. By the end of the night I won't know who I am or what I do any more. You don't work for the KGB by any chance?"

She ignored his gentle sarcasm. "If you worked for the *Times* you'd have known John. He writes a daily showbiz column for them. He's the epitome of the extrovert, he knows everyone and everyone knows him.'' She noticed the lingering doubt in his eyes. ''When I heard you were coming I made some discreet enquiries about you at the newspaper. John's never heard of you.''

She stopped talking when the waiter arrived with the food, then picked up the conversation again after he had left.

''You probably think I'm making this up. We can phone John if you like: he'll be putting the finishing touches to his column for the morning edition. You can speak to him yourself.''

Whitlock stared at his plate, his appetite suddenly gone.

''Also, if you'd really been a journalist you'd have known what a 'stringer' is. You didn't. A 'stringer' isn't just a freelancer—it's a correspondent based away from head office whose local contacts give him an on-the-spot usefulness which far surpasses that of a reporter sent out from head office.''

''So how come you know so much about journalism?''

''I used to date John when he was stationed in Berlin. He was supposed to be the paper's foreign correspondent but instead of filing everyday reports like the other journalists he became obsessed with chasing after so-called spies and spent most of the time commuting between East and West Germany hoping to land the big scoop.''

''And did he?''

She put her hand to her lips, trying not to laugh with

her mouth full. "Sorry," she said after swallowing. "He wrote a story, with pictures to back it up, about an American general supposedly handing over documents to a beautiful KGB agent on Hamburg's Kennedy Bridge. The KGB agent turned out to be a Reeperbahn hooker and the documents a couple of hundred marks for services rendered. He was hauled back to New York and given that column to keep him out of any more mischief."

Whitlock smiled politely, his mind still reeling from the way she had dissected his cover story, piece by piece, until there was nothing left for him to hide behind. Nothing like it had ever happened at UNACO. He felt humiliated. Outclassed and outmanoeuvred by a pretty face—or rather by what lay behind it. As he watched her eating he knew what would have to be done if she tried to expose him publicly. His hand brushed against the holstered Browning Mk2 . . .

"What intrigues me most of all is how you managed to get someone like the editor of the *New York Times* to agree to back up your cover story."

He could have answered that in one word. Philpott. He had a sneaking suspicion Philpott had members of staff whose sole function was to dig up the personal indiscretions of those people who could be beneficial to UNACO, then use them as a form of blackmail to get what he wanted. It was only a theory but it had always amazed him, and the other field operatives, how Philpott could come up with solid cover stories at such short notice. Solid, that is, until now . . .

"Is there something wrong with the *Sauerbraten*,

sir?'' Franz asked anxiously at Whitlock's shoulder. "You've hardly touched it."

"On the contrary, my compliments to the chef. I think I've got a touch of indigestion." He looked at Karen. "Acidity, I believe?"

"Can I get you something for it, sir?"

"No, thank you, just take the plate away."

"Would you like anything else, sir?" Franz asked as he reluctantly removed the plate from the table.

"Coffee and cognac," Karen said quickly.

"For two?" Franz asked.

Whitlock nodded.

She waited until they were alone then rested her elbows on the table, her clenched hands under her chin. "I know how you must feel but I had to be sure you weren't another journalist out for a story."

"I hope you're satisfied."

"I'm satisfied you're not a journalist. I don't know who you're really working for but it must be a pretty influential organization to have the editor of the *New York Times* over a barrel."

After the coffee and cognac were served she delved into her handbag and withdrew a folded sheet of paper which she held out to him.

"What's this?" he asked, taking it from her.

"Look."

He unfolded the paper. It was a scale drawing of a miniature microphone, perfectly reproduced, which was in reality no larger than a sugar cube.

"A bug. What's it got to do with me?"

"That bug's stuck under my desk. I came across it by chance a couple of months ago. That's why I slipped you the note this morning. I had to speak to you in private.'' She rubbed her face and when she dropped her hands her eyes had welled up with tears. ''You're my last hope, C.W.''

He handed her his breast pocket handkerchief and studied her carefully as she dabbed her eyes. Gone was the confident, self-assured woman and in its place an uncertain, frightened child. She was either on the level or a damn good actress. He decided to leave his options open.

''I'm sorry,'' she said, gripping the handkerchief in both hands. ''I just feel so helpless.''

''You want to talk about it?''

She held her coffee cup between her palms and met his eyes. ''Have you ever heard of the term, 'diversion'?''

He sat forward attentively. ''MUF?''

''There's a difference. Diversion's a general euphemism for theft. 'Materials unaccounted for' is the specific term used for any kind of discrepancy between the book inventory and the actual inventory.''

''What exactly are you trying to say?''

''That there's nuclear material being siphoned off without it affecting the inventory system.''

''Have you reported it?''

She sat back in her chair. ''I can't report suspicions and that's all I have at the moment.''

''Why are you telling *me* this? What makes you think you can trust me?''

''I need outside help. You're my only chance. I can't confide in anyone at the plant. I couldn't be certain they weren't involved somehow in the diversion. Anyway, an attempt's already been made on my life.''

''They know you suspect?''

The waiter returned with a fresh pot of percolated coffee and refilled their cups.

Karen added some milk to her coffee and stirred it. ''I kept a diary in my desk recording all my thoughts and suspicions. One night it was stolen. Two days later someone tampered with the brakes of my car.''

''Did you report it?''

''Naturally, but the plant manager was convinced it was only something to do with the Friends of the Earth. I've never gone along with that theory. Our views may be poles apart but they're not saboteurs. No, it was an inside job.'' She took a sip of coffee. ''They've also managed to get into my house while I was at work. Nothing's ever been taken; all they did was rearrange the lounge furniture. I suppose it's their way of saying they can get at me whenever they want. I'm frightened C.W., I'm really frightened.''

He was perturbed by her capricious behaviour. He felt like a boxer who had been pummelled mercilessly against the ropes, on the verge of defeat, only to see his opponent's corner throw in the towel. It never happened in boxing. He thought back to his options. Was she acting? Was she, in fact, part of the team responsible for the plutonium thefts? Was she the bait to lure him into a trap? Or, on the other hand, was she on the level? Was she genuinely reaching out to him as a last source of help? Was she really in fear of her life? They were all questions which both puzzled and disturbed him, yet at the same time he knew she was the key to helping him expose the diversion at the plant. He had to stick with her, irrespective of where her true loyalties lay.

"You don't believe me, do you?"

"You're putting words into my mouth," he replied defensively.

"And you're evading the question."

He dabbed his mouth with the napkin. "I don't disbelieve you."

"The classic reply. You come to the reprocessing plant posing as a journalist but really you're on some undercover assignment for a powerful organization, maybe for a government. I hardly think you went to all this trouble just to check the plumbing. We both know why you're here. I thought I'd be helping you by telling you what I did. I want to help you, C.W., can't you see that?" She leaned forward and gripped his wrists. "If the plutonium were to fall into the wrong hands the results could be catastrophic. It would also give the anti-nuclear group some propaganda to use against us." She smiled apologetically and released his hands. "I believe passionately in the future of this industry but what chance have we got when an avaricious few are using it for their own crazy purposes?"

"Can you give me a list of the employees you think are involved in the diversion?"

"I'll have it for you first thing in the morning."

"I intend writing the story I came here to find."

"Of course, you need to keep your cover intact."

"As I said to you earlier, I'm a freelance writer. The article should appear in the *Times* a couple of days after I get back to New York. Perhaps your friend could send you a copy." He called for the bill.

When Franz arrived with it Karen deftly plucked it from the sideplate and held up a hand to silence Whitlock's protest. "It's the least I can do. Anyway, the company's paying."

She slipped her hand through the crook of his arm once they emerged into the foyer and they walked in silence to the lift to go down to the basement car park.

The change in temperature was immediately noticeable when the lift doors parted and she tugged her shawl closer around her shoulders as the cold night air swirled around them.

"Where are you parked?"

"In the corner, it's all I could find," she replied. "It's pretty busy tonight. Probably a conference."

They took no notice of the black Mercedes as it slipped noiselessly out of the parking space behind them, the driver's foot hovering over the accelerator. It crept forward, slowly building up speed, and when it was twenty yards behind them the driver pressed the accelerator to the floor. Whitlock shoved Karen out of the way and had to fling himself on to the bonnet of a BMW as the Mercedes flashed past, missing him by inches. The driver spun the wheel as the Mercedes reached the end of the row of parked cars and it skidded sideways, the left corner of the rear bumper crumpling in a flash of sparks as it glanced off the wall. The driver changed down gears and sped up the ramp, smashing through the boomgate, and disappeared out into the street.

Whitlock hurried over to where Karen was huddled

against a pillar, her head buried in her arms. He crouched down beside her and put his hand lightly on her shoulder. She put her arms around his neck and pressed her face against his chest. He became aware of someone behind him and was reaching for his Browning when he saw the uniform. He let his hand drop.

"Are you all right?" the boomgate operator asked anxiously.

"We're okay, thanks."

The man moved off to summon his superiors who, in turn, would summon the police.

"Are you all right?" Whitlock asked as he helped her to her feet.

"I'm okay," she replied in a shaky voice. "How about you?"

"I'll survive," he replied with a grim smile. "Have you ever seen that car before?"

"Never. Did you get a look at the driver?"

"No, it was all too quick," he lied.

Not that he had seen much. A Caucasian face partially shaded by a trilby. It wasn't much to go on but he was determined to keep the information to himself.

"And the number plate?"

"Blacked out with masking tape," he replied. "There's no point in us hanging around here any longer. The last thing we need is to have the police involved."

"I'll make you some coffee at my place," she said, taking her car keys from her handbag.

"Thanks anyway but I want to get back to the hotel and soak my shoulders in a hot bath. It's already getting a bit stiff. Anyway, you've got that list to prepare. The car won't be back tonight.''

She kissed him lightly on the cheek. ''I owe you one.''

''You don't owe me anything. Now, go on. I'll see you in the morning.''

As he walked to his car he was already planning his report for Philpott. Top priority would be a thorough screening of Karen Schendel. As he left the underground car park, the driver of the black Mercedes parked in the shadows of a driveway opposite pulled out into the road, and followed the Golf Corbio at a safe distance.

SIX

Largo Antiks was a small, nondescript antiques shop on the corner of Beethoven and Dreikönigstrasse in Zurich. It was run by two balding, bespectacled men in their late thirties, neither of whom was called Largo, whose extensive knowledge of antiques had made it one of the most popular and profitable shops of its kind in the whole canton. Both men worked for UN-ACO. The shop was a front for UNACO's European headquarters. It had been bought with a United Nations grant of 1980 on the understanding that all profits would be channelled discreetly into a numbered Swiss bank account to be used exclusively by UNICEF.

A bell jangled above the door when Philpott entered the shop, followed by Sabrina and Kolchinsky. The assistant behind the counter acknowledged them with a curt nod and his eyes flickered towards an area of the shop hidden from the entrance. Philpott understood the gesture and browsed through the antiques until the lone customer had left the shop. The assistant then ushered them through the doorway behind the counter, removed a sonic transmitter from his pocket and pointed it at the empty bookcase against the opposite wall. He activated the transmitter and the bookcase swivelled outwards to reveal a concrete passage behind. Sabrina always got a kick out of the swivelling bookcase; it was like something out of a Boris Karloff film. So much more interesting than Philpott's drab wall panels at the United Nations headquarters. They set off down the passage and the assistant sealed them in before returning to the shop.

Half a dozen unmarked doors lined the passage, behind each of which was a soundproofed room where highly skilled UNACO personnel operated some of the world's most advanced and sophisticated computer systems in the struggle to put a stop to the alarming rise in international crime. Philpott led them to a pale-blue door at the end of the passage. He pressed a buzzer. An overhead camera panned each face in turn before the door was opened. It led into the plush office of Jacques Rust, head of UNACO's European operation.

Rust closed the door by remote control then activated his mechanized wheelchair and approached them. He was a forty-two-year-old Frenchman with a distinctly handsome face and sparkling blue eyes. He had spent fourteen years with the French *Service de Documentation Extérieure et de Contre-Espionage* before becoming one of Philpott's first field operatives when UNACO was founded in 1980. He had been paired off with Whitlock. When Philpott received official permission to increase his field operatives from twenty to thirty he put Sabrina with them to form the original Strike Force Three.

Less than a year later Rust and Sabrina were on a routine stakeout at the Marseilles docks when they had come under heavy fire from a gang of drug smugglers and Rust was hit in the spine, leaving him paralysed from the waist down. He was initially given a senior position at the Command Centre in the United Nations but when the head of the European operation died in a car crash (which was subsequently proved to have been an accident and not sabotage as originally thought) Philpott surprised many of his team by appointing him, and not Kolchinsky, as the dead man's successor. It had been a shrewd, but wise, choice and the ties between Zurich and New York had never been stronger.

"Colonel, I wasn't expecting you until tomorrow," Rust said as he shook hands with both men. "You should have let me know you were coming earlier, I'd have had a car waiting at the airport for you."

Philpott eased himself into an armchair, leaning his cane against the wall. After graduating from Sandhurst Military College with the coveted Sword of Honour he had first seen active duty in Korea where he suffered a serious leg injury while attempting to rescue a wounded colleague. It had left him with a pronounced limp in his left leg. "We took the morning flight on SwissAir. Sabrina was there to meet us."

Sabrina kissed him on both cheeks then ran her hand lightly over his hair. "How many times must I tell you, don't cut your hair so short. It shows your receding hairline.''

"Still as complimentary as ever," Rust added drily.

"Oh, I've got something for you," she said, handing him the FN FAL magazine clip now sealed in a plastic bag. "There's a set of prints on it. Your boffins shouldn't have too much trouble in coming up with a name.''

Rust phoned out on his internal line for someone to fetch the clip. He replaced the receiver and looked up. "Anyone for coffee before we start?"

All three declined.

"There's been a new development since I received your telex yesterday. An avalanche's blocked the track outside Sion and first reports say it won't be cleared before daybreak. That means the train's going to be delayed there overnight.''

"Why do I get the feeling this is more than just coincidence?" Philpott asked as he tapped the dottle from his pipe into the ashtray beside him.

Rust smiled. "The snow's very loose on the Wildhorn at this time of year and all it took was a small charge to start the ball rolling, if you'll excuse the pun. I thought we might need the extra time to help consolidate our position. Although judging by the telex you've already tracked down the plutonium.''

"Perhaps," Kolchinsky said, entering the conversation for the first time. "The Geiger counter picked up levels of radiation but we already knew those kegs had been stored in that particular freight car. Now it contains a sealed crate belonging to Werner Freight. What we don't know is whether that crate contains the kegs. If we jump the gun and point a finger at Stefan Werner without sufficient evidence and it turns out we were in the wrong he's got enough sway to splash UN-ACO across the front page of every newspaper in Europe.''

A light flashed on the desk and after checking the video camera Rust activated the door. He handed the plastic bag to the white-coated technician and asked to be told the moment the fingerprints were identified.

''I don't think he would,'' Sabrina said after the technician had left.

''What?'' Philpott asked, the lighter poised over the mouth of his pipe.

''Stefan. He's not a vindictive person. If he knew it was a matter of international security I'm certain he wouldn't object to having the crate opened.''

''Stefan?'' Rust said raising his eyebrows. ''I didn't know we were on first-name terms.''

''I went out with him a couple of times when I was at the Sorbonne.''

''You never said you knew him,'' Philpott said sharply.

''I went to a couple of parties with him, that's all.''

''How well did you know him?''

''I never slept with him if that's what you mean, sir,'' she shot back angrily. ''We were friends, that's all. I haven't seen him since I left Switzerland five years ago.''

''What kind of person was he?'' Kolchinsky asked.

''Ambitious,'' she replied. ''Very ambitious. His work was his life.''

The telephone rang and Rust snatched up the receiver. He gave a thumbs-up sign then replaced it and manoeuvred his wheelchair round behind his desk where he tapped his security code into the IBM computer linked up to the central data bank elsewhere in the building.

"We're in business," he said when the relevant entry appeared on the screen. "The fingerprints check out to one Kurt Rauff."

"What have you got on him?" Philpott asked.

"You British have a term for him. An international milk thief."

"A petty villain in other words," Philpott replied with a hint of irritation in his voice. "What was he mixed up in?"

"This and that. He had a number of convictions, all small sentences. Pickpocketing, cheque fraud, embezzlement."

"Hardly your gun-toting sniper," Sabrina said.

"Not so quick, *chérie*," Rust replied, holding up a finger. "It seems he's elevated himself into the big league these past four years. He was involved in gun-running for the likes of Dauphin, Giselle and Umbretti."

"It's audacious enough for any of them," Philpott said, biting the stem of his pipe thoughtfully. "Any luck yet with the two men Mike saw on the train?"

"We've come up with a few names. Most of them correspond with the list your boys drew up at the UN. I've got men asking around."

"May I see that telex?" Sabrina asked.

Rust pointed to it lying on his desk.

She read it through then looked up at Philpott. "You

haven't mentioned that the black-haired man has different coloured eyes.''

"What?" Philpott replied in bewilderment.

"Didn't C.W. tell you, sir?"

"I didn't speak to him. He called at night and spoke to the duty officer. That's the description he passed on to me."

"Jacques, you might . . ." she trailed off seeing Rust's grim expression.

"One brown, one green, *n'est-ce pas*?"

She nodded slowly.

Rust stared at the screen. "His name's Joachim Hendrique."

"Balashikha," Kolchinsky whispered, ashen-faced.

"Balashikha? The KGB's training school for Third World terrorists?" Philpott asked, staring at Kolchinsky.

Kolchinsky nodded. "Run by Directorate S, the most feared division within the KGB itself."

"There's no mention of Balashikha here," Rust announced after scanning the screen.

"I'm not surprised. The true identity of Balashikha graduates is known only to the most senior members of Directorate S. The whole place is shrouded in secrecy."

"So how do you know about him?" Philpott asked.

"Hendrique was reputed to have been the best student ever to graduate from Balashikha. That kind of information tends to leak out to other members of the KGB hierarchy. Accidently-on-purpose, if you get my meaning."

"Was he one of the names on the list?" Philpott asked Rust.

Rust shook his head. "The only known photographs of him are a series of blurred snapshots taken by the CIA official in Nicaragua. The features must have been too indistinct to program into the computer. The identikit can only match faces already stored in the memory bank."

"Yet you knew who he was the moment I mentioned his eyes," Sabrina said, sitting forward, her interest stimulated.

"He once tried to kill me. It happened while I was still with the *SDECE*. We'd received a tip-off about a shipment of cocaine due in at Nice aboard a South American freighter, so when it was unloaded we were able to apprehend the gang without much of a struggle. A couple of them made a break for it. I chased one into a warehouse where he managed to double back and attack me from behind. He knocked my gun from my hand then pushed me up against the wall, pressing his own gun into my stomach. He was wearing a balaclava so all I could see was his eyes. One brown, one green. He pulled the trigger but the chamber was empty. Most criminals would have panicked at that moment. He just laughed. Then he hit me with the butt of his gun and the next thing I remember is coming round to find my colleagues crouched anxiously beside me. He'd escaped. I'll never forget those eyes as long as I live."

"If you never saw his face . . ."

"Having differently coloured eyes is rare enough but he also had the distinctive physique of a bodybuilder,"

Rust said, cutting in across Kolchinsky's words. "It's the same man, Sergei, I'd stake my career on it."

"What does it say about him?" Philpott asked, pointing to the VDU.

Rust read through the text, translating the salient points from French into English. "He was born in Chad in 1947 and raised by missionaries. He ran away to sea at fifteen and made a name for himself as a good, but sadistic, fist fighter. He next surfaced in Amsterdam in 1969 as an insurrectionist amongst the more seditious members of the hippy community and was instrumental in provoking clashes between them and the police. He was never caught. He went to ground and wasn't heard of again until 1975 when word reached the CIA that he was training the Marxist MPLA soldiers in Angola. After Angola he went to Nicaragua where he fought with the Sandanistas until the downfall of Somoza in 1980. Since then he's become involved in illegal gunrunning operations across Europe. He's also known to deal in drugs in and around Amsterdam where it's rumoured he lived on a houseboat somewhere in the Jordan area. His favourite weapons are a .357 Desert Eagle, which he always carries on his person, and a Franchi Spas shotgun. There's one point that isn't in his dossier. He never works for himself. He merely employs the muscle and makes sure the whole operation runs according to plan."

"You have to give him credit for his choice of weapons, especially the Desert Eagle," Sabrina said.

"Can you put a name to his accomplice?" Kolchinsky asked.

Rust opened the file on his desk and ran his finger down the list of suspects. One name caught his eye and he programmed it into the computer. "Akkid Milchan. Thirty-seven years old. Six feet five. Egyptian. Mute. His face was scarred in an explosion aboard a Liberian tanker in 1979. He also lives in Amsterdam and has been working, off and on, for Hendrique since 1982."

"At least now we've got an idea who we're up against. Jacques, you said this Rauff has been mixed up with the likes of Dauphin, Giselle and Umbretti. Find out if any of them has been linked to Hendrique over the past few months. I also want Werner checked out, but for God's sake be discreet." Philpott crossed to a map of Europe on the wall as Rust reached for the telephone to relay the orders. "Sabrina?"

She sprang nimbly to her feet and approached him, her hands thrust into the pockets of her baggy camouflage pants.

"The train's stuck at Sion," he said, prodding the name on the map with the end of his pipe.

"And will be until morning," she added.

"Precisely," he said, giving her the kind of look a great thespian might give an impish soubrette who had just delivered his punchline. "I know it's been a long day but I want you to drive to Sion tonight. You've got a berth reserved on the train so you'll be able to get some sleep once you get there. Mike needs to be filled in on the latest developments."

"You think Stefan's involved, don't you?"

"Not necessarily, but I do think the crate contains the kegs."

"What makes you so sure, sir?"

"Instinct."

She smiled. "You sound like Mike."

Rust manoeuvred his wheelchair out from behind the desk and stopped in the centre of the room. "Anyone hungry? I know this little restaurant round the corner that serves a delicious *choucroute garnie*."

"I'm famished," Philpott said, then turned to Sabrina. "Have something to eat with us before you go."

"Thank you, sir, but I'll grab a bit on the way there."

"*Friture de perchettes* served in butter sauce? Your favourite, *chérie*," Rust said, then kissed the tips of his bunched fingers.

"Another time, Jacques. I want to get to Sion as soon as possible."

Rust pulled on his jacket, then led the way out into the passage and through a side door into the street, the antiques shop now being closed. Sabrina zipped up her anorak as she stepped out into the cold night air and rummaged in her pockets for the keys to the Audi Coupé.

"Come on, I'll escort you to your car."

Philpott gave her a reassuring smile, then he and Kolchinsky disappeared around the corner in search of the restaurant.

"Want a push?"

"It'll be like old times again with you watching my back," Rust replied with a grin.

"And look what happened," she said bitterly.

He looked round at her. "Why can't you accept that it wasn't your fault? If you'd stuck your head out to give me covering fire you wouldn't be pushing this wheelchair. You know damn well I've never blamed you for what happened that night; it was one of those risks we had to take. Anyway, why must this discussion always crop up whenever we see each other?''

She remained silent.

"How's Mike these days?" he asked, broaching the silence.

"Fine," she answered absently.

"Send him my regards," he said as they reached the Audi Coupé.

"I will." She unlocked the driver's door, hugged him and quickly climbed inside.

He waited until the Audi Coupé had merged with the evening traffic before making his way to the restaurant. Philpott and Kolchinsky were seated at the table nearest the trellised entrance of the small cocktail bar.

"You didn't have to sit here just because of me," he said, giving the barman the customary wave. It meant he would have his usual.

"It saves you weaving through all those tables and chairs," Kolchinsky replied.

"This is my very own Monza," Rust said, extending his arms.

"How long before you get some feedback on Werner and the others?" Philpott asked.

"It'll be brought to me as soon as it comes through. You suspect Werner, don't you?"

"I certainly think his company's involved somewhere along the line. If it does turn out he's personally involved I've got a feeling it's going to be difficult as hell trying to prove it.''

"Herr Stefan Werner."
Heads automatically turned to look when the toast-master made the announcement.

Werner was in his late forties with a short, stocky physique, thinning brown hair and a neatly trimmed russet moustache that tapered down over the corners of his mouth. He had a charismatic quality about him that had long made him one of Europe's most eligible bachelors. He entered the palatial ballroom and took in his surroundings, mentally assessing the wealth of his hosts. He ignored the mottled marble floor, the neo-Doric pillars and the intricately carved oak ceiling. His only interest was in the collection of paintings lining the oak-panelled walls. Houses could be paid off gradually; paintings had to be bought outright. He regarded it as a fairly accurate way of weeding out the pretenders from the cream of Europe's opulent élite.

The hostess broke away from a clique of friends and bustled towards him, arms outstretched. They embraced fleetingly. She was the granddaughter of some forgotten Prussian nobleman and she and her husband had once owned a beautiful sixteenth-century castle overlooking the town of Assmannshausen in the Rhine Valley before selling it in favour of their present mansion on the outskirts of Berlin. They insisted it had been a step up the social ladder; he secretly disagreed.

"I'm so glad you could make it tonight, Stefan. You know how popular you are with the *single* ladies."

"You flatter me, Marisa," Werner replied with an

affected smile. "You know how much I enjoy your parties. I'm only sorry I had a prior engagement, otherwise I'd have been here much earlier."

He had long since mastered the art of tactful lying.

"You're here, that's the main thing. I believe you were at the theatre?"

"At the Philharmonie actually. A recital of Handel's *Messiah* by the Berlin Philharmonic and the Schönberg Boys' Choir. I missed it the last time round."

"It sounds as if you enjoyed it," she said, leading him across the room.

"It's not enjoyment, it's ecstasy," he replied, and helped himself to a glass of champagne from the tray of a passing waiter.

He caught the tail end of a whispered discussion behind him regarding his worth and was horrified to hear the group settle on a figure of 150 million pounds. Had they trebled it they would have been nearer the truth. Not only did he own Werner Lines, a worldwide shipping empire with more than 140 vessels in commission, but he had also branched out into the freight industry over the past four years and succeeded in cornering an important section of its competitive market by buying out a succession of small, struggling companies and amalgamating them under an experienced board of directors answerable only to him. With his freight company working hand-in-hand with his shipping line he was able to undercut his competitors by offering their clientele the kind of package deals no company director could resist. His success rate was obvious by the number of struggling competitors, many of whom he subsequently bought out to add to his ever growing empire . . .

"Stefan, I nearly forgot to tell you. There's someone here to see you."

Another of her unattached friends who always seemed to find their way on to the invitation list whenever she was certain he would be at one of her soirées. He knew she only had his best interests at heart but he had yet to meet one of these women whose interest in him stemmed beyond his bank balance. Anyway, his standing in society was far too high to have it blackened by the indiscreet infidelities of a wife bored with her husband's success. He had seen too many prominent European industrialists toppled from their pedestals by tabloid revelations of the pathetic vanity of their wives, frivolously whittling away the family money on a succession of oversexed gigolos. Bachelorhood suited him perfectly.

"He arrived half an hour ago and said he wanted to see you urgently. He said I should say 'Brazil, 1967' and you'd understand."

"Where is he, Marisa?" he asked, gripping her arms.

"I put him in the study. Is he Russian?" she asked, stressing the last word.

"Yes, an old friend of mine."

"I suppose he's with the KGB," she said, chuckling.

His eyes narrowed menacingly but he quickly checked himself and smiled. "You've been watching too many late-night movies. No, we're in the same line of business."

"Is he married?" she asked with a mischievous glint in her eye.

"No, but I doubt you'd find too many takers here willing to give up the delights of the West for a Russian dacha."

"Perhaps we could get to him to . . . defect, is that the word they use?"

"I doubt you'd get him to do that."

"I'll get one of the staff to show you the way."

The butler led him down the hall to a veneered door which he opened. "Can I get you anything, sir?"

"No, thank you."

The butler bowed curtly and closed the door behind him.

Benin embraced Werner then held him at arm's length. "You're looking well, my friend."

"I can afford to," Werner answered with a smile. He crossed to the sideboard. "Scotch?"

"Please." Benin eased the velvet curtains apart and looked out over the brightly lit garden. "Is it safe to talk here?"

Werner poured two measures of scotch and handed one of the tumblers to Benin. "Quite safe. Any news of the man Hendrique saw? Or the one at the Mainz plant?"

"Nothing yet, but I've got a team working around the clock so it should only be a matter of time before they come up with the answers." Benin moved to the writing desk and stared absently at the framed family photograph then turned back to Werner. "I've come here to ask you to direct operations from on board the train."

"And Hendrique?" Werner asked.

"He'll take orders from you."

"You know how independent . . ."

"He'll do as he's told!" Benin cut in sharply, then lowered his voice. "I've tolerated his insubordination in the past but he knows exactly what will happen to him if he doesn't toe the line this time. I think you'll find him very cooperative."

"That will be a first," Werner said with surprise. "How did you manage it?"

"I've built up a dossier on his drug and arms deals over the past few years. If he steps out of line this time I'll see to it that the dossier falls into the appropriate hands."

"The authorities?"

"Since when has he ever been frightened of the law? You no doubt heard about the raid on a Venezuelan freighter outside Amsterdam a couple of years ago when a gang impersonating the harbour police impounded over a million pounds worth of acapulco gold?"

"Hendrique?"

"Correct. He thought the cannabis was being shipped in by a small-time Dutch gangster trying to muscle in on the Amsterdam syndicate. He couldn't have been more wrong. It was a Mafia shipment."

Werner whistled softly.

"The Mafia immediately put out a contract on the gang. It's still valid." Benin watched Werner light a cigarette before continuing. "I spoke to Hendrique on the phone before I left East Berlin. The train's due out of Sion at nine tomorrow morning. It's next stop's

Brig, the last station before the Simplon Tunnel. Board
the train there, he's expecting you."

"I'll have a company helicopter refuelled and ready
for take-off within the hour."

"There is one more thing," Benin said, and picked
up an attaché case from beside his chair. He handed
it to Werner.

Werner knew what it contained even though he had
never seen it before. He swallowed nervously and unlocked it. Then, almost reluctantly, he opened it. It
contained a silver box no bigger than a pocket calcu-
lator, cushioned in the centre of a layer of spongy
foam.

"There's a miniature computer built into the roof of
the lid."

Werner squinted at it. A narrow blank screen above
a row of the numbers one to nine. "What are the coordinates?"

"One-nine-six-seven," Benin replied.

"I should have guessed," Werner replied, and
reached for the numerical keys.

"Don't touch it!"

Werner jerked his hand away as though the keyboard
had given him an electric shock.

Benin smiled apologetically. "It can only be opened
once."

Werner felt a drop of perspiration trickle out from
under his hairline and he wiped it away before it could
run down the side of his face.

"It must only be used as a last resort."

"I'll buy that," Werner said, then closed the case
and locked it, after memorizing the combination.

Benin held out his hand. "Good luck, my friend."
Werner shook it firmly.

Benin left the room. Werner placed the attaché case beside the chair then poured himself a stiff Scotch from the crystal decanter on the sideboard.

Graham tossed the paperback on to the opposite couchette and made his way to the dining car. It was deserted except for a sleepy-eyed steward who glared at him as though he were trespassing.

"Coffee," Graham said as he sat down.

The steward gave him a look of indifference then disappeared through one of the swing doors.

The train had already left Sion when the avalanche struck and with the possibility of further minor falls it had retreated to the sanctuary of the station where the passengers were told it would remain for the rest of the night. The station restaurant had promised to remain open until midnight and the dining car would be open all night for light snacks and beverages, all courtesy of the company.

Graham glanced at his wristwatch. Almost one o'clock in the morning. The steward deposited the steaming hot cup of coffee on to the table in front of him, slopping some into the saucer in the process.

"Are acts of God designed to show us just how mortal we really are?"

Graham glanced round, startled by the voice behind him.

Hendrique, having rejoined the train at the previous station, Vetroz, was staring out of the window behind

Graham. "Sorry if I startled you. I take it you are English-speaking?"

"Yeah."

"Do you mind if I join you?" Hendrique asked, indicating the two chairs opposite Graham.

"Sit down."

Hendrique snapped his fingers to wake the dozing steward. *"Cameriere! Un cappuccino, per favore."*

The steward scrambled off the bar stool and disappeared through the swing door.

"You Italian?"

Hendrique pulled one of the chairs away from the table and sat down. "No, but it's one of the languages I've learnt to speak over the years."

"I'm impressed," Graham said with a thinly veiled sarcasm. "How many in all?"

"A handful," Hendrique replied with a shrug. "I find I can blend in better with the locals if I understand their language. How about you? Are you interested in languages?"

"Just one. American."

Hendrique waited until the steward had deposited the coffee and left the dining car before speaking. "You look like the sort of man who enjoys a challenge."

Graham was intrigued. "Perhaps."

"I've devised a board game to alleviate these kind of boring situations. The object is to bluff your opponent into submission. There is a catch, however. We play for pain, not money. The squeamish would doubtless see it as sadistic; I see it as a test of character and inner strength. Interested?"

"As you said, I look like the sort of man who enjoys a challenge."

"Excellent." Hendrique got to his feet. "I'll fetch it from my compartment. I won't be a moment."

Graham had barely finished his coffee when Hendrique returned with a brown leather attaché case. He put the case on the table and opened it. After removing the contents he closed the lid again and placed the case on the floor beside his chair.

It consisted of a two-inch-thick wooden board, its fifteen-by-eight-inch surface divided into equal sections by an indicator running the length of the board with the figures one to ten printed on it. On either side of the indicator was a set of three lights positioned equidistantly beneath each other and a metallic pressure pad raised fractionally above the level of the board. A metallic bracelet was attached to a circuit underneath each of the pads by a length of flex on opposite sides of the board.

Hendrique, using two paper napkins to protect his hands, removed the strip light from its socket on the ceiling of the carriage directly above the table then unravelled a length of flex and secured the two crocodile clips at the end of it to the respective overhead power points. He fitted the plug at the other end of the flex into the socket at the side of the board.

"The rules are quite simple. We each attach a bracelet to our wrist then press the palm of our other hand on to the metal pad. Once the pad's level with the board it activates the electrical circuit and the game begins." Hendrique ran his finger the length of the indicator. "This monitors the level of current passing through the circuit at any given time. The number one will automatically light up as soon as we activate the circuit and the current increases gradually as the numbers get progressively higher. One to five light up in green, six to eight in amber, nine and ten in red. I think the colours are self-explanatory. The winner is the one who can out-bluff his opponent and keep his hand on the pad the longest. We play the best of three, hence the lights. As soon as the loser pulls his hand off the pad the light on his side comes on. That's it.''

"How much time is there between the numbers lighting up?''

"Five, six seconds. That's the one drawback of the game, it's over so quickly.''

"It's still ingenious,'' Graham said.

"It beats Monopoly.''

Hendrique removed the cloth and affixed the board to the table by means of its four powerful suction pads. They each snapped a bracelet around their wrist and locked it, placing the miniature keys in the centre of the board. Hendrique nodded and they pressed their hands down simultaneously on to the metal pads. Graham immediately felt a tingling sensation in his hand which quickly spread up his arm and into his chest. Although Hendrique was staring at him Graham was more interested in monitoring the progress of the indicator. As it changed from green to amber the current intensified sharply and before he could stop himself Graham instinctively jerked his hand off the pad. He wasn't expecting the jarring shock that shot through his other arm but the shortness of the flex prevented him from pulling it more than a few inches off the table.

"I'm sorry," Hendrique said without sounding very convincing. "I forgot to tell you: if you forfeit a game you incur an extra penalty of a shock transmitted through an electrode on the inside of the bracelet."

"It doesn't help to be wise after the event," Graham said tersely.

"There's something else. The aftershocks intensify three-fold each time. If you've got a heart condition we should stop now. A shock nine times stronger than the one you experienced could kill. Actually, it has in the past."

"Let's play."

"I didn't explain the rules properly at the outset so it's only fair we should start again . . ."

"I don't need to be nannied," Graham interposed. "You're one game up."

"As you wish," Hendrique replied, and placed his hand back on the pad.

This time Graham held Hendrique's stare. The colour on the indicator changed from green to amber and Graham's eyes narrowed fractionally, his stare unremitting in its intensity. Hendrique found himself unable to hold Graham's gaze and in his disorientation he turned away, unconsciously easing the pressure on the pad. The shock seared through his arm and he grabbed at the bracelet as though trying to tear it from his wrist. He closed his eyes until the pounding in his head had subsided and wiped the sweat from his forehead with the back of his hand.

"I make that one game all," Graham said with evident satisfaction.

Hendrique sucked in several deep breaths but said

nothing. It was the first time he had conceded a game since building the device three years earlier. He sat forward and placed his hand on the pad, his palm still tingling from the effects of the shock.

The last game had reached eight. Graham already knew he could reach ten without pulling off. Hendrique had been right: it was a test of inner strength.

They both pressed down on the pads. Hendrique, having learnt from his mistake, concentrated on the indicator instead of on Graham's face. Graham also watched the indicator and winced more out of irritation than anything else when green five increased to amber six. Had Hendrique warned him at the beginning about the current intensifying when crossing the colour boundary the game might already have been over. Seven. Eight. He clenched his jaw as the pain barrier seemed to break with every passing second. Red nine. His hand began to shudder and his eyes watered. He felt a strange moment of camaraderie with Hendrique. Then the moment was gone. Red ten. Graham's back arched agonizingly and he used every last ounce of inner strength to keep himself from wrenching his hand off the pad. He caught a glimpse of Hendrique through the distorting haze of pain. Hendrique's head was tilted back, his mouth open in a silent scream. In that split second Graham knew he had won. Hendrique was on the brink of defeat. Safe in that knowledge Graham braced himself then pulled away from the pad.

He remembered nothing else.

* * *

Graham sat in the deserted dining car for some time after regaining consciousness, his trembling fingers gently massaging his temples as he tried to overcome the throbbing in his head. When he did finally get to his feet his legs were unsteady and he had to stick close to the tables for support on his way to the door. He entered the next carriage, his hand gripped tightly around the railing, and moved slowly down the corridor until he reached his own compartment. He yanked the door open and stumbled inside.

The communicating door opened immediately and Sabrina came in, the Beretta gripped in her hand. She moved to the compartment door, peered out into the deserted corridor, then closed and locked it.

"Have you been drinking?" was her first reaction on seeing him with his head buried in his hands.

He jerked his head up, startled by her voice, then winced at the pain resulting from the sudden movement. "What are you doing here?"

"I'm your partner, remember?"

"You know what I mean," he snapped, and again the pain reverberated through his head.

"The boss sent me back," she replied dismissively and crouched down in front of him. "What happened?"

"My head," he muttered.

She disappeared back into her own compartment then returned with a glass of water and two paracetamol.

"I thought you never touched painkillers," he said, staring at her open hand.

"You do, and I bet you didn't bring any."

He took the tablets from her and swallowed them with a mouthful of water. Then he sat back and closed his eyes.

She sat on the opposite couchette and picked up the paperback he had been reading. Another James Hadley Chase. Not her kind of author. She read very few thrillers; they reminded her of her work.

"You wouldn't like it."

"I know," she replied and dropped it on the couchette. "What happened to your head?"

He told her about his confrontation with Hendrique.

She shook her head in disbelief when he had finished. "It's not the first time you've put your life at risk for the sake of a challenge and I'm sure it won't be the last time either."

"You don't understand, do you? It's not the actual challenge that counts; it's the psychology behind it. In that kind of one-to-one confrontation with two people of roughly the same strength, the one with the stronger willpower always wins. Take two boxers for example. Both men are the same strength and weight but it's the one who's psyched himself up properly beforehand who's going to win. Expertise and experience count for nothing if a fighter isn't mentally prepared before he enters the ring. Intimidation invariably leads to defeat."

"You lost, so where does that leave your theory?"

"I didn't lose, I let him win. There's a big difference. I merely inverted the theory."

"In other words when the two of you confront each other again you know you can beat him. He only thinks he can beat you."

"At last," he said.

"But what happens if I'm the one who ends up confronting him?"

He stared at her. "Only you can answer that question."

She pondered his words then got to her feet. "Let's see your arm."

"My arm?"

"Where the electrode came into contact with your skin."

"It's nothing," he muttered, but still pulled up the sleeve of his sweatshirt to reveal the inflamed area on his inner wrist.

She told him about the latest development from Zurich while dressing the wound, filling him in on the backgrounds of Hendrique and Milchan as well as relaying Philpott's instructions.

"And Jacques sends his regards," she concluded as she secured the bandage with a strip of sticking plaster.

He sat back and massaged his temples, his eyes closed. "You're very fond of him, aren't you?"

"I always have been, ever since we first started working together."

"Was there . . ." he trailed off and opened his eyes. "Forget it."

It was a side of Graham she had never seen before. He seemed more open than usual. She assumed it was only a temporary lapse in character while he nursed his head but she still determined to keep the conversation going for as long as possible.

"Was there ever anything between Jacques and me, is that what you were going to ask?"

"It's none of my business."

"Why not? You're my partner, for God's sake," she shot back.

He winced. "Don't shout."

"Sorry," she said with an apologetic smile. "And no, there was never anything between us. He was the brother I never had, a confidant I could turn to for advice if I ever needed it."

"Has there ever been a special guy in your life?"

"Well, there was Rutger Hauer . . ." she said, then giggled. "Never anyone special, no. I had a few casual relationships after I left the Sorbonne. These days work takes up most of my time."

"Do you ever see yourself getting married?"

"It isn't very high on my list of priorities but I guess I'd change my mind soon enough if I were to meet the right person."

"That's what it's all about. The right person."

She knew what was going through his mind. He had never spoken to her before about his wife and son.

"Carrie was the right person," he said at length.

"Where did you meet her?"

"At *Elaine*'s."

"The bar on Second Avenue?"

"Yeah. I was there with a few of the guys from Delta. We'd just been given leave after the fiasco of Operation Eagle Claw, the so-called attempt to rescue the American hostages from our embassy in Teheran back in 1980. She was there with some of her girl-friends from Van Cleef and Arpels; that's where she used to work. We managed to persuade them to come and sit with us and she ended up next to me. Well, we just got talking and she agreed to have dinner with me the following night. We were married five months later." His smile was sad. "She was really shy. It went back to her childhood when she had been teased by her schoolmates about her stammer. She'd overcome it by the time she was eighteen but it still surfaced when she got excited about something."

"And when was your son born?"

"A year, almost to the day, after the marriage. She always wanted Mikey to go on to university and become a doctor or a lawyer. I only ever wanted him to grow up to become a pro-ball player. I took him to the first Giants game when he was three. He took to it like a duck to water and from then on he'd grill me for hours on end about the various types of plays, especially when we were watching it on TV. I'd always imagined that one day I'd be able to turn to the guy beside me at the Giants Stadium and say 'That's my kid playing down there.' I'd have been the proudest father in the history of the game."

"Did he look like you at that age?"

"The spitting image according to my mother." He pulled out his wallet, opened it, and handed a picture to her. "That's the last photograph of them I ever took. It was still in the camera when . . . they were abducted. I nearly didn't have it developed but now I'm real glad I did. I've got an enlarged print of it on my bedside table."

She stared at the photograph and immediately saw why he had been attracted to Carrie. She was squatting down in the photograph and Sabrina estimated her to have been a little over five feet with a slender petite figure and a pale, milky complexion. She had the kind of wide, alluring brown eyes the Fifties' authors would have described as "big enough to drown a man." Mike Junior was standing beside her in a Giants sweatshirt, a football tucked under his arm. He had a cheeky mischievous face and his fine blond hair came down almost to his shoulders.

"He looks like he must have been pretty naughty," she said, and handed the picture back to him.

"As naughty as most five-year-olds I guess," he replied, pocketing the wallet. "I still lie awake at night trying to justify the decision I made in Libya. I sacrificed my family for the sake of seven terrorists who were planning bombing raids in some of America's major cities. My order to attack undoubtedly saved a lot of other innocent lives but it still doesn't give me peace of mind. Morally it was right, personally it was wrong. There's no in-between."

"As you said earlier, the only person who knows their true inner strength is themselves. It's something you'll have to come to terms with yourself."

"Thanks."

"Thanks?"

"For not patronizing me like everyone else. You talk more sense than all those psychiatrists put together." He glanced at his wristwatch. "Come on, time to get some sleep."

She stood up and stifled a yawn. "How's the head?"

"Buzzing," he replied, turning the couchette over to get at the narrow bed.

"I'll see you in the morning," she said, moving to the communicating door.

"Sabrina?"

She paused as she was about to close the door and looked back at him.

"The man who had Carrie and Mikey kidnapped was trained at Balashikha."

"It wasn't . . ."

"No, it wasn't Hendrique." The cynicism seemed to flood back into his eyes. "You asked me earlier what would happen if you were the one who ended up confronting him. Don't worry, you won't. He's mine."

She felt a shiver run up her spine as she closed the door behind her.

SEVEN

The man who joined Hendrique for breakfast the following morning was Eddie Kyle. He was a stocky, forty-year-old Londoner with a pale skin and crew-cut red hair. He had a long criminal record at Scotland Yard and was currently on their wanted list for a variety of crimes, the most serious being the murder of an East End gangster. The murder had been ordered by Hendrique, for whom Kyle had been working during the last five years. He was also an experienced pilot of both helicopters and light planes and flew exclusively for Hendrique, ferrying both arms and drugs in and out of Amsterdam on a regular basis.

"Everything's been arranged," Kyle said.

"Excellent." Hendrique looked up as Sabrina entered the dining car. "Is that the woman who shot Rauff?"

Kyle pretended to gaze around the carriage, his eyes lingering on her for a moment. "That's her all right."

"Are you sure? You said her face was partially hidden under an anorak hood."

Kyle grinned. "I never saw her face properly but I'm not likely to forget a figure like that. It's her all right. What a pity."

"Getting sentimental in your old age?" Hendrique asked disdainfully.

Kyle stared at her image reflected in the window beside him. "What I had in mind has nothing to do with sentimentality."

"She killed Rauff and she'd have killed you if your luck hadn't been running. We're dealing with a professional, not one of your dumb Amsterdam whores. Remember that next time, it might just save your life."

The anger in Hendrique's voice was enough to wipe all expression from Kyle's face. He was subdued for the remainder of breakfast.

Karen Schendel looked up and smiled at Whitlock when he knocked on the open door.

"Morning," she said in a friendly voice, then pointed to the desk to remind him about the microphone.

"Morning."

He gestured for her to move aside so he could take a closer look at the microphone. She eased her chair back but made no move to stand up, filling the silence with small talk as he crouched down, his head twisted at an angle to peer underneath the desk. It was as she had drawn it. The kind that cost about a hundred dollars on the black market. Sophisticated but very compact. His eyes flickered over her legs sheathed in fine black stockings. There were exquisitely shaped, even better than Carmen's legs. The thought of his wife jarred him guiltily out of his fantasy and when he glanced up Karen was smiling at him. He was about to apologize, remembered the microphone, then moved round to the other side of the desk and sat down.

"Coffee?" she asked.

"I had some before I left the hotel. I'd like to get started if you don't mind."

"Not at all," she replied as she shuffled her papers into a neat pile.

She waited until they were clear of the office before speaking again. "How's your shoulder this morning?"

He wriggled his arm. "No after-effects, yet. I soaked it in a hot bath last night; it should be okay now."

"I was worried about you."

The sincerity in her voice surprised him.

Once inside the lift she pressed the button for the floor she wanted and handed him a folded sheet of paper. On it were four names written neatly underneath each other.

"They're my four suspects. Especially Dr. Leitzig. I've arranged for you to meet him first."

"What's his position?"

"He's the senior plant technician. That entails overseeing the entire reprocessing operation."

"Does he do the monthly stocktaking?"

"Along with the plant manager and other members of the scientific staff. It's very strictly controlled."

"Is he involved in writing up the stocksheets?"

The doors parted and they emerged into another carpeted corridor.

"No, that's all done by computer. As I said last night, it's diversion as opposed to MUF. The plutonium's being siphoned off before the figures reach the computers."

He grabbed her arm as she was about to knock on a frosted-glass door halfway down the corridor. "You've made a lot of accusations but you haven't come up with a single shred of evidence to back them up."

"I told you, I don't have any evidence . . ."

"Then what are your grounds for these suspicions?"

"You don't believe me, do you?" she snapped. "You don't believe me."

"Right now I don't know what to believe. You've got to give me something constructive to work on, can't you see that?"

Her eyes were blazing. "All I have to do is make one phone call to the plant manager and I can blow your cover."

"And what good would that do either of us?" he asked calmly.

She sighed deeply and nodded. "I'm sorry, C.W., I'm just not used to confiding in the people around here. I'll tell you everything I know after you've seen Leitzig. Agreed?"

"Agreed," he answered reluctantly, wishing he had more to go on before meeting Leitzig.

Karen knocked on the door, then opened it without

waiting. A middle-aged woman looked up from her typewriter and smiled at them. The two women spoke rapidly to each other in German, their conversation punctuated with laughter.

Karen finally turned to Whitlock. "It's back to German I'm afraid. She doesn't speak any English."

"And Leitzig?"

"He does but it's a case of getting him to speak it. He can be very stubborn at times. I'll see you later."

He exchanged a polite smile with the secretary after Karen had left, then picked up the only magazine on the coffee table and leafed through it, his interest not overly stimulated by a computer programming manual written in German.

The inner door opened. The man who emerged was in his late fifties with short grey hair and round, wire-framed glasses.

Whitlock stood up and shook the extended hand, unwilling to speak until he knew which language Leitzig intended to use.

"I am Dr. Hans Leitzig."

Whitlock was relieved that it was English.

"I am on my way down to the reprocessing area. Perhaps you would like to come along so you can see the plant in operation?"

"Thank you, I would," Whitlock replied.

"Which hotel are you staying at?"

"Europa."

"Good choice," Leitzig said, then spoke briefly to his secretary.

Whitlock studied him. He could have been the driver of the Mercedes at the Hilton Hotel, but then so could the majority of Mainz's male population. It had all happened so quickly.

"Karen was telling me you are writing about the workforce rather than about the plant's operational side. I think that is a good idea, especially in the light of the bad publicity the industry has had since Chernobyl."

"My sentiments exactly," Whitlock said, hoping the sycophancy came through in his voice.

Leitzig led him to the changerooms where they pulled on white overcoats. Whitlock had to be reminded to clip on his compulsory dosemeter badge.

"How much of the reprocessing area did Karen show you yesterday?"

"She was unavailable. I was shown around by her assistant. He didn't bring me down here at all."

"How much do you know about the reprocessing operation?" Leitzig asked as they left the changerooms.

"Not much, I'm afraid," he lied.

"It is not too difficult to understand. Come on, I'll show you where it all starts."

Leitzig led him through a succession of corridors until they reached an area marked STORAGE PONDS with a no-entry sign beside it and the words AUTHORIZED PERSONNEL ONLY in black paint underneath. Leitzig fed his ID card into one of the steel doors. It swung open to reveal a lime-green cavern over three hundred feet long and another eighty feet high above the waterline. The water, Leitzig told him, was thirty feet deep. Two sets of catwalks spanned the length of the cavern and four smaller catwalks led out into the water, all of them enclosed by safety railings.

Leitzig pointed to the row of steel containers submerged in the water, and described how they had been transported to the plant in 100 tonne flasks with walls fourteen inches thick.

"How long are they stored here for?"

"Ninety days here, and another ninety days at the nuclear power station prior to transportation."

"So presumably the water acts as a coolant?" Whitlock asked as he looked over the railing at the water fifty feet below him.

"Correct. It acts as a shield for the operators. We'd already be irradiated if the water wasn't there to absorb the radiation emitted by the fuel."

"Sobering thought," Whitlock muttered, then followed Leitzig out of the cavern.

Next they went into the main building where part of the reprocessing cycle took place. They watched from behind a protective glass partition, seemingly erected to shield the visiting public from any of the harmful gamma rays. Leitzig explained that it was actually there to blot out any outside noises which might distract the skilled operators from their delicate and sensitive work. All work was carried out using remote-controlled equipment and monitored on closed-circuit television screens.

"After the quarantine period's over," he went on, with an air of simplifying an impossibly complex process, "the containers are transferred into the decanning cave through a series of sub-ponds leading off from the main storage pond. Once inside the cave, which is constructed of concrete walls seven feet thick, the fuel element can be observed both on closed-circuit television and through specially designed windows built into the walls. Each window is filled with a solution of zinc bromide which, although transparent, is able to absorb the short wave-lengths of gamma radiation. The element is first placed on the stripping machine where the contaminated cladding is cut away, then dropped on to a conveyor belt to be stored under water in concrete storage silos. The bare fuel rods are then loaded into a transfer magazine, which can hold up to thirty-eight rods at any given time, and dissolved in nitric acid. The nitric acid solution is then mixed with an organic solvent and the uranium and plutonium are separated from the waste products. The waste products, which contain radioactive fission products, iron from the plant machinery and chemical impurities from the fuel, are then reduced by evaporation and stored near the plant in tanks at temperatures of 50°C. The acid solution enters another section of the plant where it passes through a second organic solvent to remove any lingering waste products, then, on coming into contact with a water-based solution, the uranium and plutonium separate, the plutonium returning to the water solution and the uranium remaining in the solvent. They emerge as uranyl nitrate and plutonium nitrate, ready to be used in the fuel cycle again.''

It was two hours later when they returned to Leitzig's office. He had his secretary order some coffee, then closed the door and sat down behind his desk.

''What's the percentage of uranium to plutonium after the elements have been reprocessed?'' Whitlock asked.

''The normal breakdown of recovered uranium's ninety-nine per cent to point five per cent of plutonium. The other half per cent is made up of radioactive waste. It may vary by point one or point two but never more than that.''

''And those statistics are transferred on to the computer?''

''Of course, but I fail to see where this question is leading.''

Whitlock smiled. ''Sorry, it's just my journalistic training getting the better of me. Can we talk about you now?''

''Ask away,'' Leitzig replied, folding his hands on the desk.

''A little background on yourself?''

''It's all very commonplace I'm afraid. I was born in a small town called Tettnang which is fairly close to the Austrian border. It's only got a population of about fifteen thousand and it's situated in the heart of asparagus country. I remember how happy I was when I was accepted at Hamburg University, because I could at last get away from my mother's asparagus dishes.'' He chuckled to himself then reached for his cigarettes and lit one. ''I went to England to work after my graduation. First at Calder Hall, then at Sellafield. I left the industry in the early Seventies and came back here to work at the Max Planck Institute of Chemistry. I spent several years at the Institute before returning to the industry. I've never regretted the decision.''

"So how long have you been the plant's senior technician?"

"Two and a half years now."

"And what do you do in your spare time?"

"Fishing mainly. There's nothing more relaxing than to drive the Land Rover into the country for a day's fishing."

"Married?"

"No," Leitzig retorted defensively then held up his hands apologetically. "I'm a widower."

"I'm sorry."

"My wife's death was the main reason for my returning to the industry. I was able to throw myself into my work, which helped to take my mind off the fact that she was gone. I used to dread going home at night; the silence and solitude were almost too much to bear."

"Why didn't you move?"

Leitzig looked surprised by the question. "I could never turn my back on our home. It contains so many memories."

"Sure," Whitlock replied sympathetically. "Any children?"

"Neither of us wanted any. I regret that now."

Whitlock thought about his own situation. What if something were to happen to Carmen? Would he end up as desolate and lonely as Leitzig?

The secretary entered with the coffee tray and made room for it on the desk. Leitzig poured out two cups and offered Whitlock milk and sugar.

A blue light flashed on the control panel on the desk.

Leitzig acknowledged it, then stood up. "You must excuse me, I am needed down in the plant."

"Nothing serious, I hope."

"They wish to consult me about something, that is all." He pointed to a red button on the control panel. "That is the danger light. It would come on if ever there were a criticality incident somewhere in the plant. Apparently it emits a deafening siren at the same time. Fortunately I have never heard it. Please stay and finish your coffee. Hopefully we will be able to finish our conversation later today."

"I'd like that."

"Fine. I shall ask my secretary to call Karen for you as it is very easy to get lost in these labyrinths if you don't know your way around."

Karen arrived a few minutes later and they walked in silence to the lift.

"I've been thinking about what you said earlier," she said as the lift doors closed. "We have to work together, it's the only way we're going to get to the bottom of this."

The doors parted and a secretary stepped into the lift. She exchanged a polite smile with them and a silence descended until the doors parted again and Karen gestured for Whitlock to follow her.

"Where are we going?" he asked.

"The computer suite," she replied, then held up the folder she was carrying. "These are photostats of the inventory stocksheets for the last two years. I've been through the figures with a fine-tooth comb but I can't find any discrepancies. Perhaps you'll be able to pick up on something I've overlooked."

She pushed open a pair of swing doors and they entered the room. It reminded him of the computer room at UNACO headquarters, with the rattling of telex machines and the incessant whirring of printers. They crossed to the bank of VDUs and sat down in front of one of them. She instinctively shielded her fingers from him as she fed in her personal security code. It was accepted and a menu of eight options appeared on the screen. She chose a number which further sub-divided into another menu. Again it asked for a security code. Once she had fed it in the screen displayed lists of figures. She pressed the "print" button. There were seventeen pages of figures and she printed them all before collecting the paper and tucking it into her folder.

"You can go through this in my office although I doubt you'll find any discrepancies. As I said, I've already been through it entry by entry."

He took her arm and led her to one side, out of earshot of the nearest analysts. "You still haven't told me about your suspicions."

"Several times when I've been working late I've seen Leitzig with a powerfully built man with jet-black hair. He was always dressed in a white overall, like those worn by the company drivers. Only he doesn't work here."

"How can you be so sure?"

"I hire the drivers. Anyway, I followed him one night."

"And?"

"He drove to a warehouse in Rampenstrasse on the banks of the Rhine. I couldn't see what happened inside but when he finally came out he was with two other men I'd never seen before. They left in a Citroën. I even tried to get into the warehouse but it was padlocked.'' She shrugged in desperation. ''I know it's not much to go on.''

''It's enough. Come on, let's take a look at those stats.''

Neither of them saw Leitzig through the circular glass window in the swing door further up the corridor. He timed his movements perfectly, slipping into the computer suite just after they'd left and heading for the nearest computer. He fed in his own security code and chose an option from the sub-menu. It read EMPLOYEE TRANSACTIONS. He fed in Karen's security code. It showed her transactions for the day, the last being seventeen pages of inventory statistics. Nothing else. He pressed ''enter'' until the main menu reappeared on the screen.

He had been suspicious of Whitlock ever since he first met him. Whitlock knew far more about the nuclear industry than he had let on; that had been obvious from the questions he had asked during the tour. If he were a journalist why would he want the inventory figures for the last two years, especially seeing that he was supposed to be writing an article on the plant's workforce? And why was Karen Schendel helping him? How much did she know? What made it even more suspicious was Whitlock's appearance so soon after the last of the plutonium had been taken to the warehouse. It was all too much of a coincidence.

Leitzig knew he had to cover his own tracks. He would have to kill Whitlock.

* * *

A light snow had fallen over Central Switzerland during the night and Werner almost lost his footing as he climbed from the taxi at Brig Station. He paid the driver, then negotiated his way carefully across the road, paused at the entrance to wipe his feet, then crossed the concourse to the platform. People looked at him, certain they had seen his face before. They had, on numerous TV chat shows across Europe, but now, with his homburg tilted down over his forehead, none of them could put a name to the face.

The train pulled into the station a few minutes later, fifteen hours behind schedule. He boarded it and made his way down the corridor to his reserved compartment. The door of the adjoining compartment opened and Hendrique peered out at him.

"Good morning," Werner said, then entered his own compartment where he tossed his homburg on to one of the couchettes, then unbuttoned his overcoat and laid it neatly on the overhead rack.

Hendrique stood in the doorway, his hands thrust into his trouser pockets. "Let's skip the pleasantries and get a few things straight right from the start. I'm not particularly thrilled about having to take orders from someone who's spent his life behind a desk but, as you're probably aware, the old bastard's got me by the short hairs and I haven't got much choice. Having said that, my men and I will do everything in our power to ensure the cargo reaches its destination. It's just another job to us."

"I'm not particularly thrilled about having to work with a drug pusher but circumstances are such that I too am left with little alternative. I suggest we put aside our personal feelings and work together as a team. We are supposed to be on the same side." Werner lit a cigarette then pushed past Hendrique and closed the compartment door behind him. "I need a coffee. Coming?"

Hendrique led the way down the corridor then paused as he entered the dining car. Inclining his head almost imperceptibly, he indicated Sabrina, who was seated at one of the tables. "That's the woman who shot Rauff."

Werner stared at her. "It can't be!"

"You know her?"

Werner nodded. "She used to be one of the most popular debutantes in Europe a few years ago. Are you sure it's her?"

"Kyle's positive."

Sabrina turned away from the window as the train eased out of the station and caught sight of Werner approaching her. "Stefan?"

Werner embraced her, kissing her lightly on both cheeks. "I can't believe it. After all these years we meet up again. It's truly a small world." He noticed her eyes flicker toward Hendrique. "I'm sorry, this is Joe Hemmings, my security adviser. Sabrina . . ." he trailed off with an embarrassed smile. "Forgive me, I'm terrible with names."

"Cassidy," she said, holding Hendrique's penetrating stare. "Sabrina Cassidy."

"How do you do?" Hendrique said coldly, then turned to Werner. "I'm sure you have a lot to talk about so I'll leave you to it. If you need me, *sir*, I'll be in my compartment.''

"He must be a bag of laughs," she said after Hendrique had gone.

"He just takes his work very seriously. May I join you?"

"Of course."

Werner ordered himself a coffee from the steward, then sat down opposite her. "I still can't get over it. It must be four or five years now since I last saw you."

"Five years," she replied after a quick mental calculation.

"The last I heard you were making something of a name for yourself on the racing track."

"Saloon car racing. It came to an abrupt end at Le Mans when I rolled my Porsche. I spent the next four months in the American Hospital of Paris. In retrospect the crash was the best thing that ever happened to me."

"In what way?" he asked in amazement.

"I learnt a lot about myself during my convalescence. I realized my life was going nowhere."

"So what are you doing now?" he asked her after paying the steward for the coffee.

"I'm a translator in New York."

"Married?"

She held out her left hand. "Nobody wants me."

"I can't believe that."

"What about you? Is there a Mrs. Werner?"

"There probably is but I still haven't met her." He sipped the coffee, then looked across the rim of the cup at her. "What brings you to Switzerland?"

"I'm on vacation," she replied, then turned to the window when it was suddenly enveloped in darkness.

"We're in the Simplon Tunnel. You enter it in Switzerland and leave it in Italy ten miles later."

"I'd have thought with your limitless resources, Stefan, you'd be travelling by air, not on some poky little train that looks like it's going to take till eternity to reach its destination."

Werner looked around, then leaned forward. "Normally I would but this is a special case. My company have patented a new design in freight containers, using a revolutionary new material. It's more durable and economical, that's all I can tell you. It has to get to Rome for further testing without our competitors finding out how it's being transported. We were originally going to fly it down but word reached us that some of our airline staff had already been bribed by one of our main competitors to give them a preview before it was to be flown out, so we had to change our plans at the last moment. We decided on the most innocuous means of transport imaginable. As you said, a poky little train. Joe Hemmings has been on board ever since it left Lausanne and I've even got a man locked in with the freight container just in case something should happen. Not that I think it will, but it's better to be safe than sorry."

"And what if something were to happen?"

"We'd take whatever steps were deemed necessary to deal with it. Industrial espionage is such a dirty business."

"So you're staying with the train until Rome?"

"That's the plan. What about you?"

"Same. At least we'll have a chance to talk about the old days."

"I look forward to it. Dinner tonight?" he asked.

"Fine. Eight o'clock?"

"I'll make the reservation, if that's what one does on a train like this." He pushed back his chair and stood up. "You'll have to excuse me, my dear, I have work waiting for me in my briefcase."

"No rest for the wicked."

"Until tonight then."

He returned to his compartment and rapped on the communicating door. The bolt was released and Hendrique slid the door open.

"Have a pleasant chat?"

"You can cut that out," Werner snapped. He took the map from his overcoat pocket and sat down. "She didn't buy the story about the freight container."

"Are you surprised? She's a professional, not some two-bit amateur sent by one of your rivals."

"Did Kyle—"

"It's all done," Hendrique cut in. "All you have to do is give the word."

Werner opened the map and traced his finger along the train's intended route. "Next stop's Domodossola. Then it stops again at Vergiate, about fifty miles north of Milan. You'll have to make the call at Domodossola, we can't afford to waste any more time."

"Excellent. That just leaves the other one. I'll deal with him personally."

"I don't want any shooting on the train."

"Who said anything about shooting?" Hendrique held out his hand. "Have you got the number?"

Werner unzipped his holdall and withdrew a newspaper. "It's written across the top of the front page."

Hendrique took the newspaper and returned to his own compartment.

The conductor rapped on the compartment door as the train drew into Domodossola station, its first stop after the Simplon Tunnel.

Hendrique opened it. "What?"

"I spoke to the driver. He says he'll wait five minutes here for you, then he's leaving."

Hendrique grabbed him by the lapels and forced him up against the narrow built-in wardrobe. "I'm paying you well to make sure my few requests are carried out without any hitches. You make sure this train waits for me, no matter how long I am."

"It's the driver . . ."

"I don't care about the driver. This train *will* wait for me. Understand?"

The conductor nodded nervously, then scurried away down the corridor.

Hendrique turned up the collar of his parka as he stepped out into the lightly falling snow and crossed the platform to the public telephone mounted in a cubicle outside the station cafeteria. He dialled the number written in red at the top of the newspaper then fed four hundred-lire coins into the slot.

The receiver was answered at the other end.

"I'd like to speak to Captain Frosser," he said in German.

"Captain Frosser's busy . . ."

''Tell him it's about the Rauff murder. I'm calling long distance from a public telephone.''

''One moment, sir.''

''Hello, Captain Frosser speaking,'' a voice said seconds later.

''The woman you're looking for in connection with the Rauff murder is travelling on a train bound for Rome. It should reach Vergiate within the hour. Her name's Sabrina Cassidy.'' Hendrique dropped the receiver back on to its cradle, then tossed the newspaper into the wire bin on the platform on his way back to the train.

Bruno Frosser stared at the receiver after the line had gone dead, then reluctantly replaced it.

''What is it, Captain?''

Frosser sat back and clasped his hands behind his head. He looked at his assistant, Sergeant Sepp Clausen, a policeman much in the same mould as he had been in his late twenties. Ambitious and determined. Except Clausen had more hair than he did at that age. Frosser, at forty-three, had barely any hair now apart from the little that curled down above his ears to meet at the nape of his neck. It had never bothered him that the little hair on his head was brown and that his thick moustache was grey or that his fellow officers constantly teased him by patting his ample stomach and asking when the baby was due. All that ever bothered him was his work and his chances of promotion.

''Where the hell's Vergiate?'' Frosser asked in his gravelly voice.

Clausen didn't know but he knew better than to say

so and reached for the atlas in the bottom drawer of his desk.

"Vergiate, Vergiate," Clausen muttered as he traced his finger down the index. There was no listing. He reached for the telephone.

"I'd like an answer today if possible."

Clausen ignored the sarcasm. He had come to learn that it was the closest Frosser ever came to humour.

Frosser stroked his moustache as he thought about the case. It was certainly one of the most baffling he had ever come across since his promotion to the Fribourg CID five years before. It had started with an anonymous caller, almost certainly English-speaking, who had tipped him off in broken German about the body in the warehouse. Then, within an hour of the local radio and TV stations broadcasting details of the murder, two boys had come forward to say they had seen the body. They had also made up an identikit of the woman they thought had called herself "Katrina". Sabrina was close enough for him. There were still too many unanswered questions, like, who was the black-haired man the boys had seen loading beer kegs into a deserted wagon the day before the murder? Barrels that weren't there when he arrived at the warehouse. Why had the skip been sprayed with bullets? Who was the second anonymous caller who had told him she was on the train? And even if she was the killer, where did the two men fit into the puzzle?

"Vergiate's in Italy, sir," Clausen announced, his hand over the mouthpiece. "It's about fifteen miles from Varese."

"That's near Milan isn't it?"

"Near-ish," Clausen replied, screwing up his face.

"Get a helicopter on stand-by. I want to fly to Vergiate as soon as possible."

"It might take some time, sir."

"So might your chances of promotion if you don't get me a helicopter pronto."

Frosser dialled the private line of a senior detective with the Milan CID he had known for the past twelve years. He wanted a deputation party waiting to board the train once it arrived at Vergiate.

"Do you want some more coffee?" Sabrina asked, pointing to Graham's empty cup.

"Yeah, why not? There isn't much else to do on this damn train."

She caught the waiter's attention. *"Possiamo avere altra caffe, per favore."*

The waiter replenished both cups and brought them a fresh jug of milk. The standard of the food had surprised them. Although the portions were small they were delicious. It reminded her of a gem of a restaurant she had found in New York's Greenwich Village. The building's exterior was bleak and the decor appeared shabby but the preparation and presentation of the food were comparable with any of the city's leading restaurants. It was one of the few places she could get away from her Yuppie friends.

"Vergiate," Graham said as the train passed the first of the signposts on the approach to the station.

"What?" she asked, her thoughts interrupted by his voice.

"We're arriving at Vergiate," he said.

"I wonder what they're doing here?" she asked, pointing out of the window.

"Who?" he asked, craning his head to follow the direction of her pointing finger.

"La polizia. There, on the platform."

"Maybe there's a murderer on board. It might liven things up a bit."

"I can think of a couple, present company excluded of course."

"Of course," he said, feigning a look of shock.

When the train came to a halt the rear end of the dining car was facing the four policemen. She suddenly became aware of the contempt and disdain on Graham's face as he stared out of the window at them. She knew he disliked dealing with the police but she had never asked him why. She decided to do so now, knowing it could well backfire on her.

"I don't like people I can't trust. There are too many cops on the take these days, especially back home. What infuriates me most of all is that these bent cops aren't protecting the public who pay their wages, they're protecting the criminals who pay their bribes."

"It's a minority—"

"Is it?" he cut in sharply. "Until they clean up their act this is one guy who'll treat cops and criminals alike."

Two of the policemen had entered the dining car and Graham watched them walk up to Sabrina, who had her back to them.

"Sabrina Cassidy?" the one wearing the sergeant's insignia asked after comparing her face to the photocopy of the identikit in his hand.

"Yes," she replied cautiously.

"I have a warrant for your arrest," the sergeant said, pronouncing each word carefully in a thick Italian accent. "Would you come with us, please?"

"So where's the goddamn warrant?" Graham snapped.

"Mike, please." She looked up at the sergeant. "On what charge?"

"Murder." The sergeant withdrew the warrant from his tunic pocket and unfolded it. "The murder in Fribourg of Kurt Rauff. You'll be deported back to Switzerland to face trial." He glanced at Graham. "Are you travelling with Miss Cassidy?"

Graham knew the drill; it was all typed out so neatly in the UNACO manual. *The success of any given mission must be regarded as paramount regardless of the plight of any individual Strike Force operative during the course of that aforementioned mission.*

"No," he said, shaking his head. "We met on the train yesterday. Her berth's next to mine."

"I would still like to see your passport," the sergeant said.

The sergeant accompanied Sabrina to her compartment and sent his deputy with Graham to fetch his passport.

Graham ferreted through his holdall and pulled his passport out from amongst his clothes.

The young policeman snatched it from him and opened it. He was satisfied the photograph was that of Graham. "Mi-kel Green," he said, reading the name in the passport.

"Michael, for Christ's sake!" Graham snapped.

The policeman waved him aside and rifled through the contents of the two holdalls. He looked somewhat aggrieved at finding nothing more lethal than a razor. The Geiger-Muller counter was in the wardrobe and Graham had the key in his pocket. The policeman glanced at the wardrobe but didn't bother investigating it any further. As Graham left his compartment he prayed there was no noticeable bulge from the holstered Beretta under his jacket. If they decided to frisk him . . .

Sabrina's hands were manacled in front of her when Graham opened the door to her compartment. The sergeant was holding her Beretta in a sealed plastic bag. He took the passport from his deputy and flipped through it before pocketing it.

"What are you doing?" Graham demanded.

"You're free to travel inside Italy. We'll decide when you can leave."

"And here I thought fascism died with Mussolini," Graham snarled. "I hope Miss Cassidy's entitled to the customary phone call usually associated with the democratic judicial system?"

"She'll be allowed a phone call," the sergeant replied gruffly.

"Is there anything you need?" Graham asked her.

"A hacksaw?" she replied with a smile. "I'll be okay. It'll be sorted out soon enough when I contact the proper authorities."

Graham took her trenchcoat from the overhead rack and draped it over her wrists to hide the handcuffs.

"Thanks," she said softly.

"Where will you be staying once you reach Rome?" the sergeant asked.

Graham shrugged. "I haven't made any definite plans. I'm not going to be accepted anywhere now without my passport."

"Report to any police station once you arrive in Rome. By then the Swiss police will know if they'll need a statement from you or not. Your passport will be returned to you then."

The young policemen gathered up Sabrina's two holdalls and disappeared out into the corridor. The sergeant hooked his arm under hers and escorted her from the compartment. Graham slumped on to the nearest couchette and rubbed his hands over his face.

Sabrina glanced over her shoulder as she alighted from the train. Hendrique was standing by one of the dining car windows, a satisfied expression on his face.

It was the first time Sabrina had ever been inside an interrogation room and what she found in Fribourg shattered the Hollywood image of four whitewashed walls with a table and two wooden chairs in the centre of a bare concrete floor and a single, naked bulb hanging from a piece of platted flex. The walls were cream-coloured and matched the beige carpet on which stood a table and two padded chairs. A fluorescent light shone overhead and the wall heater behind her made the room even warmer than her berth had been on the train.

She had refused to answer any of Frosser's questions on the helicopter which had flown them back to Fribourg. Once there she had, on Philpott's instructions (her one phone call), kept up her silence for fear of incriminating herself. Frosser had spent a frustrating thirty minutes with her in the interrogation room and her only response to his barrage of questions had been a quiet *"ja"* at the outset when asked if she understood German. It turned out he spoke no English. She actually felt sorry for him. He was obviously a good and dedicated policeman yet he was floundering in something that was completely over his head. He had enough evidence against her, in the form of the Beretta, but he was still struggling to establish a motive for the killing. It was also something of a test case for Philpott. It was the first time a UNACO operative had been held on a murder charge anywhere on the European continent.

An operative had been arrested in Morocco two years earlier for the rather clumsy killing of a Chinese double agent and after the negotiations had failed Strike Force Three, then still containing Rust, had carried out a daring midnight raid on the prison to release their colleague. As demanded by Philpott, no Moroccan was hurt in the incident. She knew hers would be a very different case. It would be down to a mixture of tact and diplomacy while ensuring the confidentiality of UNACO at all times. It was in nobody's interests to have her face a murder charge in the full glare of international publicity. If one journalist got the faintest whiff of UNACO's official existence . . .

The door opened and Frosser entered, his tie loose at his throat and his waistcoat unbuttoned under his open jacket. He tossed a dossier on to the table and sat down.

"One of the bullets taken from Rauff's body has been positively identified as having come from your gun. That makes a very strong case for the prosecution. You're not doing yourself any favours by remaining silent.''

She stared at the wall opposite her.

He opened the dossier and tapped her passport. ''Forensics have confirmed it's a fake. Whoever made it for you is a very skilled craftsman. It also puts a new slant on the investigation. I don't believe it was a crime of passion anymore.''

She was relieved to hear it. Not only had she been appalled by the very idea of her agreeing to meet someone like Rauff at a deserted warehouse but some of Frosser's insinuations and innuendoes had nearly provoked an angry outburst from her on more than one occasion.

''The other bullets match the FN FAL found in the warehouse. It has been wiped clean.''

She was about to speak then snapped her mouth shut. Hendrique had thought of everything, even to the point of substituting one FN FAL for the other.

''What were you going to say?''

She continued to stare at the wall.

''I've been underestimating you all along. When I first saw you I automatically thought: beautiful woman, crime of passion. I even conned myself into believing those anonymous calls were part of some eternal triangle. Not any more. You, an American with a forged passport, and Rauff, a criminal connected with several of Europe's most influential racketeers. I must have been blind. It wasn't any crime of passion, it was a hit.''

She preferred the idea of a hit to her shooting Rauff in some jealous rage. Even so, Frosser was still guessing.

''It was a hit, wasn't it?''

She drained her coffee cup then folded her arms on the table and stared at the wall again.

There was a knock at the door and Clausen, Frosser's assistant, came in. "It's all set up, sir."

Frosser stood up. "Please come with me Miss . . . Cassidy."

She was sandwiched between the two men as they walked the length of the corridor. She knew what was going on the moment they opened the unmarked brown door. Eight other women stood silently in front of a black backdrop. An identification parade.

Frosser left Clausen to organize the line-up and went into the adjoining room where he sat down on a wooden chair, his mind on the latest developments in the investigation.

"Ready sir," Clausen said as he entered the room.

Frosser got to his feet and looked through the one-way glass, a powerful spotlight now illuminating the nine women standing motionless in front of the sombre backdrop.

"Bring in the first boy," Frosser said.

Clausen opened an inner door and a policewoman ushered in one of the children.

Frosser smiled at him. "Marcel, right?"

The boy nodded nervously.

"There's no need to be frightened, they can't see us." Frosser led Marcel closer to the window. "I want you to look very carefully at those ladies and tell me if you see the one you spoke to at the warehouse. Take your time."

Marcel pointed. "That's her. The pretty lady."

"Which number?"

"Three."

"Are you sure?"

"Yes."

"Thanks," Frosser said and ruffled Marcel's hair.

Clausen led Marcel out and ushered in Jean-Paul. He also pointed out Sabrina.

Clausen ushered in the third witness, a young man with ragged blond hair and a crucifix earring.

"Herr Dahn," Clausen introduced him to Frosser.

"I believe you spoke to Sergeant Clausen about the identikit photo in the newspaper."

Dahn nodded. "I'm sure it's the same woman who spoke to Dieter the day before he died."

"Dieter Teufel. You worked with him at Lausanne station, I believe?"

"It depended on the shifts, but I was there the morning she spoke to him."

"Take a look through the window and tell me if you see her."

"That's her," Dahn said without hesitation. "Number three."

"Are you absolutely certain?"

"Would *you* forget her? She was there with another man but I don't remember what he looked like."

"Do you know what they were talking about?" Frosser asked.

"He said she was asking about train schedules but knowing him he was probably trying to chat her up."

"And you didn't see her again?"

"No, I didn't."

"Thank you for your time," Frosser said, opening the door.

Dahn reluctantly turned away from the window and left the room.

Frosser told Clausen to disband the identity parade and then escorted Sabrina back to the interrogation room.

"The case against you is getting stronger by the minute," Frosser said after she had sat down. "You've been positively identified by two witnesses as having been at the warehouse when Rauff was murdered. Does the name Dieter Teufel mean anything to you?"

Had he been a less experienced policeman he would have failed to notice the split-second flicker of her eyes as she unconsciously reacted to the name. It was as good as an admission as far as he was concerned.

"He was killed under a train the day after you were seen talking to him. It was initially put down to an accident but now I'm not so sure. Could he have been pushed?" He let the question hang as he crossed to the wallheater to turn it down. "I've got enough evidence to convict you but there are still too many unanswered questions. I'm going to get my Lausanne colleagues to re-open the Teufel case. If I can pin a second murder charge on you you'll be inside for life. And I mean life."

She bit the inside of her mouth, a nervousness creeping into her thoughts for the first time since her arrest. If she was charged and the case went to court, which must be a possibility depending on how Philpott intended to handle the situation, there was enough evidence to convict her of at least wounding Rauff. The Beretta had been found in her possession but it would be far more difficult for the prosecution to connect her to the FN FAL found in the warehouse. If, however, Frosser managed to plant a seed of suspicion in a jury's mind that she was somehow implicated in Teufel's death (it would be virtually impossible to charge her with it), the evidence hinging on the FN FAL could sway the jury against her. It could mean the difference between attempted murder and murder. A murder conviction would land her in a maximum security prison, out of UNACO's reach.

She prayed that Philpott had a few aces up his sleeve.

"The commissioner will see you now, Colonel Philpott," the pretty blonde secretary said after acknowledging the intercom on her desk.

Philpott pressed his cane into the soft pile of the pale-blue carpet and eased himself to his feet.

The man warming himself by the artificial fire as Philpott opened the office door was in his early sixties, with thick white hair combed back from a face creased with the lines of responsibility from sixteen years as head of the Swiss police. Reinhardt Kuhlmann immediately stepped forward to offer Philpott an arm to lean on.

"Stop fussing." Philpott said irritably. "It's only a stiff leg."

"It wasn't bothering you the last time I saw you."

"That's because we were in Miami in the middle of summer. It's the cold that makes it so damn stiff and bothersome." Philpott sat in the nearest of the two armchairs.

"Coffee?" Kuhlmann asked.

"Not if you've still got some of that Hennessey cognac tucked away somewhere," Philpott replied, extending his palms towards the fire grille.

"You've got a good memory considering you haven't been up here for eighteen months," Kuhlmann said with a smile.

"Some things in life are worth remembering. Your cognac's one of them."

"You sound like the voice-over for a TV commercial," Kuhlmann said and poured a measure of cognac into a balloon glass.

"Aren't you having one?" Philpott asked as he accepted the glass.

"No alcohol. Doctor's orders."

"What's wrong?" Philpott asked with an anxious frown.

"Ulcers," Kuhlmann replied with a dismissive flick of his hand.

"You're pushing yourself too hard."

"That's good coming from you," Kuhlmann said and sat in the other armchair.

"Why can't you accept retirement like everyone else? You've got a wonderful wife, not to mention your two sons and their families. I know they'd all want to see more of you."

"Neither one of us is the retiring kind, Malcolm, and you know it. How's Marlene?"

Philpott stared at the cognac. "Our divorce came through earlier this year."

"I'm sorry, old friend, she's a good woman."

"I wouldn't disagree with that. She was the perfect tonic after my messy divorce from Carole. At least there weren't any ugly courtroom scenes this time round. We're still good friends.''

"That's the main thing," Kuhlmann sat back and crossed his legs. "I've made some initial enquiries about your operative. It's not going to be easy, Malcolm.''

Philpott placed the balloon glass on the table beside him. "Meaning?''

"Meaning it's not going to be a matter of conveniently dropping the charges. Not only is the investigating officer one of the country's leading detectives but the local press have also latched on to the case because of your operative's film star looks. It makes a great front page story.''

"Don't imagine for one second I intend to sacrifice one of my best operatives just to satisfy this country's gutter press.''

"She killed a man . . .''

"She wounded him, his colleague killed him.''

"She still shot him. This is Switzerland, not the OK Corral.''

"He was pointing a semi-automatic at her. What was she supposed to do? Ask him nicely to put it down? It comes back to the same old story: you've been opposed to UNACO ever since its inception.''

"I've been opposed to gun-toting foreigners shooting up my country," Kuhlmann retorted angrily.

"I can see your point. After all, your city financiers don't need guns to launder dirty money.''

Kuhlmann held up his hands. "This isn't getting us anywhere. You've got to understand my position, Malcolm. I can't just wave a magic wand and get her off.

Even if I could get Frosser to drop the charges how could I justify it to the public? There's too much evidence against her. The press would crucify the whole legal system. My hands are tied.''

Philpott glanced at his wristwatch. ''It's three o'clock. You'd better have managed to untie them by six.''

Kuhlmann stood up, fury evident in his eyes. ''Is that a threat?''

''It is if you feel threatened. You're the police commissioner, Reinhardt, use some of the authority that's been vested in you.''

''This is Switzerland, not Russia. Frosser has quite properly arrested your operative for attempted murder. I can't overrule his actions without a valid reason and I don't think you'd want me to tell him about UNACO, would you?''

Philpott took a sip of cognac and rolled it around in his mouth, savouring its smooth taste, then tilted his head back and allowed it to trickle down his throat, its warmth spreading through his body.

''I see you're determined to force my hand, Reinhardt. As you're probably aware I'm answerable only to the Secretary-General and if you and I haven't come to an acceptable agreement by six o'clock tonight I intend to call him personally and ask him to intervene on my behalf. I doubt he'd even bother consulting your ambassador at the United Nations: he'd be straight on to your President's private line to quietly remind him that Switzerland is one of the signatories on the original UNACO Charter. Furthermore, once this assignment's been successfully completed detailed reports will have to be sent to the leaders of all those countries our operatives have entered. That includes your President. I write the report and I might find myself sorely tempted to highlight the lack of Swiss security if one of my operatives is rotting in one of your jails because she defended herself against a known criminal toting a semi-automatic rifle. It's up to you how I word my report.''

Kuhlmann moved to the window of his sixth-floor office overlooking Bahnhofstrasse, Zurich's financial metropolis, and stared out over the River Limmat running through the heart of the city centre. His voice was bitter when he spoke. ''Intimidation, blackmail, threats, not to mention your apparent willingness to bend the law to suit your own purposes. You've become just like the very criminals UNACO was set up to combat.''

''It's not by choice, Reinhardt, but the only way to deal with this new breed of criminal is to fight him at his own game. I'm only sorry I've had to resort to some of those tactics today but my operatives are more than just employees to me. Marlene used to say I loved UNACO more than I loved her. She was nearly right. It's not UNACO as such, it's the people who work there. Especially my field operatives. They're like a family to me. Sabrina personifies the kind of daughter I would love to have had and now that she's in trouble I'll move heaven and earth to get her back safely into the fold.''

''Even if it means sacrificing our friendship?''

Philpott got to his feet and reached for his cane. ''I'll call you at six tonight.''

''You never answered my question,'' Kuhlmann said.

''Didn't I?'' Philpott replied, then closed the door silently behind him.

EIGHT

As the train pulled into Milan station Graham had to look twice at the priest standing on the platform to believe who it was. Kolchinsky was holding a bible in one hand and a battered bag in the other. He waited patiently until all those who were disembarking had done so then climbed aboard and headed straight for Sabrina's former compartment. It seemed to be locked from the inside, the curtains drawn across the window. Already taken. He opened the door of the adjoining compartment and stepped inside, glad to be out of the narrow corridor where passengers were pushing and jostling for the tenancy of the few remaining unoccupied compartments.

"Is this berth free?" Kolchinsky indicated the empty couchette.

"Come in, Father," Graham said with a smile as

he appraised Kolchinsky's attire. "Haven't you forgotten your crozier?"

Kolchinsky glanced behind him, then closed the compartment door. "I can do without your sarcasm. I was hoping to take the compartment beside you but it's already been taken."

"By me. I thought it might come in handy," Graham said and tossed the key to Kolchinsky. "If this were a movie I'd say you'd been horribly miscast. A KGB priest?"

"Ex-KGB," Kolchinsky retorted.

"And what happens if you're asked to bless someone? You know how religious these Italians can be."

"Then I'll do it. This used to be my main KGB cover and they made sure I was prepared for any eventuality."

"You're full of surprises," Graham said, then leaned forward, his face serious. "What's happening about Sabrina?"

Kolchinsky told him of the latest developments, including Philpott's ultimatum to Kuhlmann.

"What if Kuhlmann refuses to back down?"

"The Secretary-General could bring pressure on the Swiss Federal Assembly to make him back down but I can't see it coming to that. He's too much of a professional. That's why he's Europe's longest-serving police commissioner. He's just in a tight spot right now. How to secure her release without incurring the wrath of the international press."

Graham caught sight of a familiar face out of the corner of his eye. "What the hell's he doing here?"

"Who?" Kolchinsky asked.

"The policeman who arrested Sabrina."

"Gun and holster," Kolchinsky said and held out his hand.

"What?"

"It's fair to assume he's here to see you. All we need is for him to find your gun and holster. Now give them to me."

Graham handed his gun and holster to Kolchinsky who deposited them in his black leather bag.

"Do whatever he asks, even if it means accompanying him to the station for further questioning. We'll get you out soon enough and I'll be here meantime to keep an eye on the other two."

"You don't even know what they look like," Graham said.

"I know what Werner looks like." Kolchinsky opened the bible in his lap. "From now on we don't know each other."

When the sergeant knocked on the door Kolchinsky looked up and gestured for him to enter.

The sergeant doffed his cap. "Sorry to disturb you, Father, please carry on with your reading. I'm here to see this gentleman."

"What now?" Graham snapped.

"Would you please stand up?" the sergeant said.

Graham got to his feet and the sergeant frisked him expertly then pulled his arms behind his back and handcuffed him. A second uniformed policeman removed Graham's two holdalls from the overhead rack and left with them.

"What am I supposed to have done?"

"You are under arrest for conspiracy to murder. You'll be formally charged by the Swiss police."

Kolchinsky closed the bible and looked up. "Murder?"

"Please don't concern yourself, Father, it's a police matter."

Graham was led from the compartment and the sergeant grabbed his arm as they reached the steps leading from the coach and ordered two of his men to clear a path through the curious onlookers who had gathered around the train after seeing the arrival of the police car minutes earlier. As they neared the patrol car the crowd to their right parted to allow a white Alfa Romeo through. It drew to a halt a few feet from the car. The driver climbed out and crossed to where Graham and the sergeant were standing. The sergeant snapped to attention. The man drew the sergeant aside and spoke softly to him. The sergeant handed him a key.

The man approached Graham. "Mr. Green, I'm Lieutenant De Sica, Milan CID. I'm afraid there's been a case of mistaken identity." He unlocked the handcuffs. "I can only offer you my sincerest apologies for what's happened. The men involved will be dealt with accordingly." He handed Graham his passport. "Again I can only say how sorry I am for what's happened. You have my name if you wish to take the matter further."

The crowd thinned out as soon as the two cars were out of sight but a few lingering onlookers hovered around Graham, muttering amongst themselves. Graham finally walked back to the train and boarded it.

"What the hell was all that about?" he asked on returning to the compartment.

Kolchinsky retrieved the Beretta and holster from the bag and handed them to him. "I'd say Commissioner Kuhlmann's just conceded."

They turned to the window as the train shuddered into life and consequently neither of them saw Werner pass the door. When he reached his own compartment in the next coach he found the door was locked and the curtains drawn across the window. He rapped angrily on the glass. An unseen hand twitched the curtains and a moment later the door slid open. Hendrique was sitting on one of the couchettes methodically cleaning the components of his Desert Eagle automatic with a strip of cloth. Kyle hovered uncertainly beside Werner.

"Do I now need permission to enter my own compartment?" Werner snapped.

"Eddie, leave us. I'll talk to you later," Hendrique said without looking up.

Werner relocked the door after Kyle's hasty departure, then sat down opposite Hendrique. Since when is my compartment the meeting ground for you and your henchman?"

"It's not," Hendrique replied, then picked up the return spring and began carefully, almost lovingly, to clean each coil in turn. "Eddie merely came here to ask if I'd seen what happened on the platform."

"And did you?"

"No."

"Too busy cleaning your gun I suppose?"

"Too busy talking to Benin on the phone," Hendrique replied.

"What did General Benin have to say?"

"His backroom boys have finally identified our two friends. Blue eyes is ex-Delta, name's Mike Graham. Her surname's Carver, not Cassidy."

Werner snapped his fingers. "Of course, Sabrina Carver. Her father was a former American ambassador. George Carver."

"And the one in Mainz is using his own name. Whitlock. They work as a team, for UNACO."

"UNACO? I thought that was nothing more than a myth."

"So they would have the world believe. It seems they go to extraordinary lengths to cover their tracks."

"So how did General Benin find out?"

Hendrique smiled coldly. "Directorate S always finds out what it wants to know."

"What happens now?"

"We carry on as before. We've already rid ourselves of the girl. Whitlock will be dealt with in Mainz, which only leaves Graham. I've already got something in mind for him."

Werner watched as Hendrique began to reassemble the Desert Eagle, piece by piece. "Killing him will only bring the authorities."

"Who said anything about killing him? We fit him up, like the girl."

"You heard what happened back at the station. That was no case of mistaken identity, the orders for Graham's release must have come from the very top. The police are going to steer well clear of him from now on.''

"If he stays within the confines of the law. Why do you think it was so easy to fit up the Carver girl? She broke the law and UNACO can't release her without blowing its own cover. We can exploit their predicament further, only this time we use an innocent victim. An Italian. That's sure to stir up enough resentment across the country. The authorities would have to indict him for murder.''

''And what's to stop UNACO from sending out more agents?''

''Nothing, but Graham's our immediate concern. As my instructor at Balashikha used to say, 'You only have to be one step ahead to win the race.' Getting Graham off our backs will put us several steps ahead. By the time more agents have been briefed and despatched out here we'll be long gone.''

''And what happens if this plan of yours should fail?''

''Then you might have to play your trump card,'' Hendrique answered and glanced up at the attaché case on the overhead rack above Werner, its handle manacled to the hollow steel pipe running the length of the wall.

Werner swallowed nervously.

''Having second thoughts?'' Hendrique asked sarcastically.

''I'll do whatever it takes to ensure the success of this operation,'' Werner replied vehemently.

''A man prepared to die for his beliefs. What a touching, but futile, gesture.''

"And what would you be prepared to die for? Money?"

Hendrique pushed the magazine into the automatic. "Money's an incentive to live. The higher the stakes, the higher the incentive to live. What good's money, or beliefs for that matter, to a dead man?"

"My company's worth in excess of four hundred million pounds worldwide. Do you think all that money gives me more of an incentive to live? My life's motivated by purpose and direction. Marxism gives me that motivation."

Hendrique stood up and slipped the automatic into his shoulder holster. "With that kind of prophecy it's easy to see why you're Benin's blue-eyed boy."

"How are you going to frame Graham?"

"I'm going to kill two birds with one stone. I'll fill you in on the details later. Right now I want you to go and sit somewhere public. The dining car, bar lounge, observation car. It doesn't matter where, just as long as you're seen."

"What for?"

"An alibi. There mustn't be any chance of you being linked to the murder."

Hendrique waited until Werner had left before going in search of the conductor. He found him in a cramped, untidy cabin situated in the rear of the coach. He declined the offer of coffee and was glad he had done so when the conductor poured some into his own chipped mug. It looked more like molasses. The conductor listened to Hendrique's plan and initially refused even to consider it, but his attitude miraculously changed the moment Hendrique took a roll of banknotes from his

jacket pocket. He peeled off five 50,000-lire notes and
the conductor suggested a couple of changes to the
plan which he felt would make it run more smoothly.
Hendrique listened silently, glad of the conductor's
knowledge of the train's layout. They ran through the
revised plan, then Hendrique handed the notes to the
conductor, who stuffed them into his tunic pocket.
Hendrique watched him leave. He picked up a dog-
eared copy of an Italian magazine from the floor and
began to leaf through it. The centrespread model reminded him of his wife.

He had met her soon after graduating from Balashikha in 1973. She had been one of the dancers in a
dreadful cabaret show in a sleazy Casablanca nightclub where the liquor was cheap and the food inedible.
They were married a month later. He had initially
thought the man who arrived minutes after the ceremony was over to be a friend of hers but the truth had
been like a slap in the face when he announced he was
her pimp. He had beaten the pimp senseless in the
registry office but despite her tearful pleas that she was
off the game he had left Casablanca the same day. He
had never seen her again.

He tore out the centrespread and ripped it into pieces
then flung the magazine angrily against the wall.
Enough time had now elapsed, so he made his way to
the adjoining coach. The conductor was down on one
knee attending to one of the ventilator shafts. He
glanced at Hendrique and nodded before replacing the
grille. Hendrique removed the ''Out of Order'' sign
from the toilet door and locked himself inside.

The door had barely closed when the first wisps of

smoke seeped out through the grille, and within seconds it had become a dense, hazy fog that quickly permeated the corridor. The conductor, who had been standing tentatively at one end of the corridor, rushed into the smoke and rapped loudly on the compartment doors, requesting that passengers make their way to the next coach until the fault could be located. He assured them there was no danger—it was just a mechanical failure somewhere in the ventilation shaft—and promised to attend to it personally so they could return to their compartments as quickly as possible. Within thirty seconds the coach was deserted. The conductor knocked four times on the toilet door and Hendrique emerged. He followed the conductor through the billowing smoke until they reached the locked compartment previously occupied by Sabrina. Hendrique peered into the adjoining compartment. It was deserted. The conductor held the bunch of keys close to his face as he struggled to distinguish the various keys but finally selected one and unlocked the door. They entered the compartment and he locked it again.

"What did you want to look for, *signor*?"

"Nothing," Hendrique replied and dipped his hands into his jacket pocket.

The conductor's look of bewilderment became one of terror when he saw the black-handled survival knife in Hendrique's hand, its five-inch blade glinting under the overhead light. Hendrique drove the knife into the conductor's soft, bloated stomach then twisted it upwards, forcing the blade up through the ribcage. A sadistic smile touched the corners of his mouth as he watched the conductor's body shudder in the final seconds before death. The conductor sagged against the cupboard then slid lifelessly to the floor. Hendrique pulled the knife from the body then reclaimed his money before entering the adjoining compartment to plant the incriminating evidence. He then disappeared back out into the thick, clinging smoke.

A few feet away in the next coach something had been nagging at the back of Graham's mind ever since he had left the compartment but he just couldn't put his finger on it. As he stared at the smoke swirling against the glass on the other side of the door he suddenly realized what had been bothering him.

He grabbed Kolchinsky's arm. "I told you something was bugging me; now I know what it was. If that smoke was caused by a mechanical fault in the ventilator shaft then surely there should be a smell of burning as well."

Kolchinsky opened the door fractionally and sniffed the air. "There's no smell."

"Precisely."

"A decoy?" Kolchinsky said suspiciously.

"And no points for guessing who's behind it. Are you armed?"

"No. My gun's in my bag," Kolchinsky said guiltily.

"No matter, I'll go first."

Graham slipped out into the smoke-filled corridor with Kolchinsky tucked in closely behind him.

"He could have wired the door," Kolchinsky said once they reached their compartment.

"Not in such a short time. Hendrique's a methodical son-of-a-bitch."

Graham still took no chances and pressed his back against the strip of panelling between the two compartments, easing the door open an inch with the tips of his fingers. He felt for the frame then ran his finger down it for any traces of wires.

"Where are you?" he called out when he had finished.

"Behind you," came the reply.

"It's clean."

Graham pushed open the door and dropped to one knee, fanning the compartment with his extended Beretta. Kolchinsky appeared out of the smoke and closed the door behind him. He bent down and dabbed a spot on the carpet with his finger.

"What is it?" Graham asked.

"Blood," Kolchinsky replied, then took his Tokarev pistol from his bag.

Graham found another spot on the couchette and noticed a smear on the wall below the overhead rack. Only then did he notice his partially open holdall. He never left his holdalls open. He lifted it down and after checking for wires he unzipped it and peered inside. He retrieved the bloodied knife. They both turned to the communicating door. Kolchinsky slid it back and Graham lowered his Beretta on seeing the conductor. Kolchinsky checked for any sign of a pulse then looked up and shook his head. They both knew what had to be done.

"The window," Graham said.

"Even if he did fit through it, which I very much

doubt, don't you think someone in the coach behind us might be a little suspicious if they saw a body landing by the side of the track? Forget the window.''

''The wardrobe?''

''Far too small.''

''We've just run out of options and once this smoke clears Hendrique or one of his cronies is going to be back with some member of staff looking for the conductor. I don't relish the idea of explaining away the body and how the murder weapon just happened to find its way into my holdall.''

''There is a possible hiding place. You've got bandages in your holdall, bring them. You'll find a Swiss Army knife in my bag, bring that as well.''

''Bandages?''

''Just do as I say, Michael!''

Graham returned with a roll of bandage and the Swiss Army knife. He squatted down beside Kolchinsky who was busy unbuttoning the dead man's tunic. ''What do you want with the bandages? He's dead for Christ's sake.''

''Hopefully I can stem the flow of blood, at least temporarily. We don't want it seeping out from under there.'' Kolchinsky pointed to a strip of plywood covering the area from the bottom of the couchette to the carpet. ''I don't know what's behind there but it's our only chance. Use the knife to pry it open.''

The plywood board was held in place by a dozen small nails and Graham was careful not to bend them unduly as he prised them loose. It seemed to take forever but in reality it took him barely ninety seconds to remove the board from its wooden frame with the loss of two nails, both bent beyond repair. He squinted into the aperture. It was empty. He looked at the dead man. Would he fit? He scrambled to his feet and peeped through the drawn curtains. The smoke was thinning.

"Well, that will have to do," Kolchinsky said, securing the bandage with a tight knot. "Let's see if we can get him in there."

They tried to push the body into the aperture but it was too small.

"Tuck his legs underneath him, that should do it," Kolchinsky said and eased the body into the opening head first.

Graham did as he was instructed but although the legs fitted with a little room to spare the feet still protruded out on to the carpet. He tried to push them against the dead man's legs but they sprang out again. Kolchinsky forced the board over the aperture and, using the heel of his shoe as a hammer, banged the nails back into place.

"The weight of his legs will push the board open again. It's only made of flimsy plywood."

"It'll take a while. Someone's going to have a trip to remember when he finally does make his appearance."

Kolchinsky, with Graham's reluctant permission, used the shirt the knife had lain on in the holdall to remove the bloodstains from the carpet. He then wrapped it around the knife and stuffed it into his own bag.

The smoke had cleared by the time they had finished. Graham left his compartment and made his way up the corridor to the ventilator shaft. It was a simple matter to remove the grille and retrieve the cannister from the shaft. He carefully slotted the grille back into place and returned to his compartment, where he tossed the cannister to Kolchinsky.

"The mechanical fault," Kolchinsky said, turning it over in his hands.

"Take note of where it was made."

Kolchinsky had to hold the cannister sideways to read the printing: "Rosenstraat, Amsterdam."

"Hendrique country."

There was a knock on the door. Kolchinsky pushed the cannister into his bag and then stood up to open the door. A youth introduced himself as the assistant conductor and looked around the compartment before turning back towards the door and beckoning Hendrique to follow him.

"I apologize for this intrusion but I was asked to act as an interpreter. This man doesn't speak any English and I remember you telling me the other night you don't speak Italian. What about you, preacher? Do you speak English?"

"English or Italian, it makes no difference."

"The conductor seems to have gone missing and several of the passengers are certain they saw him go into the compartment next to this one when all that smoke was about. We tried the door but it must be locked from the inside. It's possible he locked himself in to try and evade the smoke and was subsequently overcome by the fumes. Your communicating door's the only other way in."

"Then we'd better check," Kolchinsky said, feigning a tone of alarm.

After unlatching the door he slid it open and entered the compartment, where he stood as if by chance on the wet patch of the carpet. The assistant conductor poked his head round the door then shrugged and stepped back. Hendrique pushed past him and stared at the spot where he had left the body. There was fury in his eyes as he looked from Kolchinsky to Graham.

"He must have recovered," Kolchinsky said.

"I'm sure he'll turn up sooner or later," Graham added, holding Hendrique's enraged stare.

Hendrique left without a word. The assistant conductor apologized for the interruption and closed the door behind him.

Graham latched the communicating door, then turned to Kolchinsky. "I don't care what the boss says, I'll kill Hendrique if he tries anything else."

"You know better than to let your feelings cloud your judgement," Kolchinsky retorted. "It's imperative that we find out where the plutonium's going. Kill Hendrique and the whole operation could be in jeopardy."

"The hell I'll be a sitting duck."

"Your re-evaluation comes up in two months' time. The Colonel would skin me alive if he knew I'd told you, but he's going to be pressing the Secretary-General to make it your last. We both feel you've proved yourself over the last twelve months. Don't do anything stupid."

Graham sighed deeply and sat down.

"I don't expect you to be a sitting duck, and neither

does the Colonel. If you're in danger of course you must defend yourself, but this is psychological stuff and you're strong enough to wait it out.''

''Like Sabrina?'' Graham said in a hollow voice.

Kolchinsky left the question unanswered.

Sabrina was officially charged with the murder of Kurt Rauff at 4:27 that afternoon. It had come as no surprise to her and even though she knew Philpott would be doing his utmost to secure her release she still felt a sense of abandonment as she watched Frosser fill in the charge sheet. She hadn't felt so alone since her terrifying childhood ordeal in the rat-infested cellar and she longed for a familiar face, even a familiar voice, to reassure her that she hadn't been forgotten.

If C.W. were here he would hold her hand reassuringly and put her at ease with his quiet, soothing voice. Despite her predicament she smiled to herself when trying to think of Graham doing the same. He would rather hold a handful of glowing embers and there would be little sympathy in his voice. He would tell her to stop feeling so damn sorry for herself. She knew which of them she would rather have with her right now . . .

She glanced at the man sitting beside her. A red-faced lawyer with thinning, wind-swept hair who had been appointed by the police to represent her. He had spent a frustrating twenty-five minutes trying to get her to speak. She had ignored him, preferring to stare at the wall. He seemed to be under the impression he was doing her a great favour by being there. She had been sorely tempted to put him in his place but knew he was worth neither the breath nor the effort. He was just another run-of-the-mill pettifogger. She knew if the case did go to trial UNACO would hire the best lawyer possible, regardless of cost, to handle her defence. Only then would she agree to cooperate.

A sharp rap on the door interrupted her thoughts. Sergeant Clausen poked his head inside and asked to speak to Frosser in private. Frosser banged his pen angrily on to the table and brushed past the policewoman at the door as he disappeared out into the corridor. A few minutes later he stormed back in, a telex clenched in his hand. He beckoned the lawyer forward and they discussed the telex briefly in murmured voices. The lawyer returned to the table.

"You're to be transferred to Zurich for further questioning."

She instinctively knew Philpott was involved in this latest development. If they were going to question her about the Dieter Teufel case she would have been taken to Lausanne, not Zurich. They had nothing to link her to any crime in Zurich. She knew Philpott must have a plan in mind and that lifted her spirits considerably.

Frosser noticed her smile and leaned over the table until his face was inches from her. "Remember one thing. Where you go, I go."

He left the room.

When he returned fifteen minutes later he was carrying a folder in one hand and her trenchcoat in the other. He tossed the trenchcoat on to the table in front of her. "The helicopter's arrived."

No sooner had she slipped her trenchcoat on than

Frosser pushed up her right sleeve and snapped a handcuff around her slender wrist. He attached the other handcuff to his left wrist and led her to the door. The lawyer picked up his briefcase and hurried after them.

She stopped abruptly and turned to face him. "And where do you think you're going?"

"Garbo speaks," Frosser said in amazement.

"I've got a chaperon," she said, jerking her manacled wrist. "I don't need another one."

"This is a very serious—"

"And I'll handle it my way," she cut in. "You're fired."

The flummoxed lawyer turned to Frosser for support.

Frosser merely shrugged. "It's her right to dismiss you."

The lawyer tried to reason with her but she turned her back and tugged on the handcuffs. Frosser led her along a narrow corridor, down a fire escape and out into the car pound at the back of the police station. The centre of the pound had been cleared to allow the Apache helicopter space to land. Its rotors were motionless, the pilot in a huddled conversation with the rookie who had been assigned to clear the cars. They looked up at the approaching figures, their eyes taking in and lingering on Sabrina. The rookie came out of his trance, saluted Frosser, then scurried back to the police building.

The pilot, a captain in the Swiss Air Police, grinned at Frosser, "I like your date, Bruno." Chuckling he clambered into the cockpit.

Frosser followed Sabrina into the cabin, partitioned off from the cockpit, and secured the door after him. They strapped themselves in as the pilot opened the throttle to start up the rotors. The pilot waited until the engine-rotor tachometer indicated the normal flying rpm, then raised the collective-pitch lever gradually to lift the helicopter off the ground. Once airborne he tilted the stick and altered the throttle power to increase the boost, then set his bearings and the helicopter banked sharply over the police station, heading due north-east.

Dusk had already settled over Zurich by the time the helicopter touched down at the prearranged rendezvous on a deserted airstrip five miles from Kloten International Airport. A black Mercedes was parked beside the disused hangar, its sole occupant waiting for the rotors to stop revolving before clambering from the car and heading across the overgrown runway to the motionless helicopter. The hatch opened and Frosser jumped the short distance to the ground, careful to keep his left arm extended so as not to wrench Sabrina after him. She ignored his offer of a helping hand and leaped nimbly from the cabin. The man showed his badge to Frosser then led the way back to the Mercedes. As the rotors started up Frosser glanced over his shoulder and gave the pilot an appreciative wave. The man held the back door open; as soon as Frosser had scrambled into the car after Sabrina he closed it, then climbed behind the wheel and accelerated the Mercedes away from the hangar. He guided it onto a stretch of abraded road, which had once been a busy

military thoroughfare before the airfield closed down
and joined up with the main highway a few miles further on.

Although the traffic was heavy there were hardly any
hold-ups and consequently the Mercedes was able to
reach the Zoll Bridge on the outskirts of the city centre
within fifteen minutes. As they entered Museum-
strasse the driver became aware of a police car behind
them, its lights flashing at him in the rearview mirror.
To begin with he was not sure what they wanted him
to do, but when the flashing headlights persisted he
pulled in to the side of the road in front of the Swiss
National Museum.

"What's going on?" Frosser demanded.

"I don't know, sir," the driver replied, then pressed
his badge against the window as the two uniformed
policemen approached the car.

One of the men squinted at the badge then gestured
for the driver to open his window.

The driver hissed angrily under his breath but com-
plied with the request. "We're transporting a prisoner
to the Bahnhofstrasse precinct. What's the problem?"

"Would you mind stepping out of the car, sir?"

"What's the problem?" the driver repeated.

"We'd like to take a look in the boot."

Frosser leaned forward to the open window. "What
do you want to look in the boot for? This is a police
car . . ."

"I appreciate that, sir, but we have our orders."

"Open it for them," Frosser snapped, then sat back.
The driver had barely climbed out of the car when

the two policemen spun him round, forcing him up against the back door.

"What the hell's going on?" the driver demanded, but when he tried to turn around he was shoved back up against the side of the car.

His hands were twisted behind his back and a pair of handcuffs snapped over his wrists.

A second police car screeched to a halt in front of the Mercedes and two more uniformed men climbed out. One wore the insignia of a lieutenant.

"Captain Frosser? I'm Lieutenant D'Angelo, sir."

"What's going on, Lieutenant?" Frosser asked in bewilderment.

"This man is one of her accomplices, sir."

"What are you talking about?" the driver shouted angrily. "I'm with the Zurich CID. The Captain's seen my ID."

"Taken from the body of the real detective," the lieutenant said.

"It contains my photo; check it if you want."

The lieutenant ignored the driver. "An APB was put out twenty minutes ago when the body of the real CID detective was found. We're just glad we got her in time, sir."

"Captain, I don't know who these men are but they're obviously in league with your prisoner," the driver said, struggling against the handcuffs.

"There is one way of proving our credibility. You received a personal telex this afternoon from Zurich, sir. Am I correct?"

"Yes," Frosser said hesitantly.

"I know who sent it." The lieutenant turned to the driver. "Do you?"

"No, but . . ."

"It was sent by the Commissioner. For your eyes only. Am I correct, sir?"

Frosser nodded.

"The Commissioner asked that the information be included in the APB because nobody apart from the two of you knew about it. He's waiting to talk to you on the radio, sir."

"Sir, it's a trap," the driver shouted.

"The telex was sent from the Commissioner's office. How could we know about it unless he released the information himself?"

"I believe you," Frosser said.

"Sir, you're being . . ."

"Book him. Murder One," the lieutenant interceded, then opened the door for Frosser.

The driver struggled furiously as he was led away, still shouting over his shoulder at Frosser.

"I'm grateful to you," Frosser said as he walked with the lieutenant to the police car. "I might have been in a lot of danger."

"That's why the Commissioner personally intervened with the APB, sir, We're dealing with a professional outfit here."

Frosser cast a sidelong glance at Sabrina. "Don't I know it."

"Help yourself, sir," the lieutenant said, indicating the radio.

Frosser eased himself into the passenger seat and reached for the radio. The three policemen closed in on the passenger door, blocking him from passing motorists. The lieutenant produced a dart gun but before Frosser could react he shot him in the neck. Sabrina grabbed Frosser's body with her free hand as he slumped forward and pushed him back against the seat.

"Hail to the cavalry," Sabrina said with a smile.

"Did you notice my giveaway clue?" the lieutenant asked as he rifled through Frosser's pockets for the key to the handcuffs.

"You said the driver had taken the ID disc from the body of the real detective. A UNACO operative would never kill a policeman, just immobilize him. Very subtle . . . Lieutenant."

"Call me Alain," he said, then unlocked the handcuff from her wrist and secured it around Frosser's other wrist. "Come on, Monsieur Rust is waiting. We'll ride in the Mercedes, with a police escort of course."

"What about the CID man?"

"Sleeping peacefully like our friend here. Once we reach the warehouse they'll be transferred back to the Mercedes and left somewhere near the Bahnhofstrasse precinct—so when they do finally wake up they'll find they've reached their destination after all."

"Deception with a smile. All part of the UNACO service." She climbed into the Mercedes beside him. "Where's this warehouse you were talking about?"

"Haven't you been there before?" Alain asked as they followed the police car over the Wilche Bridge.

"I didn't even know it existed."

"Not many people do. It's Monsieur Rust's pride and joy."

Alain swung the Mercedes into Limmatquai. The road, running parallel to the river, was lined with an assortment of converted restaurants, singles bars, nightclubs and even the occasional brothel spilling over from the Niederdorf, the city's red-light district, situated only a few yards away. The atmosphere reminded her of Greenwich Village: a Bohemian's paradise. They passed the baroque town hall and the gothic water church with its exquisite stained-glass windows, then crossed the junction on the Quai Bridge and Ramistrasse into Utoquai, lying on the gently swelling banks of Lake Zurich.

All three cars turned into a deserted side street off the Utoquai, the road littered with bricks and masonry from the friable walls of the derelict buildings to either side. A hoarding at the entrance to the street warned: FALLING MASONRY. CARS PARKED AT OWNERS' RISK. A second hoarding further on was more ominous: UNSAFE STRUCTURES. DANGEROUS. KEEP OUT! The leading police car slowed on nearing the cul-de-sac and swung on to the short ramp of the last warehouse, stopping inches from the battered corrugated-iron door. The driver spoke into the radio, identified himself with a password, upon which the door was opened electronically from within the warehouse and the three cars drove inside. Sabrina had been expecting to find the warehouse alive with activity. Instead it was gloomy and deserted. The two unconscious policemen were put in the back seat of the Mercedes and Alain gave her a wave before reversing it out into the street. The corrugated-iron door banged shut again. A rusty cage elevator ascended into view at the far end of the warehouse, and when it came to a halt Philpott and Rust emerged.

"Are you all right, *chérie*?" Rust asked anxiously.

"Fine. You left it pretty late though." She gave him a mock-reproving look. "So what exactly is this place?"

"UNACO's European Test Centre," Philpott replied.

"Like the one on Long Island?"

"Run on the same principle, only this one is smaller." Philpott tapped his cane on the concrete floor. "It's all under there."

"We own the whole street even though this is the only building in use," Rust added.

"So you erected those hoardings?"

Rust nodded. "There's nothing structurally wrong with any of these buildings. They're derelict, that's all. We initially had a problem with parked cars but after several were damaged by falling masonry word quickly spread around the city not to risk parking here."

"Don't you mean 'thrown' masonry?" she asked.

"Nobody was hurt, *chérie*, only the insurance man's pocket. We had to protect our privacy. We even went as far as to scatter debris across the street to give the impression that the buildings were unsafe."

"Designer rubble in other words," she said, poker-faced.

Philpott and Rust winced simultaneously.

"I couldn't resist it," she said, grinning.

A red light on the wall beside the elevator suddenly began to flash, its pulsating beam sweeping across the dimly-lit warehouse.

"What's that for?" she asked.

"Watch," Rust replied.

A circular section of the floor descended a few inches then parted, the two halves disappearing underneath the surrounding floor. Within thirty seconds there was a hole, fifty feet in diameter, in the centre of the warehouse.

First the rotors, then the fuselage, of a Lynx helicopter came into view. It was resting on a section of floor being raised from underneath the warehouse by a powerful hydraulic press. Once it came level with the floor it locked into place.

"I'm impressed," she said. "What else does it do?"

"It's going to take you to Italy so you can rejoin the train," Philpott said brusquely. "Now get in, you're already behind schedule."

The pilot reached over and pushed open the passenger door. She paused before climbing into the cockpit and turned back to Philpott. "Thank you, sir."

"Thank me by smashing this conspiracy."

She nodded, then scrambled in beside the pilot and secured the safety harness over her body.

The pilot waited until Philpott and Rust had descended in the cage elevator before starting up the rotors.

She craned her neck to peer through the window at the roof. "When does it open?"

"When I'm ready for take-off. It works on the same basis as the floor." He pointed to a holdall at her feet. "That's yours."

She unzipped it and looked inside. "Whose idea was this?"

"I don't even know what it is. Monsieur Rust asked me to give it to you."

"I might have guessed," she said and held it open for him to see.

"Is it what I think it is?" he asked, unable to hold back a smile.

"Exactly."

He chuckled, then put the radio microphone to his lips. "Sierra-Lima-Uncle 127, ready for take-off."

"Roof activated," came the reply.

There was a pause, then another voice came over the radio. "Emile, this is Jacques Rust. Don't forget the parcel."

"Parcel already delivered, Monsieur Rust." The pilot offered the mike to Sabrina. She took it from him.

"I'll get you for this, Jacques."

"I'll look forward to it, *chérie. Au revoir.*"

"*Au revoir,*" she replied with a smile and handed the radio back to the pilot.

She sat back as the helicopter started to rise.

Frosser sat alone in the captain's office at the Bahnhofstrasse precinct, a second mug of coffee on the table beside him. Although it had been an hour since he had woken in the Mercedes his head still ached with the after-effects of the tranquillizer dart and his wrists still bore the red grooves from where the handcuffs had dug into his skin. He had sent the CID driver home; the kid had done his best. The brunt of the blame rested squarely on his own shoulders. What frustrated him most of all was that he had no legal jurisdiction in Zurich and could therefore take no active part in the operation mounted to try and recapture the woman.

There was a knock on the door but he was unable to distinguish the silhouette through the frosted-glass panel.

"Come in," he called, then held out his palms towards the two-bar heater at his feet.

He shot to his feet when the door opened. Reinhardt Kuhlmann looked tired and drawn. The dark bags under his eyes stood out against his pale face and his windswept hair hung untidily over his ears and forehead. He raked the hair away from his eyes and unbuttoned his cashmere overcoat.

"Let me take that for you, Commissioner," Frosser said.

"I'll keep it on, Bruno, I won't be here very long," Kuhlmann replied and forced a weak smile. "Sit down, sit down."

Frosser perched anxiously on the edge of the chair. He knew Kuhlmann would have something to say about the events leading up to the woman's escape but he had never expected him to come in person. It only seemed to add to the seriousness of the situation.

"I've just got off the phone to Captain Moussay," Kuhlmann said, glancing at the nameplate on the desk. "A handful of witnesses have already come forward to say they saw two police cars escorting a black Mercedes along the Limmatquai. None of them knows where the cars went."

"It's a start, sir," Frosser said optimistically.

"He won't get any further. We're dealing with professionals here. As good a policeman as he is, he'll

flounder about for a few days then the investigation
will begin to wind down and within a couple of weeks
it will become just another dossier in the mound of
unsolved cases. That's where I want it to stay.''

Frosser looked bewildered. ''I don't follow you,
sir.''

''I want the case shelved. Both here and in Fribourg.''

Frosser stared at the heater and thought about the
telex from Kuhlmann earlier that afternoon. ''You set
me up, sir.''

Kuhlmann moved to the window and looked through
the slats of the Venetian blind at the city lights spread
out like some vast picture postcard. ''I had no
choice.''

''You knew they were going to snatch the woman.
You risked my life . . .''

''Your life was never at risk. I knew they'd snatch
the woman but I didn't know how or where they'd do
it.''

Frosser shook his head slowly. ''I can't believe it,
sir, you deliberately set me up.''

''She had to be released but the charges could hardly
be dropped with the amount of media coverage this
case has already attracted.''

''*Had* to be released?''

''Had to be released,'' Kuhlmann repeated. ''I don't
like it any more than you do but there are times when
pride has to be swallowed.''

''Who was she?''

''It's classified. All I can tell you is that she's an

undercover operative. She was on assignment when she shot Rauff.''

"What if I choose not to drop the case?" Frosser challenged.

"I know for a fact that a promotion's in the pipeline for you. It has been for the past four months in case you're thinking it's some kind of pay-off. Don't throw away your future over the death of some insignificant criminal, Bruno, it's not worth it."

"No, sir, I guess not." Frosser got to his feet. "Consider the case closed."

Kuhlmann left the office.

Frosser raised the mug in a toast. "Here's to equality and justice."

The coffee tasted bitter.

NINE

Graham drank down the last mouthful of coffee then sat back contentedly. "I'll say this for the Italian railways, the food's great."

"Delicious," Kolchinsky confirmed between mouthfuls of cassata.

Graham looked past him at the end table on the other side of the dining car. "Werner's just paid for the meal. They'll be leaving any minute now."

"There's no point in tailing them while the train's moving. They can't go anywhere." Kolchinsky consulted his wristwatch. "When are we due in Piacenza?"

"The waiter said around 8:30."

"Ten minutes," Kolchinsky replied, then spooned the last of the ice cream into his mouth.

Graham called over the waiter. "Can we have the check?"

"Il conto, per favore," Kolchinsky said when the waiter frowned at Graham.

The waiter nodded, then left.

Werner and Hendrique got to their feet and walked down the aisle between the rows of tables.

"Excuse me, aren't you the gentleman who was with Sabrina?" Werner asked, pausing to look down at Graham.

"Sabrina?"

"The young lady who was arrested at Vergiate."

"Yeah, I was with her, but we'd only met the night before. I didn't even know her name. Do you know her?"

"I did once. A long time ago."

"Why don't you sit down?" Kolchinsky said, indicating the two vacant chairs on either side of the table.

"Why thank you, Father," Werner said and sat down beside him. He introduced himself and Hendrique, using the alias Joe Hemmings.

"Father Kortov," Kolchinsky said, shaking Werner's hand.

"What part of Russia are you from?" Werner asked.

"Moscow originally but I was forced to leave. I work in America now."

"Yes, the Russian authorities are notorious iconoclasts."

Graham took the bill from the waiter and mentally worked out what he owed. Kolchinsky paid the balance.

"A drink perhaps?" Werner asked and indicated that the waiter should stay.

"What does one drink after a meal in Italy?" Kolchinsky asked.

"The favourite liqueurs are Amaretto and Sambuca."

"Amaretto? That's almond flavour, isn't it?" Kolchinsky asked, feigning ignorance. "Liquor isn't one of my strong points."

"I should hope not, Father," Werner said, chuckling. "You're quite right though, it's an almond liqueur."

"That would be nice, thank you," Kolchinsky replied.

Werner looked at Graham. "How about you Mr. . . . ."

"Green. Michael Green. Nothing for me."

"Are you sure?"

"Positive."

"Due Amaretti, per favore," Werner said to the waiter, who then hurried away.

"Any sign of your missing conductor?" Graham asked Hendrique.

Hendrique shook his head.

"I'm sure there's a perfectly logical explanation for his disappearance," Werner said, breaking the uneasy silence.

The waiter returned with the liqueurs.

After paying for them Werner held up his glass. "To the future."

"I'll drink to that," Kolchinsky said, touching glasses.

Werner took a sip. "I can't imagine Sabrina involved in anything as sordid as murder. She always struck me as the epitome of refinement."

"Murder has no class boundaries," Hendrique said.

"True enough, but I still can't imagine her as a murderess."

"Perhaps she's a spy," Hendrique countered with a faint smile.

"Piacenza, Piacenza," the assistant conductor announced from the doorway.

Werner drank down his Amaretto, then stood up. "I think I'll turn in and read a few chapters of my book. Nice to have met you both. I'm sure we'll meet again."

Kolchinsky gripped the proffered hand. "I'm sure we will. And thank you for the drink."

"My pleasure," Werner replied with a curt bow.

Hendrique pushed back his chair and followed Werner out of the dining car.

"We know they know and I'm pretty sure they know we know. It's a stalemate. And if they know we know they're almost certainly going to change their plans. We have to be ready for that." Kolchinsky finished his Amaretto and put the glass in the centre of the table.

"Right," Graham said without any conviction. Kolchinsky had left him behind after the first sentence. He stifled a yawn and got to his feet. "You coming?"

"Sure," Kolchinsky replied.

They reached the compartment as the train came to a halt in the brightly illuminated Piacenza station. The corridor windows were facing the platform and Graham scanned the assortment of passengers waiting to board the train.

"There's a nun out there," Graham called out over his shoulder.

"Come in and close the door," Kolchinsky urged. "If she sees me she's sure to want to talk. Come inside."

Graham entered the compartment and slid the door shut. "This waiting game's playing on my nerves. We're running out of time and those bastards could give us the slip any time. Who's to say they're even going to Rome? All they need to do is uncouple the freight car and we've lost them."

There was a knock at the door.

Graham unholstered his Beretta and slipped it into his jacket pocket, then peeked through a hairline crack between the two drawn curtains. "It's the nun, she must have seen you from the platform."

"That's all we need. You'd better open the door."

"We could ignore her," Graham suggested.

"We can't ignore her. Open the door, I'll speak to her."

Graham shrugged and did as he was told. The nun picked up her holdall and came in, her head bowed.

"This compartment's already occupied, Sister. I'm sure . . ." he tailed off when she looked up at him. "Sabrina?"

"I'd say we've got the same tailor," she said, removing her black-rimmed glasses. "One Monsieur Jacques Rust."

Graham locked the door. "What the hell's going on? How did you get out of custody? How did you get here for that matter?"

She held up her hands defensively. "Give me a chance to sit down and I'll answer all your questions."

"Fancy a coffee?" Kolchinsky asked.

Her smile answered the question.

"You can get something to eat later. The dining car's open till ten. I've no idea why, there are barely enough passengers for a first sitting," Kolchinsky said on his way out in search of coffee.

When he returned it was with a small tray on which was a cup of hot coffee and a slice of chestnut cake with freshly whipped cream. She refused the cake so he ate it while she described what had happened, from the time of her arrest at Vergiate to the helicopter flight from Zurich.

"This is for you, Sergei, from the boss," she concluded, taking a sealed envelope from the holdall and handing it to Kolchinsky.

Kolchinsky slit the seal open, read the contents of the letter and then burned it. "The Colonel wants us to impound the plutonium as soon as possible. He feels it's too dangerous to play this cat and mouse game with them any longer, especially with Hendrique on the loose with such an array of weapons. This train's only so big and innocent people are likely to be hurt if he's not stopped."

"One has already. The conductor."

Kolchinsky nodded and explained the incident briefly to Sabrina.

She glanced at the communicating door. "Make sure you point out which couchette he's under before I turn in. I'd hate to sleep on him."

"I'm sure he wouldn't mind," Graham said sardonically.

She gave him a contemptuous smile then turned to Kolchinsky. "Have you got a plan in mind?"

"It's the outline of a plan. Whether it's feasible is quite another matter."

Graham and Sabrina listened to him in silence then the three of them thrashed out the details until they were in agreement how to implement it.

Sabrina then went through to the dining car and while she ate she thought about C.W. and wondered how he was progressing with his investigation in Mainz.

The telephone rang.

Whitlock rolled over sleepily in bed and fumbled in the darkness for the overhead light switch. He knocked something over and by the noise it made on hitting the carpet he knew it was the quarter-full glass of water he had left on the bedside table before going to sleep. He found the switch then lifted the receiver to his ear, his forearm shielding his eyes from the dazzling light.

"Hello?" he muttered, stifling a yawn.

The voice at the other end was little more than a hoarse whisper.

"Hello?" he said irritably. "You'll have to speak up."

"C.W.?" the voice was barely audible.

"Yes, who's speaking?"

"Karen."

"It's . . ." He squinted at the bedside clock with

one eye. "God, it's 2:40 in the morning. What do you want?"

"He's outside."

"Who?" he asked, struggling to sit up in bed.

"The man in the black Mercedes who tried to run us down at the Hilton. He's on the porch. Please help me."

He heard the sound of breaking glass over the telephone.

She screamed.

"Karen! Karen!" he shouted into the mouthpiece. "Are you there?"

"He's getting into the house," she whimpered. "He's going to kill me."

"Lock yourself in one room and barricade the door. I'll be there as fast as I can."

"C.W., please . . ."

"Karen, get off the phone and do as I say!"

He cut her off and immediately called the police, who promised to send a car round to her house without delay. He dressed quickly and pocketed the Browning as he hurried from the room. After getting brief, but accurate, directions from the night manager at the reception desk he ran out into the car park to where the Golf was parked. He started it up first time and sped out into Kaiserstrasse, heading south towards the Rhine. The wheels shrieked as he swung into Rheinallee, a promenade running parallel to the river, then over the Heuss Bridge into the eastern side of the city. He lost his bearings and had to double back to the bridge, much to his frustration, then sped up Boetcke-strasse, past the dominating castle on his left (which the night manager had specifically mentioned), and almost missed Hindenburgstrasse but managed to negotiate the bend at the last possible moment. The Golf mounted the kerb but he quickly regained control of the wheel and pulled up behind the police car, its rooflights flashing, in front of the old Roman Catholic church. He leaped out and sprinted up the driveway but was prevented from entering the house by a uniformed policeman. He looked past the policeman at the slivers of broken glass strewn across the hall carpet then explained who he was in hesitant, but comprehensible, German. The policeman called out to an unseen colleague in the lounge and Whitlock was allowed to enter.

Karen was sitting on the edge of the sofa in the lounge, a dressing gown tied tightly around her, a white handkerchief in her hands. It was only when she looked up that he could see the bluish welt under her left eye. She ran to him and hugged him fiercely, tears spilling down her cheeks. Just as suddenly she pulled back and smiled sheepishly. He squeezed her hand reassuringly and led her back to sit with him on the sofa. The policeman, sitting in an armchair beside the sofa, questioned Karen a while longer then turned his attention to Whitlock and asked him a few routine questions. When the fingerprint man announced he was through dusting the front door the policeman got to his feet and promised Karen a police car would pass the house at regular intervals for the rest of the night. She saw him to the door and waited until he had driven away before returning to the lounge. Whitlock handed her the compress lying on the coffee table and she reluctantly held it against the swelling.

"Coffee?" she asked softly.

"I'll make it, you just keep the compress in place."

The kitchen was compact, with built-in pine cupboards and a pine table in the middle of the floor with matching benches on either side of it. She sat down on one of the benches and watched as he prepared a fresh brew of percolated coffee. He unhooked two mugs from the row against the wall, poured coffee into each, then took a carton of milk from the fridge and put it on the table.

"Thanks for coming so quickly, and for calling the police," she said after he had seated himself opposite her.

"I'm only sorry I wasn't able to prevent that," he said indicating her eye. "And keep the compress on."

"It's uncomfortable," she replied with a grimace.

"It's meant to be. What happened tonight?"

"I was woken up by a noise outside and when I came downstairs I saw the Mercedes parked in the driveway. I'm sure it was the same one that was used to try and run us down at the Hilton. Then I saw a shadow on the porch. I know I should have called the police but I panicked and you were the first person who came to mind. He smashed one of the panes in the front door while we were talking . . ."

"Yeah, I heard it," he said grimly.

"I ran to the bathroom but the bolt's very flimsy. He broke down the door and then hit me. When he heard the police siren in the distance he fled. Thank

God there was a police car in the vicinity to respond to the call.''

"What did he look like?''

"He was wearing a balaclava. I'm scared, C.W., I'm really scared.''

"Do you want me to stay with you tonight?''

"Very much,'' she said squeezing his hands.

He pulled away. "As a night watchman.''

"You're married, aren't you?''

"Six years now.''

She smiled sadly. "Why are the best men always married? It's not fair.''

"I'm sure the single guys say the same about women. I did, until I met my wife.''

"Have you got children?''

"We've never wanted any. Maybe we'll regret it some day.''

"I never regretted having Rudi. I'll always have the memories.'' She studied his face as he stared thoughtfully into space. "Your wife's a very lucky woman.''

"Lucky? In what way?''

"To have a husband who doesn't cheat on her the moment she's out of sight. Not many men would turn down the chance of sleeping with me.''

He was surprised by the arrogance in her voice. It seemed out of place after what she had just been through.

She noticed his frown. "I know I'm beautiful. Is that such a crime? It's not vanity, it's just honesty.''

"There's nothing wrong with believing in yourself,'' he said tactfully.

"More coffee?''

"No, thank you." He got to his feet. "Get some sleep. I'll be on guard down here."

"I'll sit with you," she said after putting the two mugs in the sink.

"No, I want you to go to bed. You'll only be in the way if he does come back. Don't worry though, he won't get past me."

She kissed him lightly on the cheek. "Thanks again. If you need anything I'm upstairs, second door on the left."

"I'll see you in the morning," he said with a smile.

"Help yourself to anything you want. There's plenty of food and I pride myself on a well-stocked drinks cabinet. It's in the lounge, I'll show you."

"No need, coffee is all I want. Now go on, off to bed."

She stifled a yawn. "I suddenly feel really tired. I guess all the excitement is finally getting to me."

He waited until she had gone upstairs before checking the windows and doors. They were all closed. He returned to the kitchen and poured himself another cup of coffee. He looked at the sleeping tablets on the sideboard. The one he had dissolved in her coffee would knock her out until morning. It would leave her with a slight headache but she would put that down to her bruised eye. He had drugged her for two reasons. She would get a good night's sleep despite her bruise, and she would also be out of harm's way should her attacker return. He switched off the kitchen and lounge lights and sat on the sofa allowing his eyes to adjust slowly to the darkness. When they had he moved to the bay window and tugged back the curtain to get a clear view of the street and the driveway. He sat down and waited.

His hand tensed on the Browning each time a set of headlights came into view, then relaxed when the car subsequently drove past the house. The Mercedes returned half an hour later. At least, that was the first time he saw it. It passed three times, slowing on each occasion so the driver could scan the house for any sign of activity. When it reappeared for the fourth time it drew to a halt on the opposite side of the road. The driver climbed out, a Mini-Uzi in his gloved hand.

Whitlock moved to the front door and pressed himself against the wall inches from the broken pane of glass. The driver would have to put his hand through to unlatch the safety chain. Although the driver was wearing rubber-soled shoes Whitlock could still hear him moving stealthily across the porch until his silhouette loomed up against the rippled-glass door. He grabbed the hand as it snaked through the broken pane and jerked it up on to a shard of glass. The driver screamed in agony as the glass sliced through the back of his hand. Whitlock quickly slipped the chain and yanked open the door, snapping the glass from the frame, and punched the driver hard on the side of the head. The blow knocked him backwards into the cane furniture on the porch. Recovering himself, the driver grabbed one of the overturned cane chairs and brought it up viciously into Whitlock's stomach then vaulted over the railing and sprinted to the Mercedes, his left arm dangling limply by his side.

By the time Whitlock reached the Golf the Mercedes had already accelerated away from the house. He started up the Golf and sped after the black car as it hurtled down Boetckestrasse towards the docklands along the Rhine. The Mercedes failed to negotiate the bend as it cut into Rampenstrasse and slammed into the side of a parked Volkswagen. Whitlock brought the Golf to a halt and waited. The Mercedes, with smoke escaping from its crumpled radiator, reversed and narrowly missed a Renault van parked on the other side of the street. The driver swung the wheel violently as the Mercedes drew abreast of the nearest side street and somehow managed to negotiate the narrow entrance without damaging the bodywork any further. He could only have realized at the last possible moment that the side street led directly on to the wharf but when he slammed on the brakes the wheels failed to grip on the wet surface and the car cartwheeled once before slewing another ten yards and disappearing over the side into the water.

By the time Whitlock had cut the engine and run to the edge of the wharf the Mercedes was already sliding backwards into the water. He stood where he was for several minutes after the car had sunk but there was no sign of the driver. He returned to the Golf and drove back to the house. After checking that Karen was still asleep he made himself a fresh brew of coffee and took his mug into the lounge. Seated on the sofa he closed his eyes and thought about Carmen back in New York.

Within minutes he had fallen asleep.

A sharp rap on the compartment door woke Graham and Kolchinsky.

Kolchinsky climbed off the couchette and peered through the crack between the curtains. He unlocked the door and slid it back.

The assistant conductor gave him a tired smile. *"Buon giorno. Correggio, quindici minuti."*

"Grazie," Kolchinsky replied and took the tray from him.

The assistant conductor closed the compartment door and headed off down the corridor, whistling softly to himself.

Graham rubbed his eyes sleepily. "Correggio?"

"Fifteen minutes," Kolchinsky said and handed him a cup of coffee.

"What time is it?" Graham asked.

"Five to four."

Graham sat up and watched Kolchinsky shave over the small washbasin in the corner of the compartment. Each stroke of the blade was timed to coincide with the train's systematic rocking. He then studied Kolchinksy's white bodysuit.

"Standard KGB issue?"

Kolchinsky met Graham's eyes in the reflection of the mirror. "No, just common sense. It's thermal, perfect for this kind of weather."

Graham stretched, then got to his feet. He was wearing a tracksuit and a pair of thick woollen socks. He dropped nimbly to the floor and effortlessly executed thirty one-handed press-ups, alternating hands. This was followed by fifty sit-ups and he completed the short programme with twenty normal press-ups before springing to his feet and dusting his palms together.

"Is that a daily routine?" Kolchinsky asked, towelling his face.

"It's part of a daily routine. There isn't time to do it all."

Five minutes later they were both dressed in suitably warm, insulated clothes in readiness for the sub-zero temperatures they would encounter on leaving the train at Correggio.

"Sabrina asked to be woken before we left. I think you should do it."

Graham shrugged and opened the communicating door. She was curled up on the couchette, her knees drawn up to her chest, her right hand trailing on the carpet. The blankets had slipped down to her waist and although she looked uncomfortable her face was serene and peaceful. He was about to shake her then abruptly changed his mind and carefully pulled the blankets up over her shoulders, tucking them in gently around her neck. He considered slipping her arm under the blankets but decided against it; the movement would almost certainly wake her.

Kolchinsky stood aside to let Graham back into the compartment. He closed the communicating door silently. "So, there is another side to the cynical Michael Graham."

"What?" Graham said sharply. "Why wake her now? She's not involved in this part of the operation. Let the kid sleep, she's had a couple of rough nights in police custody. Come on, the train's slowing; we must be nearing Correggio."

By the time they reached the end of the corridor the train had already pulled into the dimly-lit station. The platform was deserted and apart from a frumpy middle-aged woman with a whimpering child they were the only passengers to alight from the train. Graham picked up his two holdalls and followed Kolchinsky through the unmanned ticket barrier into the deserted concourse.

"I'll call Zurich and get them to send through a helicopter as quickly as possible."

Graham sat on the nearest bench and watched Kolchinsky cross to the row of public telephones against the far wall. A prostitute entered the station from the street and approached Graham. She was a teenager with an attractive face marred by an excessive amount of make-up and a slender figure accentuated by the tight-fitting black leather jacket and mini-skirt. She rested one of her feet on the bench.

"*Buon giorna, come si chiama?*" she purred seductively and traced her finger over his lips.

He batted her hand aside and glared up at her. "I'm not interested. Take a walk."

Although she understood no English the tone of his voice was enough to warn her off. She walked back towards the entrance leading out into the street.

"Who was that? A prostitute?" Kolchinsky asked when he returned.

"Yeah, a baby-pro," Graham said dismissively.

"A baby-pro?" Kolchinsky asked, frowning.

"Jailbait. A hooker who's still under the legal age of consent." Graham gestured towards the telephones. "Did you get through to Zurich?"

Kolchinsky lit a cigarette then nodded. "We've had

a stroke of luck. One of our helicopters is in Milan. It should be here within the hour.

"Where do we meet it?"

"We don't. Zurich said they'll have a hired car waiting at the landing place so the pilot can come through and pick us up."

Graham glanced at the prostitute standing in the entrance. "When I see a tramp like that I guess I should appreciate Sabrina a little more."

"I think you do already, only you won't admit it. Take tonight for instance, on the train."

"I covered her up because the last thing we need at this stage of the assignment is her going down with pneumonia. You're making a lot out of nothing, Sergei."

"Am I?" Kolchinsky replied. "She thinks a lot of you, you know."

Graham stared at his feet. "We're so different. She's the epitome of the little Yuppie girl. A slave of fashion, living in the affluent part of the city, eating out at all the chic restaurants, driving a Mercedes Sports bought for her by Daddy. That's another thing, her father's done everything for her. He bought her a flat, bought her a sports car, influenced the Secretary-General . . ."

"No!" Kolchinsky interceded sharply. "She's here on merit and you know it. You've seen her shooting, she's in a class of her own. I'll tell you this, you were the envy of every Strike Force member when you were brought in to replace Jacques. They'd have done anything to be in her team."

Graham got to his feet. "There's a pinball machine over in the corner. It'll help pass the time."

He was still playing the machine when the helicopter pilot arrived forty minutes later. Kolchinsky took him across to meet Graham.

"Are you ready, *Tommy*?"

"I'm impressed," Graham said without taking his eyes off the machine. "I didn't know they showed films like that in Russia."

"I saw it at the Odeon in Leicester Square. I hated it."

"I'm not surprised, it's hardly a film for geriatrics."

"Thank you very much. Actually I . . . went with one of the secretaries from the Russian Embassy. She wanted to see it."

"Enough said," Graham replied and clocked up his seventh free game. "Okay, I'm ready . . ."

They left the station and climbed into the hired Peugeot 305. It was a short journey to the makeshift airfield, a flat strip of snow-covered grassland on the outskirts of the town. Graham grabbed his two holdalls and made his way towards the Lynx helicopter. Kolchinsky spoke to the pilot through the open driver's window then walked across to where Graham was waiting.

"Ready?"

"Ready, but why isn't the pilot warming up the helicopter?"

"Because he's not flying it. I am."

"You are?" Graham said with surprise. "Since when do you fly helicopters?"

"Since I got my licence twenty years ago."

Graham exhaled deeply then moved over to the helicopter and climbed in beside Kolchinsky.

"You're quite safe, I assure you."

"I don't doubt it," Graham said, strapping himself into the seat. "I just never knew you could fly these contraptions. I suppose the KGB trained you?"

"On the contrary. I learnt to fly while I was serving as a military attaché in Stockholm. It was something to alleviate the boredom."

The pilot, who had been directing the Peugeot's headlights at the helicopter, returned Kolchinsky's wave, then swung the car round and headed back towards the highway.

"How long before we catch up with the train?" Graham asked once they were airborne.

"You're sitting on the map."

Graham tugged the map free and opened it out on his knees. He traced his finger along the dotted black line representing the railway track. "If my memory serves me correctly it was due out of Modena at 4:45. It's now—" he pushed back his cuff to reveal his gold plated Piaget watch "—5:17. How long was it due to stay in Modena?"

"Fifteen minutes."

"Then it should be somewhere around Castelfranco Emilia right now, about twenty-five miles away."

"We're slightly ahead of the schedule Zurich radioed through to the pilot. That means we should catch up with the train before it reaches Anzola d'Emilia. Are you with me?"

"You knew all along, why didn't you just say when I asked you?"

"Just testing," Kolchinsky replied with a smile.

Graham folded the map and slipped it behind the seat. He unclipped his watch and turned it around in his hands. "Carrie gave me this for my thirty-fifth birthday. We went to the theatre that night. She'd booked the tickets five months in advance. She even got me to wear a tux."

"You in a tuxedo? I can't imagine it."

"Neither could I, but she was determined to make a night of it. We took in the show on Broadway then went on to Christ Cella's where I had the best T-bone steak I've ever tasted, and we ended up drinking Irish coffees at Fat Tuesday's until three in the morning. What's more she paid for everything. God only knows what it must have cost her but she refused to let me touch my wallet. She kept insisting it was my night. It was the last time we ever went out together. I was sent to Libya ten days later."

"Vasilisa loved the theatre. We'd go at least once a month but I haven't been now for over seven years, not since she died. It wouldn't be the same without her."

"I know what you mean," Graham said, then snapped the watch around his wrist.

Kolchinsky checked the Air-Speed Indicator then glanced at his watch. "We should be over the train in a couple of minutes."

Graham zipped his parka up to his neck and pulled on a pair of gloves.

"Don't forget the balaclava," Kolchinsky reminded him.

"I don't intend to, it's in my holdall."

"Michael, you don't—"

"I know, it's dangerous as hell but we agreed last night that it's essential to the success of the operation. Don't worry, I'm your man. The boss has always called me a daredevil, now it's time to live up to the image."

"You've always lived up to it."

"You look more nervous than me. Christ, all you have to do is hold this baby steady. I'm the one who has to rappel in the pitch dark onto the roof of a moving train."

Kolchinsky handed him a miniature headset consisting of an earphone and microphone connected by a thin strip of durable wire. Graham slipped it on then clambered into the cabin where he pulled the balaclava over his head.

"Train a hundred yards ahead," Kolchinsky said into his mouthpiece.

Graham unlocked and opened the hatch, flooding the cabin with a rush of glacial air. After checking that one end was securely bolted to the cabin floor he flung the rope ladder out through the open hatch. He looped his hand through the wallstrap and leaned forward precariously, trying to catch a glimpse of the train. He could vaguely make out its outline in the helicopter's dimmed undercarriage lights. It was at least sixty feet below them.

"I'm going to need more light," he said.

"Look in the black box behind you, there should be a Halolight in there."

Graham unclipped the box lid and opened it. He found what he was looking for. A disc-shaped light attached to a leather headband which could be adjusted according to the wearer's specification. It had been created in the UNACO laboratories along the lines of the Davy lamp. He fitted it around his head then ensured the light was positioned in the centre of his forehead.

"Ready," he said, moving to the open hatch.

There was a brief silence before Kolchinsky spoke. "Altitude thirty-eight feet. Ready."

Graham turned his back on the open hatch and took a firm grip on the section of rope ladder lying on the cabin floor. He stepped out into the bitterly cold night air. Although the wind was negligible the rope ladder was swaying from side to side due to the concentrated buffeting of the rotors above him.

"How are you doing?" Kolchinsky asked.

"The rotors are whipping up a bit of a hurricane out here. No chance of switching them off, I suppose?"

He heard Kolchinsky's chuckled response in his earpiece.

Each step was a carefully planned manoeuvre, easing his foot off one rung and on to the next where he had to feel for the right grip before committing himself. There was an element of cautious apprehension in his movements, but no fear in his eyes. He had long since come to regard fear as man's most negative characteristic. With fear came hesitancy, stupidity and uncertainty, any of which could cost a life. He had witnessed it countless times on the battlefields of Vietnam where he had come to learn so much about himself. He regarded fear as nothing more than a chimera and the only way to negate it was an absolute belief in one's own ability. It was a principle he had carried

over into his training of Meo tribesmen in Thailand
after his injury in Vietnam. His critics accused him of
brainwashing his troops with little consideration for
human life, especially when it was revealed he used
live ammunition during the weekly obstacle course.
His answer had been simple. The only way to combat
fear was to confront it, and believe enough in oneself
to overcome it. Figures released after the war showed
that over a two-year period his troops had not only
suffered the least casualties but had also been awarded
the most medals for bravery out of all the Meo battal-
ions in Thailand. His only regret was that the figures
hadn't been released any earlier. Most of his critics
were dead, the victims of the fear syndrome he had
tried so hard to make them understand.

The ladder was swaying wildly by the time he
reached the halfway point. He could see a couple of
lights further down in the train, presumably in the
coaches, but the front of the train was shrouded in a
veiled mist as the first lights suffused the distant horizon. Carrie had always maintained there was nothing
more beautiful than a New York sunrise. He had disagreed. Beauty to him was the symmetry of the perfectly delivered curve ball in baseball or the angled
precision of a flawless touchdown pass in football. He
put those thoughts from his mind and concentrated on
the next rung of the ladder. The train was less than ten
feet away and he was already planning how he would
land and get to the bulky padlock securing the door
on the side of the freight car.

"Michael, I'm picking up something on the radar,
dead ahead."

The powerful spotlight underneath the helicopter illuminated the whole train. They both saw the stone bridge thirty yards away.

"Take me up!" Graham shouted into the mouthpiece.

"I'm going down," Kolchinsky replied and dipped the helicopter towards the roof of the rear freight car.

"It's too dangerous . . ." Graham started, then felt his dangling legs touch the roof.

The helicopter tilted and the rope ladder swung away from the freight car. As the momentum swung him back over the car he let go, landing heavily on the roof.

Kolchinsky immediately nosed the helicopter upwards, desperately trying to avoid the bridge. He couldn't clear it in time and the right landing pad struck the stonework and buckled. Stones and masonry tumbled on to the track below as part of the bridge disintegrated from the force of the impact. He managed to regain control of the helicopter but there was a grating sound emanating from one of the Rolls-Royce turboshaft engines and seconds later black smoke began to pour out from the upper fuselage where they were located.

Graham had fallen heavily on his shoulder and instinctively grabbed on to a ridge in the freight car's roof. It had saved his life. Had he rolled off the roof he would have been flung against the steel stanchion erected to support the reinforced archway. He lay on the roof, momentarily winded, his face screwed up in agony as the pain throbbed through his left shoulder.

"Michael! Michael!"

He winced as Kolchinsky's raised voice seemed to reverberate through his head.

"Michael!"

"Stop shouting," Graham shouted.

"Are you all right?" Kolchinsky asked anxiously.

"I'm alive. My left shoulder hurts like hell though."

"Abort . . ."

"Forget it," Graham snapped.

"What chance have you got against Milchan with an injured shoulder?"

"I'll shoot the son-of-a-bitch, it makes no difference. I'm going in."

"One day you'll surprise us all by actually obeying an order."

"Don't count on it," Graham replied. "What happened to you? I heard a bang as I went under the bridge."

"I hit it. I've had to land in some field, the engine's damaged."

"And you?"

"Whiplash, that's all. If your shoulder's bad I want . . ."

Graham didn't hear the rest. He pulled the headset out from under the balaclava and tossed it away. He realized he was sitting in the dark and flicked on the switch of the Halolight. Nothing happened. If it had been damaged he knew he could forget about trying to get into the freight car until daybreak. He gave it several taps with his forefinger before it finally came on. As he moved, a sharp pain shot through his left arm and he pulled it protectively against his body. He waited until the throbbing subsided then made his way

to the edge of the roof where he grabbed the top rung
of the metal ladder and began to descend the side of
the freight car. Despite the almost unbearable pain in
his shoulder he managed to reach the padlock and attach a small magnetized transmitter to it before climbing back up to the roof. Once he was there he removed
a matchbox-sized detonator from a pouch on his belt,
extended the aerial and turned the dial to the transmitter's wavelength. There was a muffled explosion as
the padlock was destroyed. He was reaching for his
Beretta when Milchan's massive hands appeared on the
top rung of the ladder. A moment later his horrendously disfigured face appeared above the level of the
roof. Milchan grabbed Graham's foot and jerked it
sharply. The bullet went wild. Milchan chopped his
wrist and the Beretta tumbled from his hand then slid
agonizingly slowly down the side of the sloping roof.
The butt snagged on the raised ventilator. Graham
ducked a wild punch and made a grab for the Beretta.
The train jolted over a fault in the line and the Beretta
came free. His fingers raked the roof in desperation
only inches from it and he cursed as it slid over the
side. He swivelled round to face Milchan, his left
shoulder now a constant source of pain. He could
barely move his left arm; it seemed dead as it hung
limply at his side. This only added to his anger and
frustration. He lashed out sideways with his foot,
catching Milchan on the side of the face. Milchan
dabbed his bleeding lip with the back of his hand then
grinned. Graham lashed out again but this time Milchan grabbed his foot and pulled him effortlessly towards the ladder.

Graham saw the punch coming but his left arm refused to respond when he tried to raise it to defend himself.

Then nothing.

The sharp rapping on the door brought Sabrina out of her deep sleep.

"*Si?*" she asked, slipping her hand around her Beretta under the pillow.

"*Buon giorno. Caffe?*" the assistant conductor asked through the locked compartment door.

"*No, grazie.*" She glanced at her bare wrist then remembered her watch had been confiscated in Fribourg. "*Che ore sono?*"

There was a pause before he answered. "*Le otto e un quarto.*"

"8:15? Oh God!" she hissed under her breath. "*Grazie,*" she called out, then scrambled off the couchette and opened the communicating door.

The adjoining compartment was empty.

"Thanks for waking me, you guys," she muttered angrily, her hands on her hips.

After a cursory wash she donned the habit and wimple, slipping the Beretta into her pocket. She went directly to the dining car, pausing in the doorway to look around. Her luck was in. Werner, Hendrique and Kyle were having breakfast, and judging by the food still on their plates they would be there for some time to come. It was the perfect opportunity for her to search their compartments, especially Werner's. He might be the kingpin but he was also the weak link. Hendrique and Kyle were seasoned criminals; Werner was a businessman. She knew if there were any clues to be found, his compartment would be the place to find them. First she returned briefly to her own berth to fetch the keys Kolchinsky had taken from the dead conductor.

Her instincts had been right: both compartment doors were locked. Knowing she had only a limited amount of time she decided to go through Werner's compartment first. The corridor was deserted. Quickly she unlocked the door and went in, fastening it again behind her. There were two pieces of luggage on the overhead rack, a small beige suitcase and an attaché case manacled to the steel pipe against the wall. She climbed on to the couchette and turned the attaché case round to face her. It had a combination lock. She knew the odds against her cracking the combination, even if she had all day, but having learnt never to discount the obvious she tried the locks anyway. They opened. Her astonishment turned immediately to suspicion. Even a harmless businessman would scramble the combination before leaving his case unattended. It had to be a trap. She took a nailfile from her pocket and traced it along the seam, checking for wires. There were none. She looked around the compartment for something with which to lever open the lid. All she could see was a newspaper so she rolled it up and stood to one side, holding it at arm's length as she lifted the lid up several inches. Nothing happened. She exhaled deeply. Discarding the newspaper she opened the lid. A silver box and a miniature console were the case's sole contents. Just as she was going to try to lift out the box she heard a key being inserted into the lock of the compartment door. She jumped off the couchette and pulled out her Beretta, aiming it at the doorway.

The door slid back and Werner froze, momentarily taken aback by the sight of an armed nun. He smiled a second later, recognizing her, and took a hesitant step into the compartment, his arms raised. Kyle followed him in but his arms remained at his side.

"Close the door and lock it," she commanded.

"Do as she says," Werner said without taking his eyes off the Beretta pointing at his chest.

Kyle locked the door.

Her eyes flickered towards the communicating door. "If Hendrique tries to burst through there you'll be the first to die."

"He has no intention of bursting in, my dear. You might be interested to know what he is doing in there, though. May I?" Werner indicated the door with one of his raised hands.

"Don't move!"

"Of course, only I thought you'd want to see your partner. Hendrique has orders to kill Graham if he hasn't heard from us in two minutes." Werner glanced at his wristwatch. "A minute's nearly up. Call my bluff if you want but Graham's death will be on your conscience for the rest of your life."

"You open the door," she said to Kyle without taking her eyes off Werner.

Kyle drew back the bolt then tapped four times on the door. It was unlocked from the other side and Kyle opened it to reveal Graham bound and gagged on the couchette opposite the door, and Hendrique standing over him holding a Franchi Spas shotgun inches from his chest.

"What have you done to him?" she asked anxiously.

"A drug-induced sleep, that's all," Werner said. "He was very aggressive, even with handcuffs on. You have thirty seconds to throw down your gun. Hendrique's very punctual, especially when it comes to killing."

Hendrique's hooded eyes were challenging, his lips curled in a contemptuous sneer.

Her determination wavered. If she surrendered her gun she would be breaching one of UNACO's fundamental principles, giving in to the demands of known criminals. And Graham had sacrificed his family to thwart a wave of terrorist bombings. She knew exactly what he would want her to do. Shooting Hendrique would be easy. But at what price if he killed Graham in return? As Werner had said, she would have to live with the decision for the rest of her life.

"Twenty seconds."

She pushed Werner aside and levelled the Beretta at Hendrique's head. His response was to press the shotgun into Graham's chest.

Kyle stepped forward to disarm her.

"Leave her!" Hendrique snarled. "We'll settle this my way."

Kyle backed off.

She looked at Graham, his head lolling on his chest, and tightened her grip on the Beretta.

"Ten seconds."

She swallowed nervously, her eyes riveted on Hendrique's face.

"Seven seconds."

Her finger tightened on the trigger and Hendrique smiled faintly to himself.

"Four seconds. Three, two, one . . ."

She let the Beretta drop from her hand. Kyle scooped it up and trained it on her back.

Hendrique traced the shotgun down Graham's chest then pressed it into his stomach.

"I've conceded, what more do you want?"

"So you have," Hendrique replied and squeezed the trigger.

Click.

"I learn so much about a person's character by calling their bluff. It also makes the contest that little bit more interesting."

"You jeopardized—"

"I jeopardized nothing," Hendrique cut across Werner's outburst. "I knew she'd back down. There's a touching loyalty amongst undercover agents, especially between partners."

"You want me to tie her up?" Kyle asked.

"Give me the gun first," Hendrique replied.

Sabrina chose her moment perfectly and brought her foot up into Kyle's midriff just as he extended the Beretta towards Hendrique. She pivoted round to face Hendrique but found herself staring down the barrel of his Desert Eagle automatic.

"It's a question of speed. Can you get to it before I pull the trigger?"

"If it's loaded," she retorted, still holding the hem of her habit above her ankles.

"You're learning, but are you prepared to call my bluff again?"

She let the hem drop and Kyle, his face twisted in pain, manacled her hands behind her back then shoved her roughly on to the couchette beside Graham.

"How did you know I was in your compartment?" she asked.

Werner pushed aside his jacket to reveal a miniature transmitter attached to his belt. "It picks up a signal the moment the case is opened."

"So you left the case unlocked on purpose?"

"That was the bait, although I was certainly surprised to see you back again. I thought another agent would have been sent out to replace you but I seem to have underestimated UNACO's powers of persuasion."

The surprise was mirrored in her eyes.

"Oh yes, we know who you're working for," Werner said triumphantly. "It took a while though to find out. UNACO isn't exactly a household name."

"Why are you doing this, Stefan? You've got everything. Money, respect, and you own one of the most successful companies in Europe. And what about all those millions of underprivileged children who've benefited from your charitable foundations? I remember the documentary NBC did on you last year. Those African kids looked upon you as some kind of Messiah sent to give them hope for the future. I felt honoured to have known you. Was it all just a sham, the perfect cover? Who would suspect one of the world's leading philanthropists of being an arms dealer?''

''An arms dealer?'' Werner said with a chuckle. ''Is that what UNACO thinks I am?'' His face became serious. ''Those foundations did start out as a cover but now they've become something of an obsession. I feel as though I'm doing something constructive while I remain here in the West.''

''You're talking too much,'' Hendrique snapped.

Werner gave a resigned shrug. ''It'll come out soon enough.''

She looked from Hendrique to Werner. ''You're KGB?''

''Correct.'' Werner patted the attaché case. ''I was hoping I wouldn't have to resort to this but you've left me with no choice. You know what's inside the case, only you don't know what's inside the metal box. Let me show you.''

He punched the four digits on the keyboard and they appeared on the narrow screen above it. 1-9-6-7. The box sprung open. Inside was a radio transmitter, no bigger than a cigarette lighter, on a rolled gold chain. He put the attaché case to one side and leaned forward, the transmitter resting in his cupped hand.

''I'm not going to insult your intelligence by beating about the bush. There are six metal kegs in the crate, as you no doubt guessed all along. Five of them contain plutonium. The sixth contains an explosive device. I couldn't tell you how powerful it is because I haven't actually seen it. All the kegs are the same weight so none of us knows which one contains the explosives. It was put together in a vacuum so it's perfectly safe as long as it remains sealed. The slightest breath of air will trigger the mechanism inside." He lifted back the transmitter's cap to reveal a small red button. "This is the only other way the device can be triggered. Press this button and . . ." He threw up his hands. "You have a nuclear explosion to rival Nagasaki, only this time right in the heart of Europe. The fallout would have catastrophic results for generations to come."

She stared at him in horror. "And you have the audacity to talk about doing something constructive by helping the underprivileged children?"

There was genuine hurt in his eyes. "Do you really think I'd *want* you to press the button, knowing the consequences? Do you? We wouldn't gain anything by destroying the plutonium after all the trouble we've gone to in accruing it. We want to prevent a catastrophe as much as you do. After all, none of us would survive it."

"So what's the price?"

"All we ask is that we're given a safe passage to our ultimate destination."

"And it's up to me to pass on this demand?"

"It's a request, not a demand."

"And if you're challenged you'll sacrifice the lot?"

"If I was cornered and saw no way out, yes." He closed the cap and slipped the chain around his neck, tucking the transmitter under his shirt. "Hypodermic?"

Hendrique fetched it from the adjoining compartment and handed it to Werner who rolled up Sabrina's sleeve, found a vein in the crook of her arm, and gently inserted the needle into her flesh. He then eased the wimple from her head, allowing her blonde hair to fall on to her shoulders.

"So angelic, so beautiful," he said wistfully, then put his hand against her cheek.

She jerked her head away.

"Goodbye, my dear Sabrina."

"Until the next time," she rejoined, her voice already beginning to slur.

"Stay with them," Hendrique told Kyle.

She shook her head, desperately trying to stave off the drowsiness, but her eyelids were becoming increasingly heavy. The compartment meshed into a kaleidoscope of hazy colours before she slumped sideways against Graham.

TEN

Whitlock could sum up his mood in one word. Despondent. What had he achieved in his three days in Mainz? His cover had been blown at the outset by a beautiful woman who just happened to have dated one of the *New York Times*'s leading showbiz columnists (a fact corroborated by UNACO); he had nearly been run over by a Mercedes, the driver of which had subsequently drowned (or so he assumed); and although he tended to agree with Karen that Leitzig was involved in the diversion he didn't have a shred of evidence against him. Each investigative avenue led to a dead end. He had to make the breakthrough, and quickly. But how?

The day could have started off better. He overslept, only waking at 9:30. Then, as he was reversing the Golf out of the driveway, the rain had started to fall, soon developing into a torrential downpour. After stopping off briefly at the hotel to change he drove to the plant on the old Frankfurt road, a route recommended to him by Karen the previous day. The traffic was negligible, most drivers preferring the spacious lanes of the A66 highway.

He stopped the Golf as close to the guards' hut as possible and opened his window fractionally to display the pass Karen had organized for him on his first day at the plant. One of the guards pulled on a raincoat, tugged his peak cap over his head, then braved the sheeting rain to approach the car.

"Morning. Whitlock, *New York Times*," he announced.

The guard ran his finger down the plastic-protected clipboard. "We have orders not to admit you."

"Who revoked my pass?" Whitlock asked angrily.

"Dr. Leitzig."

"Why?"

"I've no idea, call him when you get home."

"I want to speak to him now!"

"Your pass has been revoked, there's nothing more to say. You're trespassing on Government property."

Whitlock flung his pass on to the dashboard and shook his head in frustration. Leitzig had snookered him. No doubt he would have a perfectly valid reason if challenged on the revocation order. And he had effectively blocked Whitlock's investigation from within the plant.

The guard rapped on the window. "I've told you, you're trespassing on Government property."

Whitlock knew the futility of arguing; the guard was probably in Leitzig's back pocket anyway. He needed time to rethink his strategy, time that wasn't on his side. He turned the Golf around in front of the boom-gate and drove away.

The guard unclipped the radio from his belt and put it to his lips. "He's on his way."

Whitlock rejoined the old Mainz-Frankfurt road—even the potholes were preferable to the long tailback on the main highway. He switched on the radio and turned the tuner until he found a music station. It was playing a bland pop song which was still better than some agricultural or political discussion in German. Rosie, his fifteen-year-old niece, would probably have liked it. He still hankered after the music of the Sixties when the singers, unlike those of today, had tuneful voices and their backing bands didn't have to vie with each other to see who could make the loudest noise. As Rosie kept reminding him, "it must get increasingly difficult to keep up with the changing face of society the older you get." She had a knack of making him feel twice his age!

He snapped out of his reverie as a pair of dazzling headlights drew even closer in the reflection of the rearview mirror. He muttered about the lack of consideration shown by some motorists and signalled for the driver to pass. The headlights remained fixed on the back of the Golf, forcing him to tilt the rear-view mirror towards the passenger seat. He opened his window and made a sweep with his arm to beckon the driver on. He even gave way, moving precariously close to the verge so that the driver could see the road ahead for himself. The headlights swung out from behind the Golf and he caught a brief glimpse of the red bonnet braided with strips of chrome. A Range Rover. It drew abreast of the Golf but Whitlock was unable to see the driver.

"Go on, go on," he shouted and waved the driver forward.

The Range Rover swerved inwards, striking the Golf broadside.

"Damn maniac," Whitlock yelled as he swung the wheel violently to prevent the Golf from veering off the road.

The gently sloping thirty-foot grass embankment to his left ended abruptly in an area of dense woodland which could easily rupture a car's fuel tank on impact.

The Range Rover struck the side of the Golf a second time and he instinctively trod sharply on the brakes, knowing he could lose control of the wheel and plummet down the embankment. He knew, though, that the Range Rover was infinitely more powerful and it would be only a matter of time before it forced the Golf off the road. The back wheels slewed sideways, away from the verge, and the Golf ended up straddled across the road. The Range Rover stopped, then executed a careful U-turn to face the stalled Golf. He reached over and unfastened the glove compartment, feeling around inside it for the Browning. As his fingers curled around the butt the Range Rover hit the Golf a glancing blow, disintegrating the right headlight in a shower of broken glass. The Golf spun round a hundred and eighty degrees, the momentum of the turn snapping Whitlock's head against the steering wheel. He struggled to sit up, his head pounding from the force of the blow. When he gingerly touched the gash across his eyebrow he could feel blood oozing on to his fingertips.

The Range Rover had turned to make another run. The Golf was immobile only a few feet from the edge of the road and the next buffet would almost certainly cartwheel it down the embankment. Whitlock tried unsuccessfully to start the engine then reached for the Browning lying on the passenger seat. The Range Rover came directly towards the Golf, aiming to strike it on the driver's door to get the exact angle to spin it round so it would roll sideways down the embankment. He waited until the Range Rover was twenty feet away before gripping the Browning in both hands and extending it through the open window. He picked an imaginary spot in the centre of the darkened windscreen and fired twice. Both bullets pierced the glass, inches apart, and a myriad of threadlike cracks branched out from the resulting dimpled holes. The Range Rover sheered off course, narrowly missing the back of the Golf, then continued down the road and disappeared around the first bend.

Then he saw the motorbike parked further up the road. It was a black Suzuki 1000cc. Its rider, dressed in white leather, kick-started the machine and streaked past the Golf.

He managed to restart the Golf and as he slipped it into gear he began to think more carefully about the Range Rover. Had he seen it somewhere before? Had Karen mentioned it to him? The more he thought about it the more he was sure someone had referred to it in passing. He had met over a dozen different workers at

the plant the previous day but he couldn't place anyone
who might have told him about it.

He snapped his fingers. "Leitzig," he said out loud.

Leitzig had a Range Rover that he used to go on
fishing trips.

Whitlock's head was throbbing by the time he found
a public telephone. His suspicions about Leitzig grew
stronger when he found out from the plant's switch-
board that he was not due at work until the afternoon
shift. He found Leitzig's home address in the direc-
tory, tore out the relevant page, and hurried back to
the battered Golf. He would assess the damage later
and use his credit card to settle up with Hertz. UN-
ACO would refund him once he returned to New York.
Kolchinsky wouldn't be pleased . . .

Leitzig lived in a run-down double-storey on Quin-
tinstrasse overlooking the Old University campus on
the eastern side of the Rhine. Whitlock parked the Golf
at the end of the street, pocketed the Browning, then
ran through the driving rain to the garage at the side
of the house. He cupped his hands on either side of
his face and peered through the cracked window. Although a piece of sacking had been erected as a makeshift curtain he could still see the red Range Rover
inside. The paintwork was damaged on the passenger
door. He couldn't see the windscreen but he had all
the proof he needed to confront Leitzig.

Next he turned his attention to getting into the
house. He scaled a rickety six-foot wooden fence behind the garage and landed nimbly in the overgrown
back yard where he remained on his haunches, Brown-

ing drawn, assessing the dangers. A veranda to his right, presumably leading into the kitchen. He made his way towards it through the knee-high grass, each squelching step soaking his feet more. A Christian Dior shirt stained with blood, a Richard James bottle-green suit saturated, and an expensive pair of Pierre Cardin slip-ons drenched. If they were ruined UN-ACO would pay for a replacement pair, whether Kolchinsky liked it or not. He reached the veranda and tried the door. It opened.

An Alsatian was blocking his way, but instead of leaping up at him in defence of its territory it merely wagged its tail then returned to its basket to sleep. He decided against patting it, on the basis that he had already tempted fate too far. He slipped into the kitchen and closed the door securely behind him then reached down and removed his shoes.

Leitzig was sitting beside a small heater in the lounge, his back to the doorway. Whitlock paused and looked around the room in amazement. It was a shrine to one woman, with pictures of her from youth through to her middle years. Dozens of enlarged photographs, each mounted and framed, covered the walls, the ornamental mantelpiece and the chipped sideboard opposite the doorway.

All his pent-up anger seemed to dissipate and his voice sounded hollow when he finally spoke. "Dr. Leitzig?"

Leitzig sprang to his feet and swung around to face him. There was a fury in his eyes. "Get out! Get out!"

Whitlock instinctively stepped back into the hallway, the Browning hanging limply by his side.

Leitzig was breathing heavily. "This is her room and I am the only other person allowed to share it with her. Nobody else!"

"Then we'll talk somewhere else. How about the kitchen?"

"Who are you? What do you want?" Surprisingly, Leitzig was hesitant.

"Whitlock. You tried to kill me half an hour ago, remember?"

"I don't know what you're talking about. Get out of my house or I will call the police."

"Please do, but don't forget to mention your Range Rover in the garage. They might be interested in matching up its damaged paintwork with the paintwork on my Golf. I'm sure they'd come to some interesting conclusions."

"I do not think you would want the police here any more than I would."

Whitlock was at the end of his patience, his equanimity finally deserting him. He grabbed Leitzig by the collar and slammed him against the wall. His voice was low and threatening. "I'm tired of playing games with you. I want some answers and I promise you I'll get them."

Leitzig shook his head. "You cannot hurt me any more than I have already been hurt. I am immune to pain now."

Whitlock shoved Leitzig aside and entered the lounge where he picked up the nearest photograph. "I'll smash them, one by one, until you tell me what I want to know."

Leitzig stared at the photograph Whitlock was about

to drop as though it were a priceless Ming vase. "Please, I beg of you, do not hurt her."

"You answer my questions and I won't hurt her."

"I will answer any question you ask. Please, please, do not hurt her."

Whitlock put the picture back on the sideboard and crossed to the heater.

Leitzig took the same picture from the sideboard and sat down in the single armchair.

"My wife," he said softly, tracing his finger over the outline of her face.

"I assumed it was. When did she pass away?"

"Three years ago. I killed her."

"You killed her?"

"She was dying from cancer. I could not bear the sight of her suffering so I killed her. I only did it because I loved her so much."

"Euthanasia," Whitlock said.

"Call it what you like but I still killed her," Leitzig continued. "I took her back to Travemunde where we had spent our honeymoon twenty-six years before. I wanted her to have the holiday of a lifetime. On the last night there I deliberately got her drunk at dinner then took her for a walk along the beach." He gripped the frame in both hands and swallowed back the emotion which was threatening to surface. "That was when I drowned her."

"And you got away with it?"

"The inquest recorded a verdict of accidental death, if that is what you mean. I did not go unpunished up here," Leitzig said, tapping his forehead. "The guilt is like a migraine. It will never go away. I have often thought about suicide but I do not have the courage to go through with it.''

Whitlock rubbed his own forehead; the throbbing was incessant. He touched the gash above his eye and was relieved to feel that it had stopped bleeding.

Leitzig seemed to notice Whitlock's dishevelled appearance for the first time. ''Do you want some dry clothes? I have plenty of sweaters and pants.''

It was a tempting offer but Whitlock was determined to remain in control. ''You stay where you are.''

''What's going to happen to me?''

''That all depends on your cooperation. How did you first get involved in the diversion?''

Leitzig stared at the photograph in his lap. ''I was blackmailed into helping them.''

''What did they have on you?''

''I will show you. Can I get up?''

''Where are you going?'' Whitlock asked.

''To the sideboard.''

Leitzig opened one of the drawers and withdrew a brown envelope which he handed to Whitlock before sitting down again.

Whitlock extracted the six enlarged black and white photographs. They had all been taken with a night lens and showed Leitzig forcibly holding his wife's head under the water. The last photograph had caught him as he was emerging from the sea, his wife's lifeless body floating face down in the water. He slipped the photographs back into the envelope and handed it to Leitzig.

''Those pictures would have put me behind bars for life.''

"Who took them?" Whitlock asked.

"I do not know but I received them two days after the inquest."

"Then what happened?"

"Nothing initially, then about six months later I was contacted at the Planck University where I was working and told to apply for the vacant post of senior technician at the reprocessing plant. With my experience I was accepted after the first interview. I found out later that my predecessor had been killed under mysterious circumstances while skiing at St. Anton in Austria. Make of it what you want but I am pretty sure he was murdered so they could put their own man on the inside."

"Did you ever see any of your blackmailers?"

"I liaised with two of them. The senior of the two was a Machiavellian type. Totally evil. A powerfully-built man with dark black hair and hooded eyes."

"And his name?"

"Hendrick, Hendricks, something like that. He was not the sort of person you asked to repeat himself."

"And the other man?"

"Canadian, called himself Vanner. Blond hair, blond moustache, always wore a trilby. He used to chauffeur Hendricks around in a black Mercedes."

Another piece of the jigsaw had fallen into place. "So when did the diversion start?"

Leitzig removed a packet of cigarettes from his pocket and lit one. "About six or seven months after I started at the plant. In the interim period I had to recruit four new technicians and although I interviewed dozens of applicants I could only take on those put up by Hendricks. They were all fully qualified so it did not arouse any unnecessary suspicion. With the five of us working together the diversion went like clockwork.''

''I've been through reams of computer print-outs but I can't find any discrepancies. You must have siphoned the plutonium off sometime during the actual reprocessing, but how did you manage it with so many other technicians around? Or were there others in on it?''

''Apart from a few guards and drivers nobody else was involved, certainly not any of my personnel. I had my team. We did not siphon the plutonium off *during* reprocessing, we siphoned it off *afterwards*.''

''Afterwards? But those figures are checked by several sources before being stored in the computer.''

''Agreed, tampering with bulk figures is virtually impossible. There is an insignificant column in the stat sheets headed 'Residual Figures', you probably did not even notice it.''

''I remember it, the figures were all pretty negligible. Karen said it was something to do with the fissile material left in the residue. It didn't make a lot of sense to me.''

Leitzig stubbed out his cigarette. ''As I told you when I showed you around the plant, the uranium and plutonium undergo several extraction stages to remove any lingering impurities before they separate to form uranyl nitrate and plutonium nitrate respectively. Naturally there is both uranium and plutonium left in the residue, albeit in very small amounts. That residue then goes under its own extraction stage to release the trapped uranium and plutonium. The amounts vary with each magazine, even if it is only a matter of grams. It all counts in the end.'' He lit a second cigarette. ''I covered my tracks right at the start by going to the plant manager and expressing my dissatisfaction at the residual extraction process. He played into my hands by asking me to supervise it personally. So I had a free hand. Over a three-day shift we could siphon off eight, maybe nine grams without it affecting the stat figures. We worked over a two-year period. Six kilograms of high-enriched, 'weapons-grade' plutonium.''

''Where is it destined for?''

''I overheard Hendricks once say it was to be shipped to a secret laboratory in Libya.''

''Did he mention the name of the ship?''

''That is all I heard.''

''Did he say what it was going to be used for?''

''Use your imagination. It could be used for nuclear warheads but it is my guess it will be converted into an atom bomb. Six kilograms is the perfect size.''

''Libya with an atom bomb? Sweet Jesus.'' Whitlock felt his head beginning to throb harder. ''I want the name of all your fellow conspirators. Technicians, guards, drivers, the lot.''

The doorbell chimed.

''Can I answer it, or am I still a prisoner?''

''You always will be,'' Whitlock replied, picking up one of the photographs on the mantelpiece.

Leitzig left the room.

Whitlock heard the door open, then the sound of a muffled cough. Most people would have put it down to some background noise but he knew exactly what it was. A gun fitted with a silencer. He dived low through the doorway and rolled across the threadbare hall carpet, the Browning fanning the area in front of him. There was no sign of the gunman. He scrambled to his feet and dashed out on to the porch just in time to see the rider in the white leathers taking off up the road on the black Suzuki.

Leitzig was slumped against the wall, blood pumping from a bullet wound in his stomach. Whitlock slammed the front door and raced into the lounge where he rifled through the sideboard drawers for some linen napkins to stem the flow of blood. Then he collected his shoes from the kitchen and slipped the incriminating photographs under his jacket. Leitzig was semi-conscious and there was nothing more he could do. After calling an ambulance anonymously on the hall telephone he left the house.

His first stop was Karen's place. He parked in the driveway and hurried up to the porch where he rang the doorbell. No answer. He reached through the broken pane of glass and unlocked the door.

"Karen?" he called out as he entered the hallway. No reply.

He checked the kitchen and lounge before making his way up the stairs to her bedroom. The door was ajar, as he had left it earlier in the morning when he had looked in on her. He poked his head around the door. She was still asleep, her sable hair spilt out across the cream pillowcase.

He left, locking the front door again after him. As he drove to the hotel he thought back over the eventful morning, looking forward to being able to contact

Philpott with a constructive report for a change. His immediate priority was a steaming hot bath and some treatment for his gashed eyebrow. Then he would have to brave the weather again to dump the Golf in one of the city's underground car parks, and get himself another car from a different hire company. A battered, paint-scarred yellow Golf would be difficult to miss, especially when it was parked near the scene of the shooting. If the police traced it to him he might not be as lucky as Sabrina had been in Zurich.

All eyes seemed to focus on him as he entered the foyer of the Europa Hotel. He smiled ruefully and walked self-consciously across to the reception desk to ask for his room key.

When the receptionist handed it to him he glanced round quickly and leaned closer to her. She also glanced round and leaned closer to him, turning her head slightly to catch what he was about to say.

"You won't believe this, but it's raining."

There was a bemused smile on her face as she watched him disappear into the lift.

The first thing Sabrina saw when she opened her eyes was a blurred face looking down at her. She rubbed her eyes and the face became more distinct.

"Mike?" she said groggily. "Mike, are you all right?"

"Yeah, I'm fine," he replied gruffly, then put a glass to her lips. "Drink this."

She took a sip of the brandy then coughed and spluttered as it burnt its way down her throat. She pushed the glass away from her face. "You know I hate the stuff."

"People respond quickest to something they hate," Philpott said from the corner of the room.

She was lying on a single bed in what was obviously a hotel room. "Where are we?"

"The Da Francesca Hotel in Prato," Philpott replied and got to his feet. "The American Embassy in Rome received an anonymous call to say you and Mike had been left unconscious in a small storage shed at Prato station. The caller also told the Embassy to call us. How did they know who you were working for? Mike didn't say anything—"

"And neither did I, sir!" she shot back, then touched her temples gingerly. "Stefan Werner's a KGB agent. They found out through him."

"Werner, KGB?" Kolchinsky said from the chair beside the door.

She turned to him and a look of concern crossed her face. He was wearing a thick foam collar around his neck, tilting his head back at an angle.

"What happened?" she asked anxiously.

"Whiplash. It's a long story. Michael will fill you in on the details later." He reached for the cigarettes on the table beside him.

She positioned the pillow against the headboard and sat up. "Can I have something to drink? My tongue feels like a piece of recycled leather."

"Coffee?" Philpott indicated the tray on top of the television set.

"Yes, please," she said eagerly.

"Milk, no sugar?"

"Yes, sir." He poured the coffee out for her and she leaned forward to take it from him.

She took several sips before putting the cup and saucer on the bedside table. Thoroughly and professionally she proceeded to tell them everything that had happened, careful to omit any references to having acceded to Hendrique's demands. It would only have been met with a barrage of criticism, especially from Graham. She had done it because of him and it was a decision she knew she would never regret.

"So this whole operation's been funded by the KGB," Philpott said once she had finished. "So much for your *glasnost*, Sergei."

"Don't tar us all with the same brush, Malcolm," Kolchinsky replied, then turned to Sabrina. "Did Werner give you any clue as to his handler's identity?"

She shook her head.

"I'll get on to Zurich and the UN right away, see what they can dig up." Kolchinsky rose carefully to his feet.

Philpott crossed to the door and put a hand lightly on Kolchinsky's shoulder. "You know the KGB hierarchy inside out; surely there aren't that many extremists who would resort to something like this?"

"More than you think," Kolchinsky replied, then left the room.

"Why didn't he phone from here?" Sabrina asked.

"Because I'm waiting for an important call," Philpott replied, then sat down in the chair vacated by Kolchinsky. "There've been some new developments in the last few hours. I'd just finished telling Mike when you started to stir."

"Why didn't you wake me up earlier, sir?"

"There wasn't any need. We can't make a move until the phone call anyway." Philpott took out his pipe and filled it from his tobacco pouch. "After we'd received the tip-off about your whereabouts I sent one of our helicopters after the train to tail it for the rest of the journey through to Rome. There was only one snag: the wagon wasn't anywhere to be seen when the helicopter caught up with the train."

"You mean it had been uncoupled?"

Philpott lit his pipe and exhaled the smoke upwards. "That's exactly what I mean. I had our men board the train when it next stopped but Werner and Hendrique had already flown the coop, having disembarked here at Prato some two hours earlier, according to the conductor. The wagon hadn't been uncoupled at Prato so every station from Modena to Prato had to be contacted to try and find out where it was."

"And did you?"

"Seventy minutes later. A porter at Montepiano— it's a town about fifteen miles north of here—vaguely recalled seeing a single wagon on one of the lines. The sighting fits in with the time the train was here in Prato. It could be a red herring but it's the only clue we've got. The helicopter team have gone to Montepiano to see what they can find out about the wagon."

"And this is the call you're waiting for, from Montepiano?"

Philpott nodded. "Once we know the plutonium's destination, hopefully you can get there first to prevent it from going any further. One of our helicopters is on

stand-by not far from here and Zurich assures me the
pilot knows the countryside like the back of his hand.''

"So you want us to go ahead regardless of Werner's
threat?''

"You know UNACO's policy—''

"Mike, that's enough! If you played by the book it
would be fair comment but you quoting the Charter is
like Stallone quoting Macbeth.''

Sabrina giggled, then clamped her hand over her
mouth. "I'm sorry, sir.''

Graham eyed her icily.

"We can't be at all sure Werner was bluffing when
he said he would detonate the plutonium if he were
cornered—but to give in to his demands would be to
condone criminal behaviour. UNACO was founded
precisely to neutralize situations like this. We can't
back down.'' Philpott sucked on his pipe. "A marks-
man shoots to kill when he's cornered a rabid dog. If
the dog's only wounded it can still bite. I think you
know what I'm saying.''

They both nodded.

Philpott indicated with the stem of his pipe the two
cream-coloured holdalls by the side of the bed. "I
managed to get them back from the Swiss authorities
last night. I'm sure you want to get changed.''

Sabrina clambered off the bed and picked up the
holdalls. "Thank you, sir, I'll appreciate being myself
again.''

"The bathroom's through there,'' Philpott said,
gesturing to the door on his right.

She went into the bathroom and closed the door behind her.

Philpott got to his feet and crossed to the window as though his proximity to the door might be misconstrued. "Why do you resent her so much, Mike? Is it because she's a woman? Or because she hasn't got your level of field experience? Or is it her shooting ability—"

"It's got nothing to do with that," Graham retorted defensively.

"Have you ever seen her on the range? I only ask because I know you like to shoot on your own."

"I know she's good; better than me," Graham said with an indifferent shrug.

"I've been thinking about the two of you for a couple of days, which was why I had these sent out from New York." He opened his attaché case and withdrew a folder. "Naturally they're confidential but as you're her partner I thought you should see them. They're the targets she used during her prelim tests. There're only a couple in here, I could hardly have the life-size ones sent out. Take a look, you might learn something."

Graham opened the folder and picked up the first target. *Beretta 92/15 rounds* had been printed in the top right-hand corner. There was a single hole in the centre of the bull the size of a quarter. The second target had *Mannlicher Luxus/10 rounds* printed in the top right-hand corner. Apart from the one stray bullet hole dissecting the circle around the bull the rest of the bullets had formed an uncanny geometric circle in the centre of the bull. It was as though she had purposefully set out to create another perfect circle within the bull itself.

Philpott pointed to the one flaw on the target. "It

was her first shot, she hadn't quite adjusted the sights properly. Nobody's perfect though.''

Graham closed the folder and handed it to Philpott. ''I never knew anybody could be that good.''

Philpott held up the folder. ''I know some of you feel she got into UNACO because of her father's influence but it wouldn't have mattered if he were the President or a hot dog vendor on Forty-Second Street—this was the deciding factor that got her into UNACO. *She* was on the range that morning, not her father.''

''May I ask you a question, sir, confidentiality aside?''

''Depends on the question,'' Philpott replied, slipping the folder back into his attaché case.

''Did her father have *any* influence on your final decision?''

''If you'd ever met George Carver you wouldn't need to ask that question.''

Graham waited for Philpott to continue. There was a lengthy pause instead. ''Go on, sir.''

''I don't need to, I've answered the question.''

Sabrina emerged from the bathroom before Graham could get Philpott to justify his answer. She was wearing a baggy white jersey and figure-hugging jeans tucked into a pair of brown leather ankle boots. Her hair was tied at the back of her head with a white ribbon.

''Why the sudden silence?'' she asked, then smiled. ''Should I have been in the bathroom for another five minutes?''

''Mike was asking about your father.''

''What about him?''

Graham glowered at Philpott as he struggled to think of something to say. He was tempted to be blunt but knew it would serve no purpose. "I was asking the boss if he'd ever met your father."

She frowned. "Have you, sir?"

"Once, in Montreal. I had been speaking at a police convention that afternoon and in the evening I was invited to a cocktail party at the home of the American Ambassador, then your father. It was the usual drab embassy party apart from one incident when a little girl in her pyjamas came running into the room determined to show everyone the gold stars the teacher had stuck in her book that day at school."

"I did that?" She screwed her face up in horror. "How embarrassing."

"What amazed me was the way you alternated between English and French when talking to your parents. I know your mother is French but you sounded as fluent as her and you couldn't have been much older than seven or eight. It's one of those things I've always remembered."

"It's just the way I was brought up. I spoke English to my father and French to my mother. You could say I had the best of both worlds. It was so strictly enforced that when I first went to sleep over at a friend's house—I must have been about nine at the time—I automatically spoke to her parents as I did to my own back home. I thought all mothers spoke French!" She sat on the edge of the bed and stared at her unpainted fingernails. "Have you heard from C.W., sir?"

"Yes, I heard from him before I left Zurich this

morning. With everything that's happened since it totally slipped my mind.''

He detailed the events from the time Whitlock had been roused from his bed by Karen's telephone call through to Leitzig's shooting some nine hours later.

''Is Leitzig still alive?'' Graham asked.

''C.W. phoned the hospital minutes before he phoned me and he was told Leitzig's on the critical list.''

''And C.W.? How bad was his eye injury?'' Sabrina asked.

''He needed five stitches. Mike also picked up an injury.''

''What happened?'' she asked anxiously.

Graham merely shrugged.

''He sprained his shoulder badly trying to land on the wagon roof. The doctor's given him painkillers. He'll be fine until we get back to New York where he can get it attended to properly.''

The telephone rang.

Philpott crossed to the bedside table to answer it. He listened intently, occasionally nodding, then replaced the receiver without a word.

''The wagon was coupled to the back of a train bound for Trieste. It's due into Trieste at 4:40. That leaves you with a little over fifty minutes. There's still a chance you can get there before it arrives. I'll call the pilot.''

They pulled on their jackets and pocketed the new Berettas Kolchinsky had left on the bed for them, each taking a spare clip as an additional back-up.

"The pilot's waiting in the foyer," Philpott said after replacing the receiver.

They hurried from the room without another word.

The helicopter covered the 190 miles to Trieste in forty minutes, touching down on a strip of wasteland directly behind the station.

Graham and Sabrina disembarked even before the pilot had shut down the engine and made their way to the terminus building. The spacious concourse was teeming with commuters and tourists. After looking around briefly she grabbed his arm and led him to the side of a newsstand a few feet away.

"I'll find out about the train from the information centre over there. It's pointless both of us going, we could easily become parted in this mêlée. I'll be as quick as I can."

With that she was gone.

When she returned five minutes later her face was grim.

"Don't tell me, it arrived early," Graham said.

She nodded. "Twenty-five minutes ago."

"More than enough time to transfer it elsewhere. Which platform?"

"Seven."

"We'll have to double back towards the helicopter and see if we can get on to Platform Seven from there. You'd think Philpott could have organized a clearance for us like he did at Strasbourg."

"This is where I play my ace." She withdrew two plastic ID cards and handed one to Graham. "I took them off the CID guys in Switzerland. All you have to do is hold it up briefly and say *polizia*. I'll deal with any dialogue.''

"There are times when I could swear you're more than just a pretty face.''

"Praise indeed.''

The gate leading on to Platform Seven was unguarded and they were able to slip through unobserved.

She pointed at the engine. "It's a *Rapido*, no wonder it got here ahead of schedule.''

"What's a *Rapido*?''

"There are different classes of trains in Italy. A *Rapido*'s an express, it only stops at the major cities. Very fast, very reliable.''

"So what would you class the boneshaker we were on?''

"That would be the other end of the scale. A *Locale* perhaps. It stops at every station.''

"Cosa desidera?" a voice called out behind them.

"Get your pass ready,'' she said to Graham.

She turned to face the approaching porter and held up the disc, careful to obscure the accompanying photograph with her fingers. She launched into a barrage of Italian and within seconds had the porter answering her questions. She thanked him once she had the information she needed and waited until he was out of earshot before speaking to Graham.

"The crate was transferred into the back of a white van almost as soon as the train arrived at the station.''

"Did he say where it was going?''

"He said he overheard one of them talking about a ship but that it wasn't mentioned by name.''

"If the plutonium's bound for Libya then Trieste's as good a port as any to load it on to a ship."

"Straight down the Adriatic and across the Mediterranean."

"Precisely. I still want to look at the freight car, though. I don't altogether trust these European porters, not after what happened at Lausanne."

They weren't expecting any kind of opposition but still transferred their Berettas from their shoulder holsters to their coat pockets as they neared the freight car. Sabrina pressed herself against the side of the car and waited for Graham's signal before sliding the door open. It was empty.

"We're only wasting time here," he said, closing the door again.

Darkness was beginning to fall as they made their way back to the helicopter. Within a couple of minutes the pilot had it airborne, heading towards the docks.

"Look!" she exclaimed as the helicopter banked low over the harbour complex.

Graham followed the direction of her pointing finger. A demarcated section of the complex, from Wharves Nine to Seventeen, dazzlingly irradiated under numerous floodlights, was painted in the distinctive colours of the Werner Company. The W-logo was portrayed on every warehouse wall, on the stem of every quayside crane, and even the bold numbering denoting each wharf had been painted in yellow with a black border. What struck them both was the cleanliness of the wharves compared to the surrounding ones. Whereas they were littered with discarded packing crates and overflowing steel drums and many of the warehouse walls were daubed with multicoloured graffiti, the fenced-off Werner wharves were free of any rubbish and the warehouses looked as though they had been painted only hours earlier. Whatever else was wrong with him they had to admit Werner was a very professional operator.

"Do you want me to put down on one of the wharves?" the pilot called out over his shoulder.

"No, the harbourmaster's office. Know it?" she shouted back.

The pilot gave her a thumbs-up sign and within a couple of minutes the helicopter had landed in a clearing. He pointed to a red-brick building some forty feet away. She followed Graham across the lawn to the building where, once inside, he sat on the bench beside the door while she approached the counter to speak to the duty officer. The duty officer consulted his logbook several times during the conversation and finally scribbled something down on a piece of paper which he then handed to her. She thanked him then walked over to Graham.

"One of Werner's freighters—" she glanced at the paper "—the *Napoli*, was berthed at Wharf Eleven up until an hour ago."

"Well, that's no good to us," he cut in.

"Give me a chance," she retorted irritably. "Anyway, it seems the *Napoli* was already running six hours behind schedule because Werner had personally instructed her captain to wait for a crate which was being brought to Trieste by train. The captain then received the go-ahead to leave the port without the crate but no sooner had the *Napoli* left than a company

Sikorsky touched down on Wharf Eleven. It was to take the crate out to the *Napoli* as soon as it was delivered to the warehouse.''

"And the helicopter's already taken off with the crate?''

She nodded grimly. "Twenty-five minutes ago.''

He banged his fist angrily on the arm of the bench.

"They're always one step ahead of us.''

"There's something else. The *Napoli*'s ladened with grain bound for Ethiopia. I can't believe anyone would actually exploit the suffering of those people for some political ideology.'' She shook her head, a mixture of anger and frustration in her eyes.

"We'll head it off in time,'' he said, trying to reassure her. "Where's its next port of call?''

"Dubrovnik. It should be there by early morning. Then Tripoli.''

"So we have to stop it before it leaves Dubrovnik,'' he said, getting to his feet. "I can't see Werner being too far away from the plutonium, so there's every chance we'll meet up with him in Dubrovnik.''

"It's not a game, Mike!'' she said, grabbing his arm as they left the office.

"I agree, it's a challenge.'' He walked several yards then turned to face her. "You're the sharpshooter, Werner's your problem. I want Hendrique.''

"It's not a vendetta either,'' she shouted after him, her words almost lost in the biting wind.

"We've got to get to Dubrovnik tonight,'' he said to the pilot.

"Dubrovnik?'' The pilot shook his head. "No chance, not tonight.''

"What the hell's that supposed to mean?"

"I've been in contact with air control. A particularly strong *bora* wind's blanketed the entire Dalmatian Coast in such a thick fog that all flights to and from the area have had to be called off until it lifts."

"This is UNACO, not a boy scout jamboree. Risks are part of our business, or weren't you told when you joined?"

The pilot glared at Graham but wisely kept his anger in check. "I'd be the first to risk it if there was some sort of visibility but I'm told the fog's so bad you can't see a hand in front of your face. We wouldn't be risking our lives, we'd be committing suicide."

"When's the fog expected to lift?" Sabrina asked.

"The weathermen predict early morning."

"And you'll fly us to Dubrovnik then?" she added.

"I'll have the airport call me the minute the fog shows signs of lifting."

Graham looked suitably put out but he said nothing, knowing the pilot was right.

"Just one thing. How would a ship be faring out there right now?" Sabrina asked.

The pilot stared out into the darkness. "It would have dropped anchor as soon as the fog closed in. Only a madman would try and navigate a ship in these conditions."

Graham and Sabrina exchanged glances, each knowing what the other was thinking.

"If you want to fly back with me to the airport I've got a car waiting there, I can give you a lift into town. We're going to have to find a hotel for the night."

"Thanks, we'd appreciate that," Sabrina said.

As the rotors started up the same thought still nagged at the back of their minds. Unknown to the other, neither was prepared to hazard an answer.

Whitlock moved to the wall mirror to straighten his tie. He found himself staring at the stitches across his right eyebrow. An inanimate object had done what no opponent had managed to do in four years of amateur schoolboy boxing. Cut him. He had already come to fancy the idea of a scar, but this one would be fairly innocuous once the hair had grown back. A scar had the ability to give a face both character and strength. He remembered the scars on his grandfather's face, three on each cheek, which had been carved into his skin by a witchdoctor using the razor-sharp point of an incisor taken from the mouth of a slain lion. It had been part of the ritual initiation ceremony turning him from a boy into a man. His grandfathers couldn't have been more different. His mother's father, the tall warrior with the scarred cheeks who used to enthrall the young C.W. with exciting stories of past Masai battles; his father's father, the short, red-faced British Army Major who was rarely seen without a thick cigar in his mouth and a bottle of cheap whisky in his hand. His father had had a three-inch scar between his shoulder-blades, the result of an inter-tribal fight, he had once told his son. It was only after his father died that his mother told him the scar had actually been the result of a drunken brawl in a Nairobi nightclub. Much as he loved her, he still resented her for telling him. It was as though a part of the African mystique had died within him.

He smiled. His Masai grandfather would have been proud of him. He glanced at his wristwatch. 8:07. He was due at Karen's house for dinner at 8:30. The last supper, as he had called it. His work in Mainz was over. It was strange to think that twenty-four hours earlier he had been pacing up and down the very same room, frustrated at his lack of progress.

He pushed the Browning into the holster under his left arm, the threat of the mysterious motorbike rider ever present in the back of his mind.

The telephone rang.

He sat on the edge of the bed before picking up the receiver. "Hello?"

"C.W.?"

"Karen, is that you?"

"Please help me, they've—"

The receiver was snatched away from her.

"Be at the plant at 8:30 or the girl dies," a man's voice snarled in German.

"I can't, my pass was revoked today," Whitlock said calmly, but hearing his heart thudding in his chest.

"You'll get in, don't worry. 8:30 at the cooling pond. Come alone; and no piece otherwise the girl gets it."

The line went dead.

Whitlock disappeared into the bathroom only to emerge a minute later, his tie draped around his neck. He retied it quickly in front of the mirror, pulled on his jacket, then made his way down into the hotel foyer. After handing his key in at the reception desk he hurried out into the chilly night air to where his new rented car was parked on the opposite side of the road. It was a white Vauxhall Cavalier. He was determined to keep this one intact. With that thought in mind he used the highway instead of the old Frankfurt road.

He noticed there was only one guard on duty instead of the usual three as he approached the floodlit plant complex. Only when he drew up in front of the boomgate did he see the Finnish-made Jatimatic machinepistol in the guard's hand. It surprised him. Not only was the Jatimatic fairly new on the market but it was also rarely seen outside the Scandinavian countries.

It was the same guard who had turned him away that morning.

"I hope you're being paid overtime for all this devoted service," Whitlock said through the open window.

The guard ordered Whitlock to unlock the back door. Once inside he closed the door and pressed the Jatimatic into Whitlock's neck.

"Your piece, and take it out slowly.'

"You told me on the phone not to bring one."

"Your piece!" the guard snapped, his finger tightening on the trigger.

"Okay, okay," Whitlock said in a placating voice and reached for the Browning.

"I said slowly."

"If I go any slower my hand won't be moving."

The guard snatched the Browning from him. "Carry on straight but instead of turning into the visitors' car park turn left and continue for another hundred metres. You'll see a white door marked Seventeen. Park there."

Whitlock followed the guard's instructions and drew up in front of the white door with "17" emblazoned across it in black paint. Underneath was stencilled: *Entrance strictly prohibited to unauthorized personnel.* As he climbed from the Cavalier something caught his eye in the reflection of the overhead spotlight. The black Suzuki 1000cc was partially hidden in the shadows of an oak tree on the perimeter of the grass embankment. The guard prodded the Jatimatic into the small of his back and he returned his attention to the white door. It opened inwards.

"Left," the guard ordered.

He did as he was told and a few feet further on found himself in front of the door to the storage pond Leitzig had shown him a couple of days earlier. The door was ajar and he pushed it open with his fingertips. He glanced over his shoulder, awaiting instructions.

The guard gestured to the metal ladder on the wall to his right. "Climb, to the top."

Whitlock was hoping he could disarm the guard on the ladder but he was out of luck. The guard waited until Whitlock was half-way up before following him, careful to keep his distance at all times. As Whitlock neared the top of the ladder he was able to see the white leather boots and pants of the motorbike rider standing a few feet away on the catwalk. He clambered up on to the catwalk and saw the rider's face for the first time.

Karen was wearing a pair of dark glasses to hide her bruised eye, her black hair contrasting vividly with the whiteness of the leather jacket.

The guard, breathing heavily, appeared on the catwalk and handed the Browning to her.

"Frisk him," she ordered in German.

The guard frisked Whitlock quickly. "He's clean."

"You don't seem too surprised to find me holding the aces. Wasn't my performance over the phone realistic enough?" she asked.

"It was the first time. What baffles me though is why you went to the lengths of a black eye if, and correct me if I'm wrong, you and Vanner were going to kill me once I reached the house."

"How did you find out about Vanner?"

"Leitzig told me, before you shot him."

"Well, the black eye was an accident. Frankie, Frankie Vanner that is, opened the kitchen door into my face in his rush to leave the house on hearing the police sirens in the distance. That's when our plan started to go wrong. We'd expected you to come alone."

"Who exactly is this Vanner?"

"Hendrique's right-hand man. He was originally supposed to have been on the train but Werner had him sent back here once you arrived." She held up her hand as he was about to speak. "My turn to ask a question."

He glanced at the muzzle of the Browning pointing at his midriff. "I'd say that's a fair request."

"When did you first suspect me?"

"I've always suspected you, even if it was just a nagging doubt in the back of my mind. It was something Leitzig said which really got me thinking. He said part of the reason for his being planted here was to employ Hendrique's four technicians to help him, along with the drivers and guards who were also involved in the diversion. You told me at the Hilton you were in charge of hiring, amongst others, the drivers and the guards. It was a matter of putting two and two together.''

''I'm impressed,'' she said without sounding it. ''You're right, of course. I employed all the staff vetted by Hendrique without any of them suspecting I was anything other than the head of the PR department. It's been the perfect cover—only four other people know about it. Werner, Hendrique, Frankie and my handler.''

''What about Leitzig?''

''Leitzig?'' she scoffed. ''One of the reasons for my being here was to monitor the diversion's progress and report it directly to my handler. If Leitzig had known I was watching him he'd probably have panicked. As far as he was concerned he was the kingpin in the plant itself. All our staff worked for him. He paid them and if any of them got greedy he'd call in Hendrique.''

''What about his predecessor? Did Hendrique kill him?''

''He wasn't greedy, he just refused to cooperate. He also threatened to expose the diversion plot before it had even begun. Hendrique killed him and made it look like a skiing accident.'' Her smile was apologetic. ''I think I've answered enough of your questions.''

She took a step back and extended the Browning at arm's length, the muzzle aimed at the centre of Whitlock's forehead. Her finger curled around the trigger.

He stared at the Browning, transfixed, knowing he could never reach it before she pulled the trigger. Her wrist flexed in the second before she fired. The bullet took the guard in the chest, knocking him back against the wall. She fired again and the guard toppled face down on to the catwalk. The Jatimatic came to rest inches from Whitlock's feet.

"You could try," she said, watching his flickering eyes. "Otherwise kick it over the side."

He brushed it off the catwalk with the side of his foot.

"This section of the plant's not in operation tonight and even if someone should go past they wouldn't hear a thing. It's soundproof. We're all alone."

Whitlock looked down at the dead man. "You've got a strange way of repaying loyalty."

"I told you, he worked for Leitzig, not for me. Anyway, he knew about my cover. I had to confide in him to get him to help me. Actually, it's worked out rather well. The guard catches you snooping in an unauthorized area of the plant and in the ensuing struggle he's shot and you lose your footing, falling to your death. It's not very original but quite effective nevertheless."

"And what if I manage to keep my footing?"

"Then I'll shoot you. It might spoil my little scenario but at least you won't have to worry about it."

"Such consideration." He moved to the railing and peered down at the tranquil water seventy feet below. "Can I ask one final question?"

"Ask."

"Who exactly are you working for?"

"KGB, Department S. I was recruited at university

and I've been working for them ever since.'' Her voice became strangely hollow. ''I've only got one regret about all of this, that we never made love last night.''

''Well, it would have saved you the bother of tonight's trip.''

''I couldn't have killed you then,'' she said quietly. ''I wanted you so much.''

''We could try—''

''Don't mock me,'' she erupted, then levelled the Browning at his chest. ''I'll shoot if you haven't jumped in ten seconds.''

He turned his head to look at the pond below, then clutched his neck, his face twisted in pain. Massaging the back of his neck his fingers felt for the sheathed stiletto he had strapped underneath his collar before leaving the hotel. He had rehearsed the move countless times on a dummy in front of his bedroom mirror back home but it was the first time he would be putting it into practice. Surprise and accuracy were vital if it were to succeed; the slightest misjudgement would cost him his life. He gripped the hilt then tilted his head fractionally so he could unsheath the knife cleanly and follow through in one fluid movement.

She saw the glint of the blade at the last second but instead of firing she instinctively tried to get a better grip on the Browning. The finely-sharpened blade sliced across the back of her hand. She screamed, dropped the Browning, then stumbled backwards clutching her bleeding hand to her stomach. He saw what happened next as if it were in a slow-motion replay. She backed against the railings and lost her footing, toppling backwards but grabbing on to one of the vertical struts with her injured hand. She managed to get her other hand around the railing, then glanced down at the water seventy feet below her.

"Don't look down!" he shouted.

Only her hands were visible above the level of the catwalk.

"Give me your hand."

"I can't, they're slipping," she screamed, her bloodied hands unable to get a grip on the smooth railing. "Help me, for God's sake help me."

He reached down between the struts and grabbed one of her wrists with both hands, but even as he took the strain the blood was already acting as a lubricant between their skins. He dug his fingers mercilessly into her flesh and in a last, desperate bid to hold on she released her grip on the now sticky railing and clasped her hands, one at a time, around his wrists. He tried to pull her up but her hands were slipping all the time. Then, suddenly, she dropped her injured hand to her side, unable to bear the pain any longer. Her wrist slipped through his hands and as she dug her fingers into his palms he caught sight of her wide, pleading eyes staring up at him. Then the contact broke. He turned away sharply as she plunged backwards into space.

He finally stood up and looked down. She was floating face down in the pond, only her white leathers visible above the surface of the water.

He removed the ID disc from the dead guard's pocket to use to open the door then picked up his Browning and made his way towards the ladder.

After locking the storage pond door behind him he

walked down the corridor and out into the night. He drove the Cavalier slowly down the driveway until he came to the boomgate where a guard emerged from the hut and glanced at his pass. Even if his pass had been revoked no guard would bother checking the list against outgoing vehicles.

"You haven't seen another guard dressed like me, have you? Only when I came on duty a few minutes ago this place was unmanned. Anyone could have got in."

"No, sorry," Whitlock replied with an apologetic smile.

The guard activated the boomgate.

Whitlock's next stop would be the hospital to check on Leitzig's condition. The last he heard, Leitzig was off the critical list. The sooner he got the names of Leitzig's fellow conspirators the sooner he could file his last report to Philpott.

Then back to New York.

Back to Carmen.

ELEVEN

An airport official telephoned the helicopter pilot at 4:15 the following morning to tell him the fog had lifted sufficiently over the Adriatic for him to attempt the flight to Dubrovnik. Within ten minutes he, Graham and Sabrina had checked out of the hotel and within twenty-five minutes air traffic control had given the helicopter clearance for take-off. As soon as they were airborne Graham and Sabrina removed wetsuits from the holdall which had been left, on their instructions, in a locker at the airport. In the confined space it was no easy task to strip down to the T-shirt and shorts they were wearing underneath their thick winter clothes and pull on the suits.

By the time they reached Dubrovnik two-and-a-half hours later the fog had already dissipated and the first shafts of dawn light stippled the darkened horizon like the initial brushstrokes of a magnificent watercolour.

The pilot pointed downwards as they flew over the section of harbour owned by Werner Freight. It was a much smaller area than the Trieste complex, comprising only two wharves and a line of warehouses painted in the company's distinctive colours of black, red and yellow. The pilot, having already radioed ahead to the harbour authorities, had established that the *Napoli* had yet to dock in Dubrovnik, its arrival time now uncertain due to the delay caused by the fog. There was currently no ship berthed at either of the two wharves.

When the pilot banked the helicopter away from the harbour to rendezvous at a predetermined spot marked on a chart which had also been included in the holdall, Graham and Sabrina slipped on their flippers and facemasks, then put their Berettas and black plimsolls into the waterproof pouches and secured them to clips at their waists. The coordinates on the chart turned out to be an area some five hundred metres off-shore. It was the perfect place for the drop. When the pilot had lowered the helicopter to within ten feet of the water he nodded his head vigorously, the signal for them to deplane. No sooner had they jumped through the open hatchway and hit the water than the helicopter ascended and wheeled away over Ploce Beach towards the airport.

They were both experienced swimmers and consequently neither had any difficulty in covering the distance to the wharf, the last hundred metres being swum underwater using snorkels to avoid detection in the beam of the powerful floodlights which were still on despite the growing light of day. Once at the wharf they rested for a couple of minutes then Graham led

the way to a rusty steel ladder at the juncture of
Wharves Seven and Eight. He climbed it until his eyes
were level with the newly tarred surface of the wharf.
The area was deserted except for a company Land
Rover parked outside the warehouse facing directly on
to Wharf Eight.

The warehouse door suddenly opened and a man
emerged, an Italian Spectre sub-machine-gun slung
over his shoulder. Graham ducked down, waiting for
the sound of approaching footsteps. There was none.
He raised his head slowly then cursed under his breath.
The man was standing on the other side of the Land
Rover, his head bent forward to light his cigarette. He
tossed the spent match aside then leaned back against
the passenger door and folded his arms across his
chest. There was no route into the warehouse without
disturbing the man and even Graham didn't fancy his
chances against the Spectre, arguably the most lethal
short-range machine-pistol on the market. He whispered to Sabrina and in reply she removed her flippers
while balancing with one hand gripped around the strut
of the ladder. She handed them to him then slipped on
her plimsolls and tucked the Beretta into the webbing
around her waist.

"Distract his attention when I give the signal."

"Oh, yeah? Have you any idea just how potent the
Spectre is?"

"Sure. It's got a fifty-round magazine and has an
effective range of a hundred-and-fifty metres." She put
her hand lightly on his arm. "He won't get off a shot.
Trust me."

She climbed up on to the wharf before he could reply and moved cautiously, doubled-over, to the near side of the Land Rover. Crouched down on her haunches, she quickly assessed the situation before giving Graham a nod. He ducked out of sight and a moment later tossed her flippers up on to the wharf. The guard swung round sharply and unslung the Spectre, waiting for the owner of the flippers to come into view. After a few seconds he frowned and took several hesitant steps towards the edge of the wharf. He stopped, now clear of the Land Rover, his back to Sabrina. She rose ghostlike from her hiding place and chopped her hand down viciously on the side of his neck. He crumpled to the ground.

"Mike!" she hissed.

Graham scrambled up on to the wharf where he helped her push the unconscious guard under the Land Rover.

"Hendrique's here," he announced, after peering through the driver's window.

She shouldered the Spectre. "How do you know?"

He pointed to the brown attaché case on the back seat. "It contains the game I played with him on the train."

"So if Hendrique's here—"

"It's fair to assume Werner's with him."

She opened the door fractionally but all she could see was several crates, each with the now familiar Werner logo stamped on the side, stacked neatly against the wall. She gripped the Beretta tightly in her hand and pushed the door open further. The shadowy warehouse was divided into three rows of stacked packing crates with two spacious passages left between them for easy vehicle and machine manoeuvrability. They slipped inside and Graham closed the door silently behind him.

"We each take a passage," he whispered.

She shook her head. "I say we stick together. There are at least four of them plus who knows how many guards. All armed."

He conceded with a shrug.

They reached the end of the passage and he was about to turn into the second section of the L-shaped building when she grabbed his arm and put a finger to her lips. They both listened but could hear nothing.

"I heard voices," she whispered.

"They've got to be around somewhere. Come on."

He pressed his back against the crates, the Beretta held barrel upwards by his face, then peered carefully into the adjoining passage. It was deserted. The section was laid out like the one they were in, with three rows of crates spanning the two hundred metres to the far wall. He indicated the middle row and they darted into one of the narrow apertures between the crates where he was able to look out into the other passage.

Werner was seated at a table with his back to them in a glass-panelled office at the end of the passage. He was playing cards with Kyle and Milchan. Hendrique was leaning against the wall, watching them. The Franchi Spas shotgun lay on the filing cabinet beside him.

"Remember what the boss said about shooting to kill," Graham said.

"I know what he said. I was there, remember?"

He lapsed into silence. She placed the Spectre on

the ground behind her, then crouched down to study the best angle for her intended shot. She rested her right wrist on her left forearm to steady her arm and lined up the back of Werner's head in the rear and frontsight.

"What's that noise?" she whispered.

"What noise?"

"It's like a rustling sound."

"Rats probably," he said indifferently. "Yeah, there's a hole in the bottom of the crate by your foot. They'll be in there."

An image of the crate teeming with bloated, scurrying rats filled her mind and she stumbled backwards out into the second passage, the Beretta clattering to the ground.

Hendrique already had the shotgun in his hand when he turned to investigate the noise. Graham launched himself at her at the same instant Hendrique fired through the office window. He felled her with a low, brutal football tackle a split-second before the shotgun cartridge ripped a jagged hole in the crate directly behind them. Hendrique kept them covered while Kyle and Milchan collected the fallen weapons, which included the Beretta from Graham's webbing belt.

As they were yanked to their feet both Sabrina and Graham noticed the contents of the damaged crates. AK47s.

Werner ignored them when they were brought into the office. He was glaring at Hendrique. "So much for your hand-picked guards. Or perhaps these two were beamed down into the warehouse by a spaceship."

For once Hendrique had no reply to Werner's sarcasm.

"I had a feeling we'd meet again," Werner said to Sabrina. "Actually you've timed your arrival to perfection. I was about to leave. My seaplane's in the hangar, refuelled and ready for take-off."

"What about the *Napoli*?" she asked.

"It's got to make up for lost time so it won't be docking in Dubrovnik after all. As for me, I'm going home. Hendrique's now officially in charge."

"So the detonator goes to Hendrique?"

"Come now, Mr. Graham, I'd hardly have expected such an illogical question to come from someone as experienced as you." Werner gave Hendrique a contemptuous look. "He's a mercenary, an arms and drug smuggler; he's ruled by money. The Socialist cause has never meant anything to him. If he had the detonator he'd probably hold it to ransom."

"That's enough," Hendrique snapped angrily.

"Well, wouldn't you?" Werner challenged, then turned back to Graham. "The detonator stays with me. It's quite simple really. If you hadn't come along when you did I'd have flown out and nobody would have been any the wiser. My defection won't be announced until the *Napoli*'s cargo has reached its destination safely, so your superiors will naturally presume I'm still within detonating distance and give the freighter a wide berth. A point borne out by your presence here now. If you hadn't taken my threat seriously you'd have already boarded the *Napoli*." He picked up a travelling bag from beside the table. "I wanted you alive on the train so you could pass on my instructions to your superiors. Now, I'm afraid, I want you dead. I'll leave that in Hendrique's capable hands.''

''Radio through to the other guards, I'll meet them round the front,'' Hendrique said to Kyle.

Hendrique strode briskly through the warehouse and out on to the wharf. The other two guards were already there, both kneeling down beside the third one.

He hauled the dazed guard to his feet and shoved him up against the Land Rover. ''You've humiliated me in front of Werner.''

''I'm sorry, sir,'' the guard mumbled, massaging his neck.

He withdrew his Desert Eagle and shot the guard at point-blank range, then swung round to face the other two guards. ''I won't tolerate failure. I want you both to stay here and for God's sake keep your eyes open.''

He removed the attaché case from the Land Rover and disappeared back into the warehouse.

''What was that shooting?'' Werner demanded when Hendrique entered the office.

''A disciplinary matter,'' Hendrique replied, then removed the board from the attaché case.

Kyle cleared the cards and the coffee mugs from the table while Hendrique removed one of the overhead strip lights and attached the crocodile clips to the power source.

''What are you going to do, play them off against each other?'' Kyle asked excitedly.

''That's not a bad idea now you come to mention it, but what I had in mind was letting Graham pit his skills against Milchan.'' Hendrique looked at Milchan. ''It's up to you.''

Milchan tapped his chest then drew his finger across his throat.

"In case you didn't understand that, Graham, you and Milchan will be playing to the death."

"And if I refuse?" Graham said defiantly.

"Then I'll be forced to shoot your beautiful assistant," Kyle said.

"Partner," Sabrina corrected automatically.

"Tie her to the chair," Hendrique said to Milchan. "She can have a ringside seat."

"I'm sorry it had to end like this, Sabrina," Werner said softly, then turned to leave, his footsteps echoing into the distance.

"I reckon he fancied you, darling. Not that I blame him," Kyle said with a twisted smile and reached out to touch her face.

She bit his hand.

"Bitch," he snarled, raising the Spectre to strike her.

Graham shoved past Hendrique and punched Kyle to the ground.

Hendrique pressed the shotgun into Graham's neck. "Tie his feet."

Milchan grabbed Graham's arm and led him to the nearest chair.

"You'll pay for that," Kyle snapped, aiming the Spectre at Graham.

Hendrique pushed the Spectre barrel towards the ground. "You're beginning to get on my nerves, Eddie. Go and do something constructive, like starting up the helicopter."

"But I want to watch," Kyle whined, pointing to the board on the table.

"We're not staying, we've got work to do. Now get the helicopter started."

Kyle reluctantly handed the Spectre to Hendrique and left the office.

Hendrique crossed to the board and placed both hands on the pads, raising one and then the other. The shock on both occasions passed harmlessly through the bracelets. He took a key from the pouch inside the attaché case and turned it through one revolution in a lock on the side of the board. A red light came on beside the lock.

"I've dispensed with the first two games. Put on the bracelets."

Both men snapped the bracelets around their wrists, locked them, then put the keys in the centre of the board.

"I've activated the death shock. Even your wetsuit won't save you, Graham."

"You're assuming I'll pull off first," Graham said.

"I know you'll pull off first. Milchan only ever plays when the death shock's in operation. He's still alive." Hendrique touched the shotgun against Sabrina's neck. "If you don't push down simultaneously with Milchan I'll kill her."

Graham glanced at her. She smiled weakly.

"Your call, Graham," Hendrique said, tightening his grip on the shotgun.

Milchan rested his hand lightly on the pad, his eyes never leaving Graham's face. Graham exhaled deeply then placed his palm on the other pad.

"Now," Graham commanded.

They both pressed their hands down on to the pads.

"Sorry I can't stay to watch you die, Graham, but we're already well behind schedule." With that Hendrique walked out into the warehouse.

Sabrina tried to loosen her tethered hands as soon as he was out of sight but Milchan had knotted the cloth over her wrists, out of reach of her fingers. She then used her momentum to shift the chair round until she was sitting with her back to the shattered window-pane.

"Mike . . . ?"

"Don't worry about me, I'm okay," he replied without taking his eyes off Milchan's face.

She glanced over her shoulder. The chair was a foot away from the window. She would have to tilt the chair back against the transom but knew in doing so she could easily impale her hands or wrists on the jagged glass protruding from it. It was a risk she had to take. She rocked the chair by propelling her body backwards and forwards, building up enough of a rhythm to topple it back against the transom. Her first thought was one of relief at not having cut herself, but the moment she moved her hand she nicked her thumb and felt blood trickle down across her palm. By carefully tapping with her forefinger she discovered she had cut her thumb on a splinter of glass about five inches long. She pressed the cloth against the splinter's serrated edge and moved her wrists up and down, using the glass as a saw. Within seconds it had shredded and she was able to reach down and untie her feet.

"What must I do, Mike? Disconnect the clips?"

The indicator read six.

"Unlock my bracelet," he replied tersely.

"Why not disconnect it at the mains?"

"Unlock my bracelet, Sabrina!"

She picked up the two keys, then another thought came to mind. "What if it's booby-trapped?"

"It's not, trust me," he replied, his face showing the first signs of pain.

She unlocked the bracelet. With his free hand he reached across and snapped the bracelet around Milchan's wrist inches below the other one.

The indicator read eight.

Beads of sweat were running down Milchan's scarred face as he stared in terror at Graham's hand on the pressure pad.

"Maybe I should prove Hendrique right and pull off first. It's not as though I've got anything to lose. What do you think, Milchan?" Graham managed a smile despite the increasing level of current passing through his body.

"Mike, don't!" Sabrina shouted. "You can't murder him in cold blood."

The indicator read nine.

"He would have murdered you in cold blood if he'd won and you were still tied to the chair. You know what they say about what's good for the goose . . ."

She took a hesitant step towards the mains cable leading to the light socket.

"Don't touch it! This one's personal."

"Killing him won't bring Carrie and Mikey back," she blurted out before she could stop herself.

The indicator read ten.

He stared at her and the pain seemed to disappear from his eyes even though his arm was shuddering from the amount of current surging through it. Then, without warning, he yanked hard on the cable, disconnecting the clips from the overhead socket.

Milchan slumped back in his chair, his chest heaving as he sucked in deep mouthfuls of air.

Graham and Sabrina had their backs to the glass panel and consequently neither of them saw the guard until he confronted them in the doorway.

"Mr. Hendrique told me to come back here and see if you needed a hand," the guard said to Milchan who was busy unlocking the bracelets from his wrist. "Looks like I got here just in time."

Milchan nodded in agreement then crossed to where the guard was standing.

"Mr. Hendrique said I was to kill them if they were still alive," the guard said, then trained his machine-pistol on them.

Milchan clamped his spade-like hands on either side of the guard's face and twisted his head violently, snapping the bones in his neck as though they were brittle twigs. He dumped the dead man in the corner of the office then tapped his own chest and pointed to each of them in turn, his mouth moving silently as he tried to express himself.

"He says now we're even," Sabrina said, reading his lips.

Graham caught him on the side of the chin with a haymaker. Milchan was unconscious before he hit the floor.

"Now we're even."

She gave Graham a quizzical look then retrieved the Berettas from the top of the filing cabinet and tossed one to him. "We might still be able to stop Stefan."

He grabbed her arm. "We're going to have a little chat once this is over. About rats."

She nodded then picked up the Spectre.

They split up once they were in the warehouse, meeting up again at the entrance where they had to step over the guard killed by Hendrique to get on to the wharf.

Day was dawning.

They heard the sound of an aircraft engine roaring into life within the confines of a dome-shaped corrugated-iron structure jutting out into the sea at the end of Wharf Eight and sprinted the two hundred metres to its wooden door where they pressed themselves against the wall on either side of it, Berettas drawn. She turned the handle slowly then jerked the door open. He dived low through the doorway, rolling twice across the concrete floor before getting in a shot at the startled guard. The bullet hit him in the neck, knocking him backwards into the water. The distraction gave Werner the few valuable seconds he needed to open the throttle and head the seaplane out on to the open water. There were half a dozen speedboats moored in the hangar. Graham was half a second behind her as Sabrina ran to a seventeen-foot 170 GTS and climbed inside.

"You know how to pilot one of these things?"

"Are you kidding?" She replied with a grin. "My father's got a forty-footer moored off Miami. I spend most of my time zooming around in it whenever I'm down there.''

She waited for him to cast off then started up the 90hp Yamaha motor and sped out of the hangar after the fleeing seaplane.

The more she thought about it the more guilty she felt about having squandered her chance back at the warehouse. Werner had been the perfect target. All she would have needed was another couple of seconds . . .

When the speedboat drew abreast of the seaplane they caught a glimpse of Werner's face through the cockpit door window, his lips moving rapidly as he shouted into the radio. She arced the speedboat across in front of the seaplane, forcing Werner to reduce speed and change direction. He was playing into her hands. The narrow extension of the harbour wall lay directly in front of the seaplane, its unmanned lighthouse flashing ineffectually as the first rays of sun glistened across the cold, uninviting water. Her plan was to shepherd the seaplane towards the harbour wall, knowing he was already too close to clear it, by hemming him in on the other three sides in ever decreasing circles. Graham held the Spectre, waiting for Werner's first mistake . . .

Werner realized what she was trying to do and desperately searched for a way out. He was so close to going home. There was only one option open to him. He had to take it. He waited until the speedboat was on the starboard side, nearest the shore, then swivelled the seaplane in a forty-five degree turn and headed out towards the open sea. Sabrina slewed the speedboat around so violently that Graham almost lost his footing, having to grab on to the perspex windscreen to prevent himself from falling overboard. The speedboat skimmed across the water as she forced the seaplane away from the open sea and back towards the wall like a sheepdog manoeuvring a maverick bellwether into its pen. Werner had the speed he wanted but he was being forced even closer to the tip of the harbour wall. In desperation he ripped the chain from his neck and pressed it threateningly against the cockpit door window. He eased the stick back and felt the landing pads lift off the water. Graham fired at the rising plane. The bullets chewed an uneven line across the fuselage and Werner jerked back from the controls, the detonator spinning from his hand. The plane, already fifteen feet in the air, went out of control. It was on a collision course with the lighthouse. Werner, bleeding profusely from a bullet wound in his right shoulder, managed to tilt the nose away from the lighthouse wall but although the fuselage missed it by inches the right wing and landing pad were sheared off as though they were made of cardboard. The seaplane pirouetted grotesquely before landing heavily in the sea. It immediately listed to the right as water rushed through an aperture caused by the buckling of the cockpit door. Werner, his body racked with pain, tried to move but found to his horror that his foot was wedged between the door and a metal strut under the seat. The seaplane shuddered as the flooded tail section dipped beneath the water.

Then he saw the detonator dangling at the end of the chain, trapped between the shattered windscreen and the dashboard. He ripped the chain free and flicked back the detonator cap. He smiled triumphantly as he looked up at the approaching speedboat.

"Stefan, no!" Sabrina screamed.

The seaplane bucked and the fuselage disappeared underwater the moment Graham fired a burst from the Spectre. The bullets ripped harmlessly into the now near-vertical nose.

Werner pressed the button.

Graham and Sabrina instinctively ducked, their eyes screwed up in anticipation of the inevitable explosion.

There was only silence.

Werner pressed the detonator a second and third time. The only noise was the water flooding into the cockpit. He closed his hand slowly around the detonator.

The cockpit, and finally the nose, slid beneath the waves.

Sabrina rested her forearms on the windscreen and watched the water bubbling angrily in the wake of the submerged seaplane. "And to think he was one of the world's leading businessmen. Christ, Mike, he was prepared to take half of Europe with him."

Graham tossed the Spectre on to the seat behind him, then ran his fingers through his damp, tousled hair. "You think he was mad?"

"Wasn't he?"

"He was a fanatic, he believed what he was doing would ultimately further his cause."

"Including the destruction of half of Europe?"

"If necessary," he said bluntly. "Fanatics are

driven by passion, not madness. Were the Japanese kamikaze pilots mad?"

"It's a form of madness."

"It's a form of extremism," he countered.

They heard the sound of rotors in the distance behind them and Sabrina slipped the speedboat into gear then turned it around to face the oncoming helicopter. It was a thirty-foot Augusta Bell JetRanger, the Werner logo displayed prominently on either side of its fuselage. Kyle was at the controls, Hendrique beside him.

When the helicopter was fifty yards away it dipped into a steep dive and Hendrique fired a burst from his Spectre through the open cockpit door. The bullets went wide of the speedboat. Graham resisted the temptation to fire at the undercarriage as the helicopter flew over the speedboat; he had only one magazine and every bullet would have to count. Sabrina swung the wheel violently and made for the sanctuary of the harbour. Kyle banked the helicopter in a wide arc and homed in on the speedboat, dipping it low overhead. Graham dropped the Spectre as he and Sabrina flung themselves to the floor, and it was lost overboard. They were down to two handguns against whatever arsenal Hendrique had stored aboard the helicopter.

Hendrique dropped the first grenade as the helicopter swept low across the speedboat's bow. Sabrina had to take immediate evasive action by slewing the speedboat to the side and moments later the grenade exploded, showering them in a fine spray of water. A second grenade, dropped from a higher altitude, exploded within a couple of feet of the speedboat and Sabrina had to use all her expertise to keep control of the wheel when the hull was pitched out of the water by the resulting wave. She zigzagged the speedboat through the water, making it impossible for Hendrique to drop a third grenade with any degree of accuracy. They reached the temporary shelter of the hangar. It was a stalemate. If they ventured out the helicopter would be waiting for them. If the helicopter descended into view its occupants would be perfect targets.

The helicopter swept past the hangar and Hendrique flung a grenade through the entrance. The speedboat was idling too far back for the explosion to do any harm but they both knew it would be only a matter of time before Hendrique started to use his Spectre. Bullets fired indiscriminately into the confines of the largely unprotected hangar could go anywhere.

When the helicopter returned Hendrique did use his Spectre, sending them both diving for cover again. Graham was the first up and he inspected the minor structural damage. Three bullets embedded in the speedboat's nose. Three bullets which could just as easily have hit them. Sabrina? Her name shot through his mind and there was a certain reluctance in his limbs to move as he turned to look behind him. She lay sprawled across the linoleum floor at the back of the boat.

Kyle was preparing for another run when the speedboat emerged from the hangar, its hull barely moving through the water, with Graham standing despondently behind the wheel. Hendrique ordered Kyle to take the helicopter lower.

''She's dead. You killed her, you bastard!'' Graham

shouted, then cast a despairing glance over his shoulder.

She opened her eyes fractionally and winked at him.

"I'm through with all this," he shouted up to the helicopter.

"Throw your gun over the side," Hendrique called down to him.

Graham's hand hovered over the Beretta in his webbing belt.

"Do it!" Sabrina hissed.

He threw it into the water.

The Augusta Bell was powered by a single 400shp Allison turboshaft engine situated in the roof of the fuselage close to the rotors. She would get only one chance to hit it so it was imperative for the fuselage to be at a precise angle before she could attempt the shot. She had to immobilize an engine she couldn't even see.

The fuselage was almost broadside on and her fingers tightened around the Beretta at her side. Any moment now and the whole target would be in sight. A distracted thought flashed through her mind. If she failed, Graham would be the first to die. In a strange way the thought gave her a renewed confidence in herself. The whole fuselage on Kyle's side was now directly above her. She extended her arms upwards and fired twice.

Graham, having been told by Sabrina in the hangar to treat the speedboat like a car, accelerated away from beneath the helicopter. She vaulted over the seat and took the helm then reduced speed and pivoted the speedboat around so they could watch the helicopter.

The rotors were already slowing and Kyle was frantically struggling to restart the engine. The helicopter dropped lifelessly from the sky and pieces of the fuselage were flung into the air as it broke into two on striking the water.

"Where the hell did you learn to shoot like that?" Graham asked in disbelief.

She shrugged modestly then headed the speedboat out towards the open sea. Neither of them noticed a second speedboat creep gingerly from the hangar, its occupant waiting until they were a speck on the horizon before setting out after them, careful though to keep his distance.

The coastguard relayed the *Napoli*'s position to Sabrina over the small radio transmitter on the speedboat and twenty minutes later they sighted the 17,000 tonne freighter in the distance. Its rusted hull was in desperate need of a fresh coat of paint and the only indication of its affiliation to the Werner empire was the company flag flying beside the Liberian flag of convenience high above the stern. As they drew closer they saw the vague outline of the company logo on the funnel underneath a fresh coat of white paint.

One of the crewmen standing by the railing pointed to the yellow "W" on the speedboat's bow and a rope ladder was immediately dropped over to the side of the ship. Graham managed to secure the speedboat to the foot of the rope ladder and as he negotiated his way up the side of the hull he was thankful the sea was still relatively calm. Hands reached out through the railings and helped him over the side and onto the deck. He then gestured for Sabrina to follow. She was halfway up the ladder when an observant crewman noticed the gentle curves beneath her wetsuit and word quickly spread across the deck that a woman was about to come aboard. When she did finally clamber on to the ship she was met with an onslaught of wolf whistles and lascivious suggestions.

"Where's the captain?" Graham demanded of the nearest crewman.

The crewman's answer was to point to the bridge.

The captain, a stout Irishman called Flaherty, eyed them suspiciously when they appeared on the bridge. The Beretta tucked into Sabrina's webbing belt didn't go unnoticed by him.

"Who are you and what do you want?"

"There's been a change of plan, you're to dock in Dubrovnik after all," Graham said.

"Just like that?" Flaherty said sarcastically. "For your information I only take my orders from one person, Mr. Werner himself."

"Stefan Werner's dead," Sabrina said, then took a step towards Flaherty, her hands extended in a pleading gesture. "It's imperative that you change course and dock in Dubrovnik."

Flaherty turned away and looked out across the sea, his finger feeling for the emergency button on the underside of the chart table. It set off a warning signal in the officers' quarters of trouble on the bridge.

"My orders are to bypass Dubrovnik altogether to make up for lost time and unless I hear differently from Mr. Werner I don't intend changing my course."

"Werner's dead," Sabrina repeated in exasperation.

"So you've said, but I've got no reason to believe you."

"I've had enough of this crap," Graham interjected and pulled the Beretta from Sabrina's belt before she could stop him. He held it inches from Flaherty's unshaven face. "Give the order to change course for Dubrovnik."

Flaherty swallowed nervously, silently cursing the apparent lethargy of his officers in responding to the emergency. "I don't know who you are or what organization you represent but I can't believe you'd actually hijack a grain ship bound for Africa. If you've got a grudge against Mr. Werner why take it out on the thousands of starving people whose lives depend on this shipment reaching the relief camps in time?"

"I said, give the order!" Graham snarled.

The helmsman glanced at Flaherty. "What must I do, sir?"

"Nothing," Flaherty replied defiantly.

The door leading on to the bridge burst open and two men entered, each toting a dated Thompson submachine-gun. Graham swivelled Flaherty around to face the sub-machine-guns, the Beretta tucked into the folds of the captain's sweaty neck.

"Mike, wait!" Sabrina said, then addressed Flaherty. "We'll make a deal with you."

"I don't think you're in any position to make a deal."

"Perhaps not, but then neither are you. Here's the deal. We release you unharmed if you give the order to drop anchor then contact the authorities personally and ask them to come on board."

Flaherty chuckled. "You want me to contact the authorities?"

"It would be to your advantage, unless you've got something to hide," she replied in a challenging tone.

"I've got nothing to hide," Flaherty answered, then gave the order to stop engines.

It would take the *Napoli* another three miles to come to a halt.

"Now to contact the authorities," Flaherty said, still amazed at the terms.

Suddenly there was the sound of feet pounding up the metal stairs leading to the bridge, then the door was wrenched open. The two armed officers swivelled round to face the intruder. Milchan stood in the doorway, his flickering eyes taking in the scene before him.

"He's okay, he works for Mr. Werner," Flaherty said, then gave Sabrina a sidelong glance. "You're becoming heavily outnumbered in here."

Milchan closed the door behind him then stood behind the two officers and banged their heads together. They both crumpled to the ground. He picked up the sub-machine-guns and extended them towards Sabrina as though in offering. She took them from him, half expecting it to be some kind of trap. No sooner had she taken them than he turned and balled his fist menacingly at Graham. He tapped his clenched fist, then his chin, and gave Graham a thumbs-up sign.

"What's he trying to say?"

"That you've got a good punch," she replied.

Milchan nodded in agreement.

"What happens now?" Flaherty asked, his voice apprehensive.

"You and I take a walk to the radio room to contact the proper authorities," Graham said behind him.

"Mike?" Sabrina said, holding out her hand. "Our fight isn't with the captain."

Graham scowled at her, then reluctantly handed back her Beretta.

Flaherty pulled a handkerchief from his pocket and dabbed his sweating face. "Who are you?"

"We're not at liberty to tell you," Sabrina replied.

Graham gestured to the door. "Come on, let's go."

"As the ship's captain I have the right to know what's going on."

"You really don't know what's in that crate, do you?" Sabrina said.

"Crate? What . . . ." he trailed off, and suddenly he looked frightened. "You mean the one the Sikorsky brought aboard last night?"

"What did Stefan say it contained?"

"Machine parts," Flaherty replied, then looked from Sabrina to Graham. "Mother of God, what does it contain? And don't say you're not at liberty to tell me."

"We don't make the rules, Captain," she said apologetically. "But the sooner we contact the authorities the sooner we can have the crate removed."

Flaherty crossed himself. "Of course. I'll take you to the radio room." He paused at the door to glance back at Sabrina. "I take it you were telling the truth when you said Mr. Werner was dead?"

"His plane crashed half an hour ago. It'll be in all the papers tomorrow."

"He was a good man," Flaherty said, then led Graham down the metal stairs.

Four crewmen appeared and carried the two unconscious officers from the bridge.

"How did you get here?" Sabrina asked Milchan.

He made undulating movements with his hand.

"Boat?"

He nodded.

"Why are you helping us?"

He bent both sets of fingers inwards and interlocked them.

She understood the sign language gesture. Friend. "But I thought Hendrique was your friend?"

He shrugged his massive shoulders then rubbed his thumb and forefinger together.

"You stayed with Hendrique for the money?" she said with a smile.

He pointed at her, than balled his fist, which she took to represent Graham, and placed his hand on the table. He then reached up his other hand and made a jerking movement, representing the flex being ripped from the light socket. He made the "friends" gesture again with his hands.

She decided against telling him about the helicopter. He was probably closer to Hendrique than anyone else.

Graham and Flaherty returned.

"How long before the boss gets here?" she asked.

"Five, ten minutes," Graham replied.

"Five, ten minutes? I thought he was still in Prato."

"So did I, but it seems he arrived in Dubrovnik an hour ago."

"I didn't know that crate was contraband," Flaherty said, getting between them. "Honest to God I didn't. You've got to believe me."

"Weren't you ever suspicious of the way Werner handled the situation? Didn't it seem strange to you that he had this obsessive interest in one particular crate?"

"Well, as I said to your superior . . ."

"Partner!" Sabrina interceded indignantly. "How many times must I say it? We're partners."

"Partner. Sorry. Well, Mr. Werner told me the crate contained machine parts for a laboratory in Libya and what with all this anti-Gadaffi sentiment doing the rounds he wanted to play down the fact that his company was actually doing business with them. He thought it might have given his opponents some ammunition to use against him. He assured me it was all above board. Who was I to argue? As I said earlier, I always considered Mr. Werner to be a good and just man."

A crewman appeared at the door. "Helicopter coming in from the south, sir."

"Has an area of the deck been cleared for it to land?" Flaherty asked.

"Yes, sir."

"You'll want to go and meet it," Flaherty said to Graham.

"Yeah," Graham replied without much enthusiasm.

"You'll be fine as long as you cooperate," Sabrina said, noticing Flaherty's dejected look.

"You can count on my cooperation," Flaherty replied.

Milchan, sitting on a wooden box in the corner of the bridge, looked up and smiled sadly at her.

"We'll put in a good word for you, I promise," she said, returning his smile.

Milchan gave her an indifferent shrug as though he had already resigned himself to the inevitability of a lengthy prison sentence.

Philpott was the first out of the Lynx helicopter after it had landed aft of the bridge. Graham indicated to the pilot not to shut down the engine then he, Philpott and Sabrina moved to the railing at the stern of the ship. Philpott listened silently as they filled him in on the latest developments.

"So you don't believe the captain's involved?"

"No, sir," Sabrina replied.

"Mike?"

"I wouldn't have thought so, sir." Graham glanced up at the bridge. "How many men have you brought with you?"

"Five."

"That's enough," Graham muttered.

"Enough for what?" Philpott replied suspiciously.

"To handle things here. Sabrina and I want to go back to the warehouse and take a closer look at those AK47s."

"You don't think this Milchan will be any trouble? These five are all on the technical staff, they're hardly trained to deal with some marauding wrestler."

"You won't have any trouble from him, sir," Sabrina said reassuringly.

"I'll see you both when the ship docks then," Philpott said.

They made their way towards the helicopter.

"Mike? Sabrina?" Philpott called out after them.

They turned, their heads ducked low.

"Well done," Philpott said.

They gave him a wave then hauled themselves into the helicopter cabin and Graham closed the door after them.

The helicopter touched down on Wharf Eight and waited just long enough for them to jump out before taking off again and banking away sharply to the left as it headed back towards the *Napoli*.

They entered the warehouse.

"I'll take this section, you take the one nearest the office," Graham said.

"How do we open the crates?"

"I saw a crowbar by the door as we came in. You're sure to find something round there."

She decided to go straight to the office; it seemed the most logical place for storing tools. She froze on reaching the doorway then slowly removed the Beretta from her webbing belt. The board had been cleared from the table. In its place was a mug of coffee, still steaming. Graham was somewhere in the warehouse, unarmed and unsuspecting.

She saw him as she turned away from the table. He was standing in the juncture between the two sections of the L-shaped warehouse. Hendrique was behind him, the shotgun barrel pressed under his chin. As she approached she noticed the deep laceration on the right-hand side of Hendrique's face, running from the bridge of his nose down across his cheek.

"That's far enough," Hendrique said when she had come to within fifteen feet of them.

She stopped.

"I must compliment you on your excellent shooting,

Miss Carver. Kyle didn't stand a chance but, as you can see, I'll have a reminder of it in the years to come."

"It's over, Hendrique," she said. "Werner's dead and the plutonium's been recovered. Even Milchan's turned against you."

"Milchan?" Hendrique said contemptuously. "You're welcome to him although I don't know what use he'll be to you. He never knew what was in those kegs—how else do you think I got him to babysit them from Lausanne to Trieste? With the amount of radiation he's been exposed to over the past few days I can't see him lasting out the month."

"You put him in that freight car knowing it would kill him?"

"Someone had to do it," Hendrique replied indifferently. "As for the plutonium, I didn't want anything to do with it anyway but the KGB had other ideas and used a little blackmail to persuade me to see it their way."

"What about those AK47s?" she asked.

"I've been using Werner Freight for three, four years now as a means of transporting arms around the world. Werner knew nothing about it. It was purely coincidental that he and I should end up working together. I'd been hoping to shift at least part of this shipment." He shrugged. "Too bad. At least I'll get away safely."

"You're not going anywhere. Not this time," she said, levelling the Beretta at Hendrique's head.

"The shotgun *is* loaded, only I don't know whether the cartridges survived in the water. Not that I think you'd shoot anyway. Graham's life isn't in any danger. I'll release him unharmed as soon as I've put enough distance between myself and the authorities."

"Shoot him!" Graham shouted as Hendrique took his first tentative step backwards.

She wavered, just as she had done on the train. The photograph of Carrie and Mikey came to mind. Carrie with her alluring brown eyes and Mikey with his cheeky, mischievous face. Innocent victims of justice. Then she remembered Graham's words after he had allowed Hendrique to win the electronic board game on the train. ". . . the one with the stronger willpower always wins. Intimidation invariably leads to defeat . . ."

She fired.

The bullet struck Hendrique above the right eye. Graham's arm swept across his chest, knocking the barrel out from under his chin. Hendrique toppled backwards against a row of crates, then slid to the ground, the surprise still mirrored in his sightless eyes.

Graham pried the shotgun from Hendrique's hand, pointed it at the wall, and squeezed the trigger. Plaster and mortar erupted into the air as the cartridge tore a jagged crevice in the wall.

Sabrina's face went pale.

He tossed the shotgun casually on to Hendrique's body. "You win some, you lose some."

For a moment she thought he was going to put his arm around her shoulders. Instead he gave her a pat on the back.

"You're okay, partner."

She watched him walk out on to the wharf then smiled to herself. Hardly a eulogy, but it was a start.

TWELVE

"Where's Graham?" Philpott asked, prodding the face of his desk clock with his fountain pen. "I bet he's doing this on purpose."

Whitlock and Sabrina exchanged glances. The thought had crossed their minds. Whereas they had arrived within minutes of each other at the United Nations building, with time to spare, Graham, ever the nonconformist, was now over fifteen minutes late. Sabrina sat down on one of the black leather couches and cupped her hands over her mouth to hide the smile as she watched Philpott's glowering face.

"Insolence isn't funny, Sabrina," Philpott said, without looking at her.

"I agree with you, sir." She removed her hands from her face to reveal a deadpan expression.

"More coffee, sir?" Whitlock asked, crossing to the dispenser.

"No, and stop pacing the floor like an expectant father."

Whitlock slumped on to the couch beside Sabrina.

A light flashed on the desk intercom. Philpott depressed the switch below the light. "Yes?"

"Mr. Graham's here, sir."

"Mike Graham, in person?" Philpott said sarcastically.

"Yes, sir," came the hesitant reply.

"Thanks, Sarah." He switched off the intercom and used the small transmitter on his desk to activate the door panel.

Graham came in carrying a cardboard box under his arm.

"Nice of you to drop by, Mike," Philpott said tersely and closed the panel again.

"I'm sorry I'm late, sir, but I've been down in the foyer for the past ten minutes trying to clear this through security," Graham said, tapping the cardboard box.

"You've got the whole day to go shopping—"

"It's not for me, sir, it's for Sabrina," Graham cut in to prevent Philpott from delivering one of his monologues on discipline.

"For me?" she said with wide-eyed disbelief.

Graham placed the cardboard box on the coffee table between the couches. He removed a folder which had been wedged under one of the flaps and placed it on Philpott's desk beside the other two documented reports submitted by Whitlock and Sabrina.

"What is it?" she asked with a hint of excitement.

"Open it," Graham replied.

"May I, sir, before we start?" she asked girlishly.

The telephone rang. Philpott waved absently to the cardboard box as he picked up the receiver.

She opened the lid and peered inside, then recoiled in terror, shifting backwards on the couch until she was pressed against Whitlock.

"What is it?" Whitlock asked, trying to peer over her shoulder.

Graham removed the cage from inside the cardboard box and she shrunk back even further against Whitlock.

"Please, Mike, take it away," she pleaded.

"It's only a hamster," Whitlock said, puzzled.

She turned her face away and put her hands up in front of her. "Mike, take it away. Please."

Graham put the cage back into the cardboard box, then squatted down in front of her. He glanced up at Whitlock. "She had a bad experience with rats as a kid which has subsequently left her with a deep-rooted fear of all rodents."

"You never mentioned this before," Whitlock said to her.

She stared guiltily at her hands.

"I don't think she realized just how far this phobia's actually developed until we spoke about it on the plane coming home. It nearly got her killed in Yugoslavia. She'll tell you what happened in her own time but I don't see why we should involve anyone else, including the boss." He turned to her. "Next time your phobia could be instrumental in getting one of us killed. As I said to you on the plane, it's all in the mind and you'll never overcome it by continually dodging it, hoping it'll go away on its own. Confront it, it's the only way.

"Rats are hardly the most domesticated of pets so I settled for a hamster, mainly because we used to have one. Well, Mikey did. Know what he called it? 'Quarterback.' We tried to tell him that it wasn't quite the name for a hamster but he was adamant, so 'Quarterback' it stayed. He loved the little guy. Many a night we'd go to tuck him in only to find the hamster out of its cage and rustling against the bedclothes. We went to a restaurant once only to have 'Quarterback' pop out of Mikey's pocket halfway through the meal."

"Oh no," Whitlock said chuckling.

"I've never paid a check so quickly in my life. All I'm asking, Sabrina, is that you give the little guy a chance. Watch him, understand him, I promise you he'll help you overcome your fear. Deal?"

"Deal," she said softly.

A sudden silence followed and they turned to Philpott, who had finished on the telephone and was browsing through one of their reports. Whitlock cleared his throat.

Philpott looked up and reached for his pipe. "I won't keep you long but seeing you're all here I thought you'd like to be brought up to date on the case. C.W., you first. The local police have made a number of arrests at the plant after Leitzig's detailed confession so I think we can safely say that network's been successfully closed down. The West German Government has promised a full enquiry into security at the plant and I've been assured that a number of heads are going to roll before it's through."

"What about my cover story, sir? Being exposed so early on could have had a damaging effect on the rest of the operation."

"Granted, but I don't see any reason to review the backstopping process. It was a million to one chance that she could have caught you out as she did. It's never happened before and I doubt it'll ever happen again. It's imperative that your cover stories are as authentic and credible as possible. I'll certainly raise the matter with the Secretary-General but as far as I'm concerned I'm happy with things the way they are." Philpott tapped the newspaper on his desk. "You wrote a good article about the plant but I never knew you were that opposed to nuclear power."

"Windscale, Denver, Three Mile Island, Chernobyl. They said it could never happen. How many have to die to prove them wrong?"

"That's the last paragraph of your article, isn't it?" Philpott asked, glancing at the newspaper.

"Yes, sir. It sums up my feelings perfectly."

Philpott consulted his notes. "Mike, Sabrina, I received the doctor's report on the two of you today. It's as we thought. The amount of radiation you've been exposed to was negligible. Your reading was slightly higher, Mike, mainly because you were in the wagon with Milchan for a short time. Even so, it's absolutely nothing to worry about."

"What about Milchan?" Graham asked.

"His report came through yesterday. He's got about six weeks at the most. There's nothing they can do for him." Philpott paused to light his pipe. "Anyway, back to the case. I've been pressing the KGB to find out all they can on Stefan Werner. A telex finally came through from Moscow this morning. I'll give you the gist of its contents. Stefan Werner wasn't his real name. He was born Aleksei Lubanov in Minsk, 1941. He was recruited by the KGB at the age of seventeen to undergo the customary ten-year training programme to prepare an agent for work abroad. He was trained at Gacznya and Prakhovka spy schools and first surfaced as Stefan Werner in Brazil, 1967. He spoke fluent Portuguese so he had no trouble in securing himself a job as a salesman at a freight company in Rio. Within a year he was running the company. He then left Brazil and bought a share in a struggling German shipping line. He bought the company out six months later and it turned out to be the foundation upon which he subsequently built his shipping and freight empire. A brilliant businessman, but a dedicated KGB agent all the same.''

''What happened about the detonator, sir?'' Sabrina asked.

''I was coming to that. All six kegs were exactly the same weight and it took our bomb-disposal team four and a half hours under vacuum conditions to find the whole thing was an elaborate hoax. Five of the kegs contained the Plutonium-IV compound. The sixth, supposedly rigged out with the explosive device, actually contained nothing more lethal than sand. It was all the work of Konstatin Benin.''

''Benin?'' Graham muttered. ''He was a co-founder of Balashikha, wasn't he?''

''Correct. He was also Stefan Werner's—or Aleksei Lubanov, if you prefer—and Karen Schendel's handler. We've proved that beyond any doubt. Sergei's on his way to Moscow right now to confront him with the evidence.''

"What about the plutonium, sir?'' Whitlock asked.

"It's already been returned to Mainz. Unfortunately the grain aboard the *Napoli* had to be destroyed but UNICEF have already sent out a replacement load. It should reach Ethiopia by the end of the week.''

The telephone rang again.

"Excuse me,'' Philpott said, then lifted the receiver to his ear. He smiled as he listened to the caller on the other end. "Well, well, well, now that *is* interesting. Thanks for calling, Matt, I appreciate it.'' He replaced the receiver. "That was the Pentagon. News has just reached them that an industrial laboratory outside Benghazi was razed to the ground by a mysterious fire in the early hours of the morning.''

"It wouldn't happen to be the same one the plutonium was bound for, sir?'' Sabrina asked.

"The very same.''

"Did we have a unit in Benghazi at the time?'' Graham asked.

"We haven't had a unit in Libya for the past five months. The only foreign vessel in the area at the time was a Russian submarine. It would seem Sergei's hint to the Kremlin paid off after all. That's the cherry on the top as far as I'm concerned.'' Philpott pulled a foolscap pad towards him. "Unlike you three I do have work to do.''

"Does that mean we can go, sir?'' Graham asked, glancing at his wristwatch.

"For someone who arrived fifteen minutes late you're certainly in a hurry to get away. What's the rush?''

"There's a game on at the Yankee Stadium, it starts in an hour's time."

"Who're they playing?" Whitlock asked.

"Boston Red Sox."

"Ouch," Whitlock said, wincing. "The Yankees are going to need all the support they can get against that kind of opposition."

"I didn't know you followed baseball?" Graham said, surprised.

"I don't really but one thing I've learnt since settling here is that baseball and football are an integral part of daily New York life. I'll have my fingers crossed for them this afternoon."

Graham patted Whitlock's arm then turned to Philpott. "Goodbye, sir."

"Bye, Mike, and well done. Well done all of you." Philpott picked up the transmitter and activated the door panel.

"How long are you in New York for?" Sabrina asked Graham as she walked with him to the door.

"I'll probably be leaving tomorrow."

"What were you planning on doing tonight?"

"Probably take in a movie," he muttered.

"Fancy some company?"

He stared at the carpet and rubbed the bridge of his nose.

"It was just a thought," she said, breaking the lingering silence. "And Mike, thanks for the little guy."

"Yeah," he said, then walked to the outer office door.

The receptionist activated it for him.

He paused to glance back at Sabrina. "I hope you like Westerns."

He was gone before she could answer.

"Come on, I'll buy you a tuna on rye at the 'Health-works' around the corner," Whitlock said behind her. "If you can spare the time, that is?"

"Meaning?" she said hesitantly, taking the cardboard box from him.

"I thought you might want to spend the rest of the afternoon getting ready for your date," he teased gently.

"That jibe will cost you a side salad and an orange juice on top of the tuna on rye," she said, affecting a supercilious tone.

They said goodbye to Philpott then walked in silence down the corridor.

"So, any idea for your hamster's name?" he asked as they entered the lift.

"Quarterback," she replied as the door closed. "What else?"

Benin had first met Kolchinsky twenty-two years before when he had been assigned to head the Surveillance Unit at the Lubianka, the KGB headquarters in the heart of Moscow. Kolchinsky had been his deputy. Their initial wariness of each other quickly developed into antipathy and one of the main reasons for Benin's transfer to the Gaczyna spy school was because of their inability to work together. Both of them were intensely ambitious but their ideologies were vastly different. Benin was a Stalinist, an extremist, whereas Kolchinsky was a moderate, always searching for reforms to kerb the often dictatorial powers of the KGB hierarchy. Kolchinsky's liberal views gained him few friends and it was known that his banishment to the West as a military attaché had been mainly for his own protection. Neither of them had changed their ideologies in twenty-two years . . .

Benin consulted his wristwatch. He had kept Kolchinsky waiting twenty minutes in the outer office. It had been a last defiant gesture of his authority. He picked up the receiver and dialled a single number.

"Send in Comrade Kolchinsky."

The secretary led Kolchinsky into Benin's office, then withdrew, closing the door behind him.

"I can see by your stomach that the West agrees with you," Benin said icily, then gestured to the foam collar around Kolchinsky's neck. "Something serious?"

"I'd be more worried about my own neck if I were you," Kolchinsky retorted and sat down.

"I take it you're here to read me my last rites?"

Kolchinsky ignored the sarcasm and opened his attaché case. He withdrew a folder, then the detonator, and tossed them on to the table in front of Benin.

"The detonator was still in Werner's hand when the body was recovered."

Benin picked it up. "I had to make him believe it was for real. I had to make them all believe it was for real. After all, reality *is* far more convincing than acting."

Kolchinsky removed a packet of cigarettes from his jacket pocket.

"I don't allow smoking in my office."

"The Politburo doesn't allow treason in their country," Kolchinsky replied, then lit the cigarette. "There is one piece of the jigsaw still missing. Your motive."

"Is this where I'm supposed to break down and confess?"

"There's more than enough incriminating evidence against you in here," Kolchinsky replied, tapping the folder. "Anyway, the KGB will have their own methods of extracting a full confession out of you. I don't think I need to remind you of those methods, you initiated many of them yourself."

Benin thought for a moment before speaking. "First the Government used this *glasnost* policy as a means of appeasing the West. Now they're tampering with our strategic nuclear defences. My plan was merely an attempt to stop them. Once the plutonium reached Libya safely I intended to leak a story to several of the West's leading newspapers that while our beloved leader was signing disarmament treaties Russia was already starting to build a new cache of nuclear weapons to replace those to be officially scrapped, using plutonium siphoned off from a Western nuclear plant and being constructed in a country allied to ours. He could have argued all he wanted but all the documented proof would have been there in black and white for the world to see. His credibility would have been shattered. Even if some Western leaders were inclined to believe his sincerity there would have been more than enough sceptics to ensure that any more arms reduction talks would be set back by several years at the very least."

"And by then a new Premier would have been in power, one vetted by you and your extremist cronies. Then you could have set about replacing all those weapons that had been signed away to make Russia the most powerful nuclear force in the world again."

"I'm not ashamed of what I've done. I did it for Russia. I did it because I love my country. We're socialist, with our own identity and our own style of government. Do you really think I'm the sole opponent to the introduction of these new reforms? The dissenters are spread throughout the Politburo and irrespective of what happens to me they'll pick up the fallen standard and continue the struggle. I wouldn't expect you to understand though, you settled for Western complacency years ago.''

''You're right, I don't understand. I don't understand fanatics like you who talk with such pride about the purity of Russian socialism. Stalin was a socialist and how many millions died in labour camps during his regime? Andropov, Shelepin, Semichastny: how much innocent blood was spilt during their terms as KGB directors? How can you justify a system where the very people it's supposed to help can't even speak out against its excesses for fear of being beaten up by thugs employed by this department? At least *glasnost* is breaking down those barriers so that people will finally have a voice. A voice of freedom.

''I'll never forget the afternoon I was at London's Hyde Park Corner and an elderly Russian Jew was invited on to the platform to speak. It turned out he'd only arrived in England the previous day and he cried all the way through the speech because he couldn't believe he was actually being allowed to voice his thoughts in public without fear of persecution. I felt ashamed of being Russian that day. If the West's taught me one thing it's that socialism can work in a democracy, unlike the socialism you advocate in this country. No, Konstantin, don't preach to me about the values of your kind of socialism.'' Kolchinsky snapped the attaché case shut and stood up. "I'll leave the folder. You'll find your telephone's been disconnected and there are two armed guards outside the door with orders to stop you should you attempt to leave before your official arrest.

"By the way, I believe you drew a blank when you tried to find out who masterminded the attempt on your life. Well, I made a few enquiries on my own before I left New York. It seems the order for your assassination came from within the Politburo itself. You've been a thorn in their side for a long time now so what better way to get rid of you than by letting the resistance movement do the dirty work for them? That's why the missile launcher got into the country so easily. Not that the resistance movement suspected anything, they thought it was all down to their own ingenuity. This is the best bit, though: Hendrique was the unwitting middleman using Werner Freight to bring the missile launcher into the country. It's a small world, isn't it?"

Benin stared at the door after Kolchinsky had left. He knew the case would never reach a court of law. There would be an official cover-up as quickly, and quietly, as possible. He also knew the choices facing him. Either die in detention, after hours, perhaps even days, of unrelenting torture, or take his own life before they arrived to arrest him.

He swivelled his chair around to face the window overlooking the breathtaking grandeur of the snow-covered Bittsevsky forest-park then reached behind him and removed his Tokarev pistol from the top drawer of his desk.

About the Author

Alistair MacLean was the bestselling author of thirty books including world famous novels such as THE GUNS OF NAVARONE, WHERE EAGLES DARE and SANTORINI. When he died in 1987 he left behind several outlines for novels. The first of these was used as the basis for DEATH TRAIN by Alastair MacNeill.